Library On Wheels
3666 Grand River
Detroit, MI 48208
313-833-5686

D1367773

JUN 2005

LOW

HUNTER'S RAIN

Recent Titles by Julian Jay Savarin from Severn House

HORSEMEN IN THE SHADOWS
MACALLISTER'S TASK
NORWEGIAN FIRE
THE QUEENSLAND FILE
STARFIRE
STRIKE EAGLE
VILLIGER

The Berlin Series

A COLD RAIN IN BERLIN
ROMEO SUMMER
WINTER AND THE GENERAL
A HOT DAY IN MAY
HUNTER'S RAIN

HUNTER'S RAIN

Julian Jay Savarin

This first world edition published in Great Britain 2004 by
SEVERN HOUSE PUBLISHERS LTD of
9–15 High Street, Sutton, Surrey SM1 1DF.
This first world edition published in the USA 2004 by
SEVERN HOUSE PUBLISHERS INC of
595 Madison Avenue, New York, N.Y. 10022.

British Library Cataloguing in Publication Data

Savarin, Julian Jay
    Hunter's rain
    1.   Muller, Hauptkommissar (Fictitious character) - Fiction
    2.   Police - Germany - Berlin - Fiction
    3.   Suspense fiction
    I.   Title
    823.9'14 [F]

    ISBN 0-7278-6139-5

Typeset by Palimpsest Book Production Ltd.,
Polmont, Stirlingshire, Scotland.
Printed and bound in Great Britain by
MPG Books Ltd., Bodmin, Cornwall.

One

In the heat of a wet July day, Müller sat in his car, watching the rivulets stream down before him. The water formed a perfect barrier, screening the occupants from the outside world. It hit the Porsche like a demented drummer high on something more than adrenalin, and who had forgotten what he was supposed to be playing.

'A vale of bloody tears,' his companion said, staring at nothing through the rain-drenched windscreen. 'Whatever is responsible – *El Niño*, *El Niña*, or whatever fucking name they want to call it – this is shit! It's supposed to be summer.'

'Don't take your frustrations out on the weather,' Müller said. 'It won't stop the rain, nor bring the sun out today.'

The man, cropped blond hair, hard face and a tan that did not come out of a studio, stared. 'Are you always like that?'

'Like what?'

'Philosophical about things.'

Müller gave a short laugh. 'Philosophical? I simply don't think it's worth getting—'

'Jesus, Müller! Allow a person the right to be pissed off about the weather.' The man tried to peer out. 'I can't see a damned thing out there.'

'Which is what we want. You can't see out, they can't see in . . . assuming anyone is crazy enough to be out in this deluge, keeping surveillance. I chose this rendezvous for that very purpose. Not even a tourist in sight when I arrived.'

'Smart of them. Which is more than I can say for us. Nice choice,' the man continued grumpily. 'Wannsee. Nice, historical ring to it.'

'I picked it for practical reasons. On a day like this, no one in their right mind would come to this shore of the lake.'

'Wannsee,' the man repeated. 'Sounds like *Wahnsinn*,

1

doesn't it? Fitting the madness of the extermination conference that was held at that villa. There was a Müller at the conference too; and *he* was a Berlin policeman.'

'I'm the wrong age to be Gestapo Müller,' Müller said, refusing to be needled. 'Finished with the weather, so now you're starting on me?'

'I don't want to be here,' the other grumbled, still trying to peer through the windscreen. 'I just hope you're right about the surveillance. When Pappi set up this meet, I was not happy. He and I have never met. Now, you've seen me.'

'And I'll forget I ever saw you, just as quickly.'

There was silence for a while, then the man reached into an inside jacket pocket, and took out a plain, postcard-sized envelope. He handed it to Müller.

'The information you need is in there.'

'How many?'

'Two.'

'*Two?*'

'Be thankful you've got any at all, Müller.'

'Thanks,' Müller said with a straight face.

The man stared at Müller with a blank expression. 'I can't guarantee you'll get anything out of them.'

'I'm not asking for guarantees.'

The man kept on his blank expression. 'These people have been living in anonymity for years; with very good reason. Many of those you're looking for are no longer alive. Rumour is, they were helped on their way.'

'Rumour?'

'Rumour,' the hard-faced man repeated. 'Let's leave it at that.' He gave Müller a searching look. 'The people you're after would dearly like to send you on your way too.'

'They've tried.'

The man nodded. 'I know. And you've managed to kill off all those they have sent openly, and not so openly. But do you notice something wrong with the picture?'

'You tell me.'

'You have not taken a single one alive. Therefore, no information. Those you don't kill, they do. When you find the time, count the people you have come up against, then count how many are still alive. Nothing that can lead back to them is tolerated. The day they find a foolproof way to get rid of you, you can start ticking off your own days. You are the thorn they need to pull, and they will not stop.'

'Don't sound so happy.'

'That's not happiness you hear. That's reality. They don't know how much you know.' The man paused.

Müller said nothing.

'Cautious. Wise.' A thin smile lived for the briefest of instants. 'When they have persuaded themselves you do know too much, their own caution may take second place to their need to succeed in their aims. You are a dangerous man, Müller . . . not because you're going about like a madman bent upon revenge; but precisely because you're not. At least, outwardly.'

The man paused again, then gave Müller another searching look. 'Pappenheim said I should be careful of you. Why?'

'I wouldn't know.'

The man looked as if he did not believe it. 'He said you could sometimes be worse than a Rhodesian ridgeback, if rubbed the wrong way.'

'You know about the lion dogs, do you?'

'They will defend their territory ferociously, sometimes to the death. Very brave, or very foolish dogs. Which are you, Müller?'

'I'm just a policeman.'

The man looked sceptical. 'My father was out there in the seventies . . .' he began, as if to explain.

'On which side?'

The man gave Müller another stare. 'I take it that's a joke.'

'It's called sarcasm.'

'Pappi was right.'

'The strange deaths of one's parents,' Müller said, 'when one was twelve years old, tend to alter the perspective a little. So where's your father now?'

The man turned to stare at the rain once more. 'When the shit hit the fan in Rhodesia, he went to South Africa . . .'

'Where it also went pear-shaped for people like him.'

'He's still out there, with my mother.'

'Tolerant, these Africans.'

3

The man shot him another blank look. 'More sarcasm, is it? In case you're wondering, I'm not like my father. I only visit for my mother's sake.'

'I did wonder about the tan. It doesn't look like sun studio.'

The man said nothing for a few moments, as if considering Müller's remark. He looked at Müller speculatively.

'I could be setting you up,' he said. 'The information I gave you could be nothing. Innocent bystanders. Bait for a trap.'

'I have considered that.'

'And?'

'If it is, you'll be a very sorry man.'

The tiniest of smiles again fled across the man's face. 'Your five minutes are up.' The man glanced about him. 'Nine-Nine-Six Turbo. Nice car.'

'I manage. Sorry you'll be getting your nice suit wet.'

The other looked at him neutrally. 'That's rich, coming from a man who wears a ponytail, an earring, *and* Armani linen.'

'It takes one to know one.'

The man did not smile. 'Tell Pappi, if he ever puts me out on a limb like this again, I'll finish the job that was bungled last May, by whoever it was.'

'I'll tell him. I'm certain he'll appreciate the sentiment.'

'Yes. Well.'

The man opened the door of the car and got out. The rain was a sudden roar.

'*Shit!*' Müller heard him say. 'This is drowning weather. Fucking rain!'

Then the door was shut, cutting out the sound as if switched off. There followed the muted thud of the door of the other car being shut angrily. It was less than a metre away.

'Friendly man who hates the rain,' Müller said to himself.

Müller did not start the Porsche but turned on the wipers briefly as the suntanned man started the big Mercedes coupe and, wheels spinning, pulled out in front of him to drive off. The windscreen remained clear long enough for him to get a second look at the official licence plate, as if to confirm what he'd seen when the tanned man had first arrived for the meet.

'No mistake about that number,' he said to himself.

To all intents and purposes, Wannsee, some 14 kilometres

south-west of Berlin, but still part of the city state, was an island. At its closest point, it was no further than a canal's width away. Five bridges – including the Glienicker of spy-exchange fame – connected it at various points to the mainland. Careful forestation had given it mixed woods that were mainly pine and oak, but included beech, birch, poplar and ash, among others. Plenty of screening for anyone not bothered about getting soaked.

Müller looked about him, but the force of the downpour gave everything a blurred look through the glass. If anyone were out there, he or she could not, for the moment, be seen.

Müller still did not start the car. Instead, he opened the envelope. On a single sheet of notepaper were the names, addresses, and telephone numbers he wanted. It had taken several weeks to get the information. He put the note back into the envelope, and put that into an inner jacket pocket. Only then did he start the car.

The 450 bhp of the enhanced Porsche Turbo barked into life. The wipers cleared the windscreen, disclosing the rain-battered surface of Berlin's infamous, beautiful lake.

Müller again scanned the immediate area. He had driven along what was in effect one of the pedestrian paths that criss-crossed the virtual island. This particular path was coastal – wide enough for a car – and was surfaced. Müller and the suntanned man had parked side-by-side, nose on to it, before a backdrop of trees, on a stretch between Kleines Tiefehorn and the rounded headland of Grosses Tiefehorn, across the water from Kladow. The path was also a popular run for cyclists; but the rain continued to pound with a vengeance. Through the briefly wiped screen, not a soul could be seen.

Not even a hardy cyclist.

The muddy area beyond the path – caused by the deluging rain – would create no problems for the four-wheel-drive Turbo; but Müller had no doubt that his reluctant informer was probably still cursing him for the spinning wheels, as he had made his way back.

Müller paused, looking to his right. An indistinct shape, fully clothed in hooded, bad-weather cycling gear, head down, was approaching in the teeming rain.

The unexpected, hardy cyclist.

'Cycling in *this*?' Müller remarked, staring at the blurred shape. 'He must be mad. Or . . .' He let his words fade.

The way Müller had parked allowed a clear view of the lake. Was the mad cyclist coming to admire it? On brighter days, the headland was a popular spot.

Choosing discretion, Müller ducked low, and drew his automatic from its shoulder holster. The big Beretta 92R was his favourite, but was a non-standard-issue weapon. He held it ready, eased his way out of the car and shut the door quietly, moving to keep the Porsche between the rider and himself. The sound of the rain greeted him like thunder.

'Now I'm the one getting wet,' he muttered. His shoes made a soft, squelching sound, barely audible within the noise of the rain. 'And muddy.'

The cyclist drew closer but did not alter the rhythm of his pace, even as he went past. He did not look at the car, though, this close, he must have heard the powerful exhaust note of the engine at idle, even above the thundering rain.

Müller peered from behind the cover of the car as the cyclist kept going. 'Anyone seeing an empty car near a path meant for walkers and cyclists only,' Müller said to himself, '*with* its engine running, would have looked. *I* would have looked . . . unless I wanted to pretend I hadn't seen it.'

The cyclist still continued without breaking pace, until he had ridden out of sight.

Müller waited a full minute in the pouring rain, looking about him, blinking the water out of his eyes, peering through the trees for signs of movement. Nothing.

The cyclist did not return.

The strange uneasiness remained as Müller slowly put the pistol away, wiped his shoes on a tuft of grass as best he could, then got back into the car. He was not yet soaked through, but his lightweight summer suit was wet enough to feel as if it would stick to the leather seat.

Still checking for the cyclist, he eased the car on to the path, turning right to head back in the direction of the infamous villa. He drove away with as little noise as possible.

'I'm coming for you,' he said quietly to the unseen people

responsible for the killing of his parents. 'No matter how long, or what it takes.'

The cyclist had turned round, and was on his way back to the spot where he had seen the Porsche. When still out of sight of the car he stopped, got off the bike, and moved a little way into the woods. He leaned the cycle against a tree then cautiously, using any convenient tree as cover, continued towards where he expected the car to be.

He stopped. 'No engine,' he muttered. 'I can't hear an engine.'

He moved on, then stopped again.

He was close enough; but the Porsche was no longer there.

'*Shit!*' he swore softly. '*Shit!* Too fucking late. And I didn't even hear it leave.' He approached the spot, stopped, and looked down at the tracks. '*Two* cars. Two fucking cars. They had already met. *Damn* it!'

Moving back into the cover of a tree, he took out a mobile and made a call.

'Yes?'

'I was too late,' the cyclist said over the noise of the rain.

There was a long silence in his ear that, in the rainy woods, was strangely menacing.

'So, you did not see the person with whom he met,' the voice at the other end said at last. It was an accusation.

'No. I came across country to make time, intending to get here first—'

'Intent,' the other interrupted, 'and achievement, can sometimes be separated by a great distance.'

The cyclist said nothing.

'You gave us a time for the meeting,' the pitiless voice went on. 'What happened?'

'The information I got must have been wrong. Wrong timing . . .'

'We have placed you where you are for a purpose. You are being handsomely rewarded. We expect results; not excuses. Do not make the mistake of believing you are indispensible.'

'He . . . he must have changed the timing,' the cyclist offered in mitigation.

'Of course he changed the timing! Müller is no fool. He would have done that instinctively. You should have foreseen it.'

'But he could have changed it to any time . . .'

'That, is your problem.'

The conversation was abruptly terminated.

The cyclist squeezed his eyes shut, and briefly turned his face upwards in the rain that still managed to crash through the foliage of the tree. The slamming droplets felt as if they were searing his skin; but he ignored them. He gritted his teeth.

'*Shit,*' he said for a third time, anger and frustration coming through.

He held the phone in such a way that it appeared as if he wanted to throw it to the ground. Instead, he put it away in a controlled manner which plainly betrayed his continuing frustration. He then returned to his bike, mounted, and made for the Rotkäppchenweg, the track that would eventually lead him back across country to Wannsee harbour.

Müller was on the *Bundesstrasse* 1, already approaching the Zehlendorf intersection with the A115 Autobahn. He was planning to take the exit that would feed him on to the A115, to head back to Berlin.

He changed his mind before the first of the three exit warning signs – the 300-metre marker – came into view, and continued along the Potsdamer Chaussee, which was itself part of the B1. The B1 was a direct, if marginally slower, route into the heart of the city, where it would eventually lead him to his home in Wilmersdorf.

The cyclist had arrived where he had parked his own car, near the yacht marina. It was a big, dark-blue Mercedes saloon that was older than the coupe in which Müller's informant had arrived; but its excellent condition was evidence of the care that was lavished upon it. Even in the greyness of the rainy day, it gleamed. The pounding droplets rolled off it like glistening marbles.

The car, parked on a surfaced area between a pair of trees,

pointed towards the rows and rows of neatly moored small sailing boats and motor cruisers. Some of the bigger cruisers were moored at the end of the rows, bows pointing landwards. Given the weather, there was barely anyone about. Three people who could be seen at the water's edge looked tiny in the distance. If there were any occupants on the boats, they had all decided to remain below.

The cyclist began to take his bike apart. It was an expensive, multi-geared sports model that had been designed for swift dismantling. It fitted easily into the boot.

He then began to remove his outer clothing. First were the waterproofs that had covered his jeans. He threw those into the boot. Next was the hooded jacket, which revealed a black leather jacket beneath. The waterproof jacket was thrown in after the trousers. He then shut the boot.

He got into the car, started it, and drove slowly away, face expressionless. The black leather jacket, worn over a white T-shirt, was a surprise.

Upon its epaulettes were the two green stars of a *Polizeimeister*; a junior police sergeant.

When the sergeant came to the intersection, unlike Müller, he joined the A115; but, like Müller, headed for central Berlin.

The rain continued to pound.

Berlin-Mitte. Friedrichstrasse. 09.15. Pappenheim sat in his office blowing a luxurious plume of smoke at the ceiling, like a dragon that had inadvertently taken a drink of water.

A knock sounded on his door.

'*In!*'

Berger entered cautiously.

Pappenheim took the Gauloise Blonde out of his mouth. There was little left of it. He gave it a regretful look, then stubbed it out in the full ashtray on his large, untidy desk.

'*Obermeisterin* Berger,' he began with the air of one who had seen too much, done too much, and was never again going to be surprised in this life. 'Stop looking at my ample self as if you expect me to fade before you. I was shot in May, not yesterday. I was not wounded, although the bruising took longer to go away than I would have liked—'

'If you hadn't worn body armour, you'd be dead.'

'I'm an *Oberkommissar*, you're an *Obermeisterin*. That means you just interrupted your superior; but I'll ignore that for now.'

She smiled at him. 'Yes, Chief.'

'Don't push your luck.'

'No, Chief.'

'To what do I owe the pleasure, Berger?'

Berger's eyes, seemingly too lively, were telegraphing something Pappenheim failed to read.

'See who I found dripping by the front desk.' She stepped back to allow someone enter.

Carey Bloomfield, in jeans, white shirt, thin-soled, slightly damp trainers, and a raincoat, speckled with rapidly drying wet patches, slung over an arm, entered the smoke-filled room. A bag was slung crosswise from a shoulder.

Pappenheim got to his feet in astonishment, then smiled with a real pleasure. He stepped from behind the desk and went towards her, hand outstretched.

'Miss Bloomfield!' he began. 'A pleasure. A pleasure to see you!' He glanced at Berger. 'Thank you, Berger.'

Berger gave Carey Bloomfield a look that was neither hostile, nor particularly friendly.

'I've got the message,' she said, and went out.

'She really dislikes me, that woman,' Carey Bloomfield said.

'Don't mind her,' Pappenheim said, shaking Carey Bloomfield's hand with enthusiasm. 'It's the weather.'

'The weather,' she repeated, not believing it. 'The very first time I ever came here, I nicknamed her Miss Hawk Eyes. Glad to see some things don't change. Hey, Pappi,' she continued, looking at him closely, 'you seem really pleased to see me.'

'I am. I am. Here. Let me take your coat. So, you made it,' he went on, 'as you promised in May.'

'I made it. Always keep my promises . . . when I can.'

She handed the coat over and he hung it on a wall hook.

'I'll remember that,' Pappenheim said. 'As for Berger, she'll soon have some news which should make her very happy.'

'Will that be good for me? Or bad?'

'Come, come, Miss Bloomfield. Be nice. She's only worried that you may have a . . . bad influence on Jens. Remember when she first met you, you were pretending to be a journalist. Now that we know you're CIA . . .'

'*Not* CIA, Pappi, as I've been repeating since I first met you guys.'

'Whatever.'

'So, what's this happy news she's going to get?'

'In his infinite wisdom,' Pappenheim began, 'the Great White Shark . . .'

'Your beloved boss *Direktor* Kaltendorf . . .'

'Not beloved by anyone here,' Pappenheim corrected, 'and still a probationary *Direktor* . . .'

'*His* bosses still don't trust him to do the job? They gave him a special police unit to play with . . .'

'It isn't quite like that. Well . . . perhaps it is. Whatever their reasons, it's a way of keeping him on his toes, which has its effect on us. He gets in our hair, as you know.'

'Do I!' Carey Bloomfield said with the air of a veteran.

'So, in his infinite wisdom,' Pappenheim continued, 'he decided we needed an extra *Kommissar* in our little part of the unit. We decided to head him off at the pass, before he could dump one on us.'

'Berger,' Carey Bloomfield said.

Pappenheim nodded. 'She's fully qualified for the job. She's already done the three years' study and passed the first and second examinations, with excellent results.'

'So, she's really just waiting for an appointment.'

'Yes. And she'll be highly recommended. As yet, she knows nothing about it.'

'Will Kaltendorf let you?'

'There are ways,' Pappenheim said dangerously.

She gave him a searching look. 'Why do I think there's more to this than you're telling me?

'So, how's the brand new lieutenant-colonel?' Pappenheim asked.

Carey Bloomfield's expression said it all. 'Nice change of tack, Pappi. The brand new lieutenant-colonel is fine, and

11

hopes to keep the rank. So, I hope you're not getting me into any trouble. They can take the silver oak leaves back as quickly as they gave them.'

'Nothing you can't handle.'

'Is that a compliment? Or should I worry?'

'You should not worry.'

'*That* worries me already.' She gave him another searching look. 'And did I just hear you say you got *shot*?'

He nodded. 'Sadly . . . yes. One night, someone jogged up behind me and put a single, silenced shot into my back. It was a powerful gun. Threw me to the ground . . .'

'Jesus!'

'My thoughts at the time were less pious. Luckily, for a reason I will never know, I'd decided to wear new body armour that I had kept in a cupboard for months. Hate wearing the things; as does Jens. But this one is very light and very strong, for wearing under your clothes. It was a fine evening. I decided to walk home and thought, if I didn't get fed up with wearing the thing by the time I got there, perhaps I wouldn't send it back.'

Carey Bloomfield was staring at him. 'You're kidding. And it saved your life.'

'I would not be here talking with you. The shooter was a pro. It was a clean, fast shot. He fired on the run, and never paused. He ran past as I fell, and kept going. He was so sure of the kill, he never looked back. Lucky for me he was so sure of himself. He might have considered a second shot – to the head – just to make certain. In which case, goodbye Pappi.'

'Jesus!' she said again. 'My God, Pappi. How could you have been taken like this? Like a rookie. You, of all people.'

'I've been annoyed with myself ever since. We'd been having some . . . exciting times. Plenty going on, and still is. I let my guard down. Not an excuse. I would not accept it from one of my people, so I can hardly accept it from myself. It was stupid.'

'We all have off-days.' She shook her head slowly, amazed he had survived. 'As you've said, lucky for you your guardian angel didn't.'

'Yes.' Pappenheim gave a rueful smile. 'Definitely working overtime that evening.'

'Who would send a hitman after you, Pappi?'

'There are a lot of people upon whose toes I have trod over the years.'

'But?'

'This one was a message.'

'Since you'd have been dead if they had succeeded, who was the message for?'

'You have one guess.'

'*Müller?*'

'I did tell you exciting things have been happening. I'll bring you up to date while we wait for Jens.'

'He's *late*? That's not like him.'

'Not late. He's been out on an early trip. He should be back soon. Let's get you some coffee.'

'Police coffee?'

'I meant outside. A treat from home. Not far from here – on our very street – we've even got a Starbucks; two, in fact, and eight in all in Berlin, at the last count. Plenty to choose from.'

'I'm not from Seattle . . .'

'I'll take that to mean yes.'

'Then I'd better have my coat back. It's raining more than cats and dogs out there.'

'No need. We'll drive.'

'But I thought you said—'

'We'll drive,' Pappenheim repeated firmly.

'You haven't had a cigarette since I got here,' she said as they walked towards a lift, along a corridor festooned with no-smoking signs.

'All in your honour,' Pappenheim said. 'But don't remind me.' He glared balefully at one of the signs. 'The Great White's work, as you know. Every corridor in this building has them. And, naturally, in the garage too.' He sighed, the longing raging through him. 'I'm cursed by that man.'

Her smile was one of sympathy. 'Smoke in the car, Pappi. I can hack it.'

'I'll smoke in the car,' he said with relief. 'Now let's hurry, in case the Great White is on the prowl.'

They got to a lift without incident, and entered quickly as it hissed open.

'I swear I heard footsteps,' Pappenheim said as the doors shut. 'Did you hear footsteps?'

She responded with an amused smile as she shook her head. 'You're hearing things, Pappi.'

Pappenheim glanced upwards, as if expecting to see Kaltendorf clamped, on all fours, to the ceiling.

'I hope so,' he said. Then the lift stopped two floors down. 'Oh no,' he added with a sigh of resignation.

But it was not Kaltendorf. A dark-haired man in his mid-twenties, in black jeans, black T-shirt, and service pistol at his belt, entered.

He nodded at Pappenheim. 'Morning, sir.'

'Morning, Hammersfeldt. Wet day.'

Hammersfeldt was staring at Carey Bloomfield. 'It isn't dry, sir.'

'Hammersfeldt has wit,' Pappenheim said to Carey Bloomfield. 'Hammersfeldt,' he added as the doors shut.

'Sir?'

'I know she's very pretty, but it's rude to stare.'

Hammersfeldt seemed to pull himself together. 'Oh! Er . . . yes, sir.' He appeared confused.

Pappenheim made no introductions as Hammersfeldt tried to look anywhere else but at Carey Bloomfield.

The lift stopped a floor later, and after a self-conscious nod at them both, Hammersfeldt got out quickly.

'Poor guy,' she said as the doors hissed shut once more. 'You embarrassed him, Pappi. Shame on you!' The incident had amused her. 'I think he got out before his floor.'

'He was staring,' Pappenheim insisted, as if in explanation.

'So, you think I'm pretty?'

'Miss Bloomfield,' he said, 'I'm too old. Save the sparring for Jens. He's better at it than I am.'

'Oh . . . I don't know, Pappi. You don't do so badly.'

Pappenheim favoured her with a brief smile. 'But I must be kind to Hammersfeldt from time to time.'

'Why?'

'He probably saved my life.'

'"Probably"?'

'He was down by the front desk when I went out, talking to the officer on duty. He saw someone in a hooded jacket run past outside. Looked like a jogger. Hammersfeldt wondered what a jogger was doing at that time of the night . . .'

'A night runner?' Carey Bloomfield suggested.

'I'll take that as a dry comment, Miss Bloomfield. Hammersfeldt drew his weapon and rushed out, just in case. It is just possible that Hammersfeldt's appearance made my would-be killer run on. Who knows?'

'Your guardian angel *was* putting in some overtime.'

'Looks like it. Hammersfeldt came up to me yelling, "*Sir, Sir! Are you alright?*" At least, that's what I've been told. I was in shock, and can't swear to it. But Hammersfeldt insists I told him to shut up. I don't remember that, either.' Pappenheim grinned. 'Even when I'm out, I'm in.' The lift stopped. 'Ground zero.'

They got out and as they entered the pristine, secure garage, light flooded the place. It was almost full. Marked and unmarked police cars and vans were separated from private vehicles.

Pappenheim led her to where Müller usually parked. Next to the empty space was a gleaming BMW 645csi in gun-metal grey.

'Wow, Pappi!' she said. 'Got yourself a hot Bimmer?'

'Hot is right,' he said, 'but not the way you mean it. This isn't mine.' He squeezed the remote to open it.

'Don't tell me Müller's switched to Bimmers and lent this to you.'

'To separate him from his Porsche, you'd need to slice off an umbilical cord.'

'Smile when you say that.'

'I'm smiling.'

'So? What's the story?' Carey Bloomfield asked as they got into the car.

'This,' Pappenheim began, 'was once used by the man who was contracted to kill Jens . . .'

'You're kidding.'

'No kid. As he has no further use for it – being dead – and

the real owners won't claim it on the grounds that it might incriminate them –' Pappenheim started the powerful engine – 'I'm using it.'

'Kaltendorf go for this?'

'I've been authorized by my immediate superior . . .'

'Müller.'

'The one. The only.'

She gave a little giggle. 'You guys are a pair. I knew guys like you at officer candidate school.'

'Guys like us,' he intoned, 'we're everywhere.'

'You're beginning to pop, Pappi. You need your smoke.'

'I do. I do.'

He drove slowly out of the parking bay, and towards the exit ramp with the wide, armoured roll-up door.

The rain was still chucking it down as the car nosed into Friedrichstrasse and turned left, heading towards Unter den Linden. A short while later, Pappenheim pulled over, and parked next to Starbucks.

'I shouldn't park here,' he said, 'but I'm a policeman if one of the traffic wardens, or a police officer, turns up.'

'Do I speak English? Or German?'

'Your German's better than mine, Miss Bloomfield,' he responded with the tiniest of smiles. 'Won't be long.'

He got out into the rain and hurried to the building to take shelter. He remained outside, and quickly fished a packet of his Gauloises out of a pocket. He lit up gratefully, took a deep, satisfying drag, shutting his eyes for long moments in the sheer pleasure of it.

Watching as he urgently smoked the cigarette to the very end, hunched slightly against the sprays of rain that encroached upon his shelter, Carey Bloomfield thought he looked like a teddy bear that had found a big jar of honey.

Pappenheim killed the glowing end with a pinch, put that into the pack, then went in, stuffing the pack into a pocket.

Carey Bloomfield relaxed as she waited for him to return. Every so often, she would idly peer into the wing and rearview mirrors. That was how she spotted the green and white patrol car drawing to a stop behind.

'If you're coming to say I can't park here,' she murmured,

'you're in for a surprise.' As far as she could tell, the driver was the sole occupant.

She watched curiously as the uniformed officer got out and walked purposefully towards the BMW. As if suddenly realizing there was no one behind the wheel, he veered off the road on to the pavement, to approach from the passenger side.

He stopped, knocked sharply on the roof with his left hand and left it there as he leaned forward to peer in. The right hand was on his sidearm.

'*Sie dürfen hier nicht stehen bleiben,*' he said to her in a firm voice as she lowered the window. The rain did not seem to bother him.

Carey Bloomfield decided to use English. 'I'm sorry. Did you just say I can't park here?'

'Yes,' he said briefly in the same language. Then his eyes widened slightly; but it was not in surprise. 'American. Miss Carey Bloomfield?'

Though alerted by this unexpected development, she could not prevent herself from responding in some astonishment.

'Yes?' she replied, the question in her voice meaning many things.

Then she noticed that he had unsnapped the retaining flap of his gun.

'What the . . .' she began.

In Starbucks, Pappenheim had been staring with devotion at a tempting chunk of chocolate cake when, from a corner of his eye, he spotted the police car arriving. He had turned to look with interest, amusing himself with the thought of how Carey Bloomfield would react.

Then he'd frowned. No partner in the car, and the number plate seemed wrong.

He had already decided to go and check, and had watched keenly as the policeman had rested a hand on the BMW.

'Excuse me,' he said to the young woman who'd been serving him. 'I won't be long.'

He was already moving as he saw the officer unsnap the restraining flap. He began to draw his own weapon from beneath his jacket. He moved with a speed that astonished

17

those who had wrongly assumed his 'comfortable' size – as he sometimes liked to describe it – would give him all the alacrity of a snail on valium.

Some of the customers gaped when they saw the gun. The young woman put a hand to her mouth. A customer by the utensil counter, who had been putting sugar into her coffee, dropped the full cup. It smashed explosively, sending sprays of hot coffee in all directions.

Pappenheim was at the door. He flung it open.

The policeman, hearing the noise, darted his head round. When he saw Pappenheim, he moved with astonishing swiftness. He immediately stopped drawing his weapon, pushed himself off the BMW, and ran back to the police car. He got in and, with lights flashing, reversed at speed against the traffic. Cars came to sliding, panicked halts.

The police car swung backwards into the nearest sidestreet. It did a rapid U-turn, and raced away as oncoming traffic parted like the Red Sea to let it through.

Pappenheim, at the BMW, lowered himself to peer anxiously down at Carey Bloomfield.

'Are you alright, Miss Bloomfield?'

'Yes. I'm OK. What the hell was that all about, Pappi?'

He slowly put his gun away, turning his head to peer through the rain, in the direction the police car had gone. He was silent for some moments.

'I'm not sure,' he said quietly as he turned back to her. 'We'll talk in the car. Did you bring your artillery?' he added.

'No. This is not an . . . official visit. You invited me, remember?'

'So I did.' But Pappenheim did not look as if he believed there was nothing 'official' tagging along. 'In there.' He pointed to the glove compartment. 'One of your favourite guns. Beretta 92R. In case he comes back . . .'

'You're authorizing me to shoot a policeman?'

'That,' Pappenheim began with certainty, 'was not a policeman. Now I'm going to finish our order. I've seen some nice chocolate cake.'

'*Chocolate* cake? At this time of the day?'

'Are you saying I'm big?'

'Hey!' she said. 'I can't talk.'

'I think there's a difference between us, Miss Bloomfield. Many women would kill to look like you and . . . Jens likes you the way you are.' Pappenheim paused. 'And if you tell him I said that . . .'

She smiled at him. 'You'll shoot me. I know. Now go get our order, Pappi. You're getting soaked.'

He glanced upwards. 'It's easing off.'

Two

Berlin-Wilmersdorf. Müller had decided that, though his clothes were now virtually dry, he would go home to change anyway.

His home was the penthouse of a classical three-storey building that had been reconstructed in the fifties to its former glory, upon its bombed-out shell. The entire building was his, inherited from his parents. Its three vast floors had been converted by his father – who had inherited the rebuilt family home from *his* father – into huge luxury apartments. The apartments on the lower floors were rented out, each with its own, separate entrance. All apartments shared the underground garage, each with three wide, allocated parking bays.

Müller waited for the steel door at the entrance to roll itself upwards. A bright red light switched to green as the door locked into place. He drove down the gentle slope of the entry ramp and into the spacious parking area, the main lights coming on as he did so. The door began to lower itself and, by the time he had parked next to a Porsche Cayenne that gleamed its newness, the entrance was again secure. Most of the cars in the other bays were sleek BMWs.

Müller got out, locked the car, and left the garage via a solid steel door with a keypad entry lock. As with the access from the street, this was his own private entrance from the garage. Each apartment had the same form of separate access. Only the garage itself remained communal.

A marbled staircase took him upstairs. He entered the high-ceilinged apartment, which boasted a large colonnaded hall with a glistening, polished floor.

He smiled as he entered, suddenly thinking of Carey Bloomfield, and remembering a jumble of her words when she had first seen the place.

If I ate off this floor, it would get sick. Do you cook? You can't have a kitchen like this and not cook. You do! Good. I hate guys like you. I can't boil water . . .

He smiled again to himself. 'Miss Bloomfield, you are an original.'

He went into his bedroom and quickly changed; then he got out his mobile, and decided to call Pappenheim.

Pappenheim brought the car to a halt on a short, wide avenue, not far from the left wing of the Bundestag, on their right. To their left was the glass-rich structure of the Paul Lobe building.

'Are you supposed to park here?' Carey Bloomfield asked.

'I'm a policeman,' he replied. 'I'm conducting an investigation.'

'Yeah. Right.' Carey Bloomfield peered out. It was still raining heavily. 'Still raining, Pappi. And it's not getting brighter.'

'So, who said I was a weatherman?'

'Didn't you grow up on a farm?'

'That was a long time ago. And anyway, the weather people get it wrong all the time.' He looked at the package on her lap. 'Time to eat,' he added with undisguised anticipation.

'Did you stop by that place just for me? Or for you?'

'I cannot tell a lie. I would almost kill for their chocolate cake.'

She smiled at him. 'Müller goes for Black Forest cake, and you like chocolate. As I've said, you two are a pair of something. Coffee smells pretty good, though.' She handed over the package. 'Enjoy.'

'There's one for you too,' he said, taking it. He opened it, and began to pass her coffee and cake over.

'Early for cake,' she said, 'but what the hell.' She glanced over to her right, at a long queue of people waiting on the steps of the parliament building. 'They must be nuts, standing in line in this rain.'

'All waiting to go in to see the glass dome,' he said. 'They come from all over, in all weathers. The chancellor's cube is just behind us, to the left.'

'Better them than me.' She took a sip of the still-hot coffee. 'Mmm. That's good.' She peered through the drenched windscreen. 'The Spree is just out front, right?'

'It is. A river runs through the government buildings,' Pappenheim added with dry humour. 'Want to see?'

'In *this* stuff? The Spree can stay where it is. I don't go to the mountain, and the mountain does not come to me. Besides, someone said I could leave my coat.'

'Someone did,' Pappenheim confirmed with a straight face. He bit into the rich chocolate cake with obvious pleasure.

'When your mouth's not full, Pappi,' Carey Bloomfield said, 'you can start telling me what the hell's going on, and why that policeman tried to shoot me. And don't forget, he actually addressed me by name.'

'That creature was not a policeman,' Pappenheim reminded her, eating through his words. 'His car had the Berlin index letter, but the numbers seemed wrong. Good enough to pass first and second glances, though. That means good organization, and access. And he knew your name. Considering you just got here, it makes things . . .' He continued eating.

'It makes things what?'

'More exciting.'

'More exciting,' Carey Bloomfield repeated. 'Great. I nearly get blown away by a wannabe cop and you say—'

The sound of a mobile phone interrupted her.

Pappenheim paused in the middle of a second bite of cake. 'Yours?'

'It's coming from your direction, Pappi.'

'Ah. Of course. Mine. Must be Jens.'

'How do you know?'

'Very few people have this number. I would not be insane enough to give it to Kaltendorf. But it's Jens. He will have tried my office first.'

Pappenheim put the cake down with a sigh, and got out the mobile. 'Yes, Jens.'

'Where are you?' Müller's voice said in his ear. 'I just tried your office.'

'Having some coffee and cake.' Pappenheim gave Carey Bloomfield a glance that said, told you.

'*Cake?* At this time of the day?'

'Don't you start.'

'Somebody told you already?'

'My. We are sharp this early in the day. "Somebody" told me, and "somebody's" having cake too. Chocolate.'

'It's early for your riddles, Pappi.'

'So . . .' Pappenheim went on, 'what pleasures await me with this call?'

'The contact was helpful.'

'Ah.'

'I'm going to check something out in Kreuzberg.'

'I think you should come back to the office,' Pappenheim advised.

'Why? The Great White throwing one of his fits?'

'Haven't seen him as yet today, thank God.'

'Then . . .'

'Hang on. Someone you should speak with.' Pappenheim handed the mobile over to a startled Carey Bloomfield.

She took the phone and stared at it, while Pappenheim made urging motions at her.

'Hello, Müller,' she said into the phone.

Pappenheim gave a little smile and went back to the serious business of finishing his cake.

A silence from the other end greeted Carey Bloomfield.

'Miss Bloomfield,' Müller said at last. 'I was just thinking about you.'

'All good, I hope.'

He ducked the remark. 'This is unexpected.'

'I had some free time. Why not see my two pals in Berlin, I thought.'

'You miss us?'

'That's a way of putting it.'

'Nothing . . . official?'

'Nothing official.'

'Can I believe that?'

'Of course.'

'I'll take that under advisement, as you would say.'

'I never say that. That's attorney-speak.'

There was another silence.

'I won't be long,' Müller said. 'Do you have somewhere to stay?'

'Is that an offer?'

'If you have nowhere to stay.'

'I'm checked into a hotel, but I can uncheck. You still got your Hammonds?'

'Naturally.'

'Here's the deal . . . I'll take you up on your offer, if you play one piece for me.'

'That's almost like the family thing we both remember from childhood, and hate. You know . . . play your recorder for grandmother . . .'

'I know. But that's the deal.' She was smiling.

Pappenheim finished his cake and raised an eyebrow at her.

'I'll take that under advisement,' Müller said. 'Can you hand Pappi back, please? Good to know you're in town.'

'Sure,' she said, meaning both. She handed the phone back.

'Something she hasn't told you,' Pappenheim said into the phone.

'Which is?'

'A fake colleague tried to shoot her.'

'*What?*'

'Thought that would get your juices flowing. So? The office? Or Kreuzberg?'

'The office.' Müller ended the call.

Pappenheim put the phone away, and turned to Carey Bloomfield. 'You two should get married. You behave like a couple already.'

'I don't marry unless I'm asked.'

'You've been asked before?'

'Yep.'

'And?'

'I said no . . . each time. I'm very picky.'

'*Each* time? How many?'

'Three. Maybe four. Suddenly you're a matchmaker, Pappi?'

Pappenheim smiled again, and started the car.

'It looks as if we won't have time for our private talk, after all,' he said to her as he slowly drove to where he could turn round. 'And, as you have explained your presence here so well, I don't have to think of a believable excuse to give to Jens.' He gave a smile that was one of relief. 'He never told me, until last May, that he'd learned about the death of his parents.'

She stared at him. 'He took all that time before telling you?'

'He wanted to sort it out within himself first. I can understand that. Not an easy thing with which to come to terms.'

'I was with him on Rügen when he found out from the dying Russian, Rachko. I really thought he would tell you.'

'As I've said . . . I can understand his reasons. After all, I had a guilty secret of my own that I'd kept from him.'

'Oh?'

'It was about the time we had flooding in the east . . .'

'The Romeo Six case.'

Pappenheim nodded as he turned the car round and headed back the way they had come.

'When it was all over – the Romeo Six thing and the kidnap of Kaltendorf's secret daughter—'

'The beautiful Solange, who was seventeen-going-on-eighteen at the time . . .'

'You say her name with teeth,' Pappenheim remarked, a little slyly.

'She has a thing about Müller.'

'She's just a child with a bad case of hero worship.'

'She's not a child anymore. She's a woman. Trust me.'

Pappenheim grinned, but made no comment about that. 'And you and Jens went down to the south of France,' he continued. 'My dark secret was that I intercepted a note to Jens while you two were down there. No sender, and just a simple message. "You may think you have won, Müller. But you haven't. Your father was Romeo Six." A direct quote.'

'*Jesus!*'

'I sat on it for a long time. I confessed after he told me about what he'd found out on Rügen. All things considered, he was very good about it. I think he was feeling a little guilty about not telling me what Rachko had said. I'll give you a quick background picture on the way,' Pappenheim went on, 'about what we've found out since then. Many . . . let's say . . . exciting things . . .'

'Exciting?'

'As in interesting, and blood-chilling. Some of it concerns you.'

'*Me?*'

'Oh yes. It will also explain why that fake policeman tried to take you out. Jens will fill in the details.'

She was again staring at him.

'Finish your coffee,' Pappenheim said.

Müller put his phone away, frowning.

Carey Bloomfield had barely arrived in Berlin and already, someone had tried to kill her.

'She'll have to stay here,' he said to himself. 'It's secure.'

Which was true enough. The massive wooden door at the street entrance was reinforced within by two full-sized sheets of steel, each ten millimetres thick. Its immovable handle, with splayed ends, was welded between the steel inlays. Infrared and movement sensors guarded the entire building. The management company – under contract from Müller and not far away – had a landline connection with monitors in their offices, which were manned twenty-four hours a day. They also had a direct connection to Müller himself.

He went into the large, almost empty room that served as his study. The two pristine Hammond drawbar organs, lids down, were highly polished islands in the vast space. One was a tonewheel B3, the other its electronic twin, the XB3. Each had a full pedal keyboard. On one wall were just two portraits: of his father, and of his mother. There were no other pictures in the room.

'She wants me to play for her,' he said to the portraits. 'Apart from the two of you, I don't normally play for anyone. But I think, this time, I'll make an exception.'

In shirtsleeves, with shoulder harness on and the Beretta in its holster, he stood with legs slightly apart, hands in pockets.

'I'm getting closer,' he went on, 'and they don't like it. They're under pressure, and are beginning to react more aggressively. They shot Pappi in May. They could not have known that he would have decided on impulse that night to wear body armour. They were trying to get to me, via Pappi.

'Today, they tried to kill Carey.' A small, reflective smile lived briefly upon Müller's face. 'She came into my life unexpectedly, and was not particularly welcome. Now . . .' He paused. 'She's becoming part of it. Won't tell her that, of course.'

The smile flitted on again, as he went out.

They were just passing the chancellor's residence, when Pappenheim's mobile rang. He pulled in to the side of the road, and stopped. A car honked in annoyance as it went past.

'Go play with yourself,' Pappenheim said with a scowl.

'Pappi!' Carey Bloomfield admonished.

'He should have been more alert,' Pappenheim grumbled as he fished out the mobile. 'Must be Berger,' he added, putting the phone to an ear. 'Yes?'

'Boss? Where are you?'

'Why are you whispering, Berger?'

Silence greeted this.

'I understand,' Pappenheim said to her.

'Better come back,' Berger whispered.

'On my way.'

They ended their brief conversation.

'Kaltendorf,' Pappenheim said to Carey Bloomfield, as he put the phone away.

'How do you know?'

'Berger was whispering,' he replied, driving off. 'That meant he was prowling around. I did hear something, after all, when we were leaving. We must have missed him by seconds.'

'How are you going to explain me?'

'We met . . . umm . . . in the street. You were on your way to us.'

'Berger's seen me. That young guy in the elevator, and the guy on the front desk . . .'

'The duty sergeant and Berger won't talk. Berger would rather have her teeth pulled without anaesthetic.'

'Urrgh! Solidarity with me, despite everything?'

'Solidarity with Jens,' Pappenheim corrected, 'and with me. No offence.'

'None taken.'

'As for Hammersfeldt, Kaltendorf won't lower himself to ask a mere sergeant in the assault team, even if he imagined Hammersfeldt might have seen me. Now for that background information I promised you.'

Berger put her phone away as she hurried along the corridor, and turned the corner towards the sergeants' office.

She found an impatient Kaltendorf waiting.

'Well, *Obermeisterin* Berger?' he demanded. 'Is he back in that cesspit he calls an office?'

'Not yet, sir.'

'Not yet, sir! Not yet, sir! That's all I ever get. Müller out on some errand of his choosing; Pappenheim smoking himself to death God knows where . . .' Kaltendorf stopped abruptly, as if suddenly realizing he was moaning to a roomful of sergeants.

He glared at Berger. 'I want them both, in my office!'

'Yes, sir.'

With a final glare, Kaltendorf stomped out.

She waited until the marching slam of the pounding footsteps had faded, before letting out a weary sigh.

'Just what I really wanted on a day like this.'

Klemp, in his thirties, a senior sergeant with a weightlifter's physique and a dangerously receding hairline, drew out a tabloid he had been reading before Kaltendorf's sudden arrival. The paper was noted more for its girlie shots than news content.

'Feeling the withdrawal, were you, Klemp?' Berger said as she moved to her desk.

Klemp grinned at her. 'Can't get through to me, Berger.'

'I know. I would need a rock drill.'

Klemp grinned again, said nothing in response, and began to give serious attention to his paper.

She glanced at her partner, Reimer, who sat at his desk with a glum expression. 'Reimer, you look worse than the day outside. What is it this time?'

Klemp looked up. 'One guess.'

'I asked Reimer, Klemp. Go back to your plastic-surgeon's fantasies.'

Klemp ducked back behind his paper.

'Come on, Reimer,' Berger urged. 'What is it?'

'It's the usual,' Klemp said, without looking up.

'Shut up, Klemp. I asked Reimer.'

'I'm the senior sergeant,' Klemp began in protest, again looking up. 'You can't talk to me like that.'

Berger said nothing, and gave the paper a pointed stare. Klemp went back to his bikini-gazing.

'So, Johann?' she went on to Reimer. 'What's eating at you?'

'Whatever it is,' Klemp said from behind his paper, 'don't make it sick.'

'Shut up, Klemp!' Berger and Reimer said together.

Klemp smirked.

'It's Nina . . .' Reimer began eventually.

'I knew it!' Klemp could not avoid saying. 'It really hurts to see a good cop like you turn to jelly like this, Johann. Dump her, for God's sake, and give us some peace!' He snapped his paper open, as if to emphasize the point.

Both Reimer and Berger ignored him.

'She's on this diet thing,' Reimer went on, accompanied by a smirking noise from Klemp.

Berger glared in his direction, but Klemp studiously kept his attention on whatever he was looking at.

'Makes you blind,' Berger said to Klemp, who made another smirking noise, but did not otherwise respond. 'Go on, Johann.'

'I think she's influenced by her mother, who's got hold of some stupid diet plan and has convinced Nina it's a good thing. I mean, Nina was . . . was like you, you know . . .'

'Watch what you say, Reimer,' Berger warned.

'Um, what I mean is, she was . . .' Reimer looked at Berger closely. 'Well, you know . . . womanly . . .' He started to draw a shape in the air with his hands, then thought better of it.

Klemp could not resist a peek. 'Careful, Berger,' he said. 'You two are partners. You don't want Reimer having the wrong thoughts when you're out there on a job, do you?'

'I know where your thoughts are, Klemp,' Berger said coldly. 'Go on, Johann.'

'Well . . . she's got . . . you know . . . thin. I'm really worried. If she fell against a cupboard, she'd sound like a snaredrum solo . . .'

Klemp guffawed. 'Go rattle those bones!'

Reimer gave him a hard look. 'It's not a joke, Klemp. She's really ill . . . but doesn't seem to know it. I've tried talking to her . . .'

'She needs a doctor,' Klemp said.

'For once,' Berger said to Reimer, 'much as I hate to admit it, Klemp could be right.'

'I'll take the bows later,' Klemp said from behind his paper.

Berger was dismissive. 'You wish. Johann,' she went on to Reimer, 'if your Nina has gone that far, she's in trouble . . .'

'And *you're* in trouble,' Klemp put in to Reimer. 'If she looks like walking broomstick, where's the fun in—?'

'Shut up, Klemp!' Reimer and Berger snarled at him.

'Why?' a mild voice enquired. 'What has he said?'

Berger and Reimer's heads snapped round. Klemp hurriedly tried to put his paper away.

'Chief!' Berger said with a bright smile. 'Didn't hear you . . .'

'I can be as quiet as a mouse when need be,' Pappenheim said to her, but he was looking at Klemp. 'Make you blind, Klemp, reading that stuff.'

'Er . . .' Klemp began, stuffing the tabloid into a desk drawer. He cleared his throat, and fell silent.

All three sergeants looked neutrally at Carey Bloomfield, who was standing just behind Pappenheim.

Pappenheim made no introductions.

'Is he in his office?' he asked Berger.

Berger knew he was talking about Müller. 'Not yet, Chief,' she answered.

'And the Herr *Direktor*?'

'He wants to see you both in *his* office.'

'I see,' Pappenheim said. It could have meant anything. 'We'll be in the *Hauptkommissar*'s office.'

'Yes, Chief.'

Pappenheim's baby-blue eyes raked Klemp. 'Don't let me spoil your reading, *Hauptmeister* Klemp. Privileges of your new promotion.'

Klemp swallowed, and said nothing.

As Pappenheim moved on with Carey Bloomfield, Reimer whispered to Berger, 'What's the CIA princess doing here?'

He was startled to see Carey Bloomfield back at the door. 'I'm not CIA,' she said to him in perfect German. 'I have a hard time explaining that.'

She smiled at him, then went off after Pappenheim.

'Shit!' Reimer said, after she had gone. 'How could she have heard?'

'It's the stuff they feed them over there,' Berger remarked.

'Ouch,' Klemp said.

'Don't mind Reimer,' Pappenheim said as they approached Müller's office.

'I won't,' Carey Bloomfield assured him. 'They're jealous of their territory. I can understand that.'

They paused at the door. Pappenheim knocked. There was no reply.

'Looks as if we'll have to wait,' he said, opening the door. 'Umm, look . . .' he went on, then paused.

'It's OK, Pappi,' she told him, knowing exactly what was coming next. 'Go have your smoke. I can wait here.'

His relief was unashamed. 'You don't mind?'

'Nope.'

'I won't be long.'

'No hurry. Take your time.'

A tiny, sheepish smile touched his features as he allowed her to enter. 'Thanks. Er . . . don't touch anything.'

'I won't.'

He pulled the door to, but did not shut it. He hurried back to his office, at something perilously close to a run.

'Pappi, Pappi,' Carey Bloomfield said to herself with an amused expression as she walked further into the large, sparklingly clean office.

Furniture – clearly not standard issue – was kept to a bare

minimum, storage units and the narrow wardrobe almost vanishing into the walls. The impression was of vast space.

She looked about her. 'If dirt got in here, it would die of fright.' She went up to the huge desk that dominated the room, and wiped an exploratory finger upon it. 'This isn't really touching. As I thought,' she continued, inspecting the finger. 'Dirt's been frightened away.'

There was not even a trace to mark the passing of her finger on the gleaming surface.

'If I licked it, I'd poison it.'

She studied the familiar model of the Hammond B3, seemingly in pride of place on the desk. The only other items there were two telephones: one red, one black.

'You're playing for me tonight, mister,' she said. 'You promised.'

The desk faced a wide window that gave an almost panoramic view of the city. On the wall next to the window was a large, mounted silkscreen.

Continuing to prowl, she went over to the silkscreen that was now hung in place of paintings she had seen there before.

'So, what's the choice this time, Müller? We've had Mondrian, Monet, Matisse . . . What's the mood this time?'

She stood, feet close together, hands in the back pockets of her jeans, behind slightly stuck out as she stretched briefly.

'Venet,' she remarked. '"Indeterminate Line II,"' she went on, translating from the French. 'Not sure where you're headed, Müller?'

'Life is a series of indeterminate lines,' came his voice from the doorway.

She jumped, whipped her hands out of the pockets and straightened self-consciously.

'Jesus, Müller! Can't you knock?'

'Er . . . it's my office.'

'So it is.' She gave him a watchful little smile that said she was pleased to see him, but with a hint of uncertainty.

Pappenheim blew a long stream of happy smoke at the ceiling, picked up a phone, and made a call.

'Ah, Hermann,' he greeted, as the other person answered. 'How are things in Thessaloniki?'

Hermann Spyros, a *Kommissar*, was head of the unit's electronics section.

'Pappi! Nice of you to ask. But I know you did not really call to ask about my eastern-Mediterranean relatives back there in the land that created democracy. You want to kidnap my genius goth again.'

'How well you know me, Hermann.'

'It so happens we're having a relatively quiet time, so she's at your service. And, even if we did have a busy time, I'm assuming she'd still have to be at your service.'

'How well you know me,' Pappenheim repeated.

Spyros gave a brief chuckle. 'If electronics wizardry translated into fast promotion, she'd be my boss. That kid is unbelievable.'

'I know it. I suppose I shouldn't ask about the German half of the family in Hamburg?'

'Ach,' Spyros said. 'Don't ask. The goth's picking up her phone. Here she is.'

'Sir?' Pappenheim heard.

'Ah, Miss Meyer . . .'

'I'm glad you called.'

'You are?'

'I have an idea, and I wanted to see you about it.'

'Well. Good thing I did call. Come on up. Meet me at the documents room.'

'Yes, sir.'

'Good to see you,' Müller said as he came further into the room. He stopped, a few feet from her.

'You too,' she said.

They looked at each other warily, as if afraid to say more.

'I saw Pappi on the way in,' Müller said. 'He told me you're a lieutenant-colonel now. Big promotion.'

'You know how it is. Sometimes, they chuck these things around. What they giveth, they can taketh away.'

'The way it is.'

'Yes. So, Müller,' Carey Bloomfield went on. 'Are we going to dance around all day? Or will you say hi properly?'

He seemed unsure of what she meant.

'Damn it, Müller!' she continued in mild exasperation. 'A brief hug is OK!'

She was about to approach him, arms beginning to open, when the pounding heels of marching footsteps were heard, distantly at first, then with increasing volume as they grew closer.

'The patter of tiny feet,' Müller said. 'My master's footsteps, I think.'

'Saved by the bell,' Carey Bloomfield commented drily, arms falling back to her sides.

He gave her a look of mild amusement as the pounding reached a crescendo and halted. A knock which was more like a banging thump interrupted what he'd been about to say. This was immediately followed by the door being flung open.

'*Müller . . . !*' Kaltendorf began.

The words died as if switched off. Kaltendorf stared at Carey Bloomfield and went into the fastest transformation Müller had ever witnessed. Coldly outraged eyes were suddenly full of warmth. He beamed. He fawned. He floated into the room, it seemed, on amazingly silent heels. He was almost on his knees with bonhomie.

'Miss Bloomfield!' he exclaimed with open delight, in English. 'How good to see you!' Hand outstretched, eager for the handshake.

Carey Bloomfield allowed him to grab her hand to shake it warmly. 'Director Kaltendorf.'

'When did you get here?' Kaltendorf asked, continuing to beam.

'Minutes ago. As I was in town, I thought I'd look up some old friends.'

'Good of you to count us among your friends.'

Müller listened to this with a neutral expression.

'Are we co-operating on a case?' Kaltendorf went on, clearly hoping this was so.

'Not a case, Director Kaltendorf,' Carey Bloomfield began to explain. 'This is not an official visit. I've got some time off, and I thought . . .'

'Why not see your friends in Berlin. Excellent! You'll be in good hands with Müller. Remember that very first meeting?'

'I do,' she remarked sweetly, glancing at Müller, who was determinedly hanging on to his neutral expression.

'Well, then,' Kaltendorf said, as if he had just presented a gift. 'I'll leave you two to it. Just looking in,' he added to Müller.

'On the way here, I spoke with Pappenheim, sir,' Müller began. 'He said you wanted to see us in your office.'

Kaltendorf was affability itself. 'No hurry. You attend to Miss Bloomfield. Enjoy your stay, Miss Bloomfield.'

'Thank you, Director. I will.'

Kaltendorf gave a little nod, and went out. He closed the door quietly behind him.

They waited until the sound of Kaltendorf's footsteps had faded for a good few seconds, before speaking.

'Did I just miss something?' Carey Bloomfield asked. 'Or was he really coming in here to bawl you out?'

'He was coming in here to bawl me out.'

'Suddenly he's sweetness and light because of me?'

'It would seem like it.'

'Saved your butt again, Müller.'

He gave her a tiny smile. 'It would seem like it.'

'What about mine?'

'Do you want a personal answer? Or a professional one?'

'Oh ho! Müller being *risqué*! Be careful. You're straying off the narrow path. The professional one will do for now.'

'If you mean that police impersonator, next time he won't be dressed as one. And yes, I'll do my best to save your butt.'

'That's a relief. Pappi has given me a background picture of what's been happening,' she went on before he could make comment, 'since I last saw you. All of that true?'

'It's true.'

She studied him closely. 'Can't leave you alone for a minute. You're always in trouble, Müller.'

'My curse.'

'Pappi said they're trying to get to you by hitting people close to you. Am I close to you, Müller?'

'I—'

The direct phone to Pappenheim rang.

'Saved by the bell again,' Carey Bloomfield said.

'Behave,' Müller said as he went to the phone and picked it up. 'Yes, Pappi.'

'We're in the rogues' gallery . . .'

'We?'

'The goth and I. You should come. Oh. And our guest. She's in this now.'

'On our way. The Great White just visited,' Müller added.

'I can't wait.'

'He was sweetness itself.'

'Are you on something?'

'It's the truth. He saw Miss Bloomfield and turned into a puppy. We're not to go to the headmaster's study just yet.'

'Oh, small mercies. Looks like she's good for you, after all.'

'I can hear something in there, but I'll ignore it.'

Pappenheim chuckled. 'You can run, but you can't hide.'

'Thank you for the witticism, Pappi.'

'Ah, those big words,' Pappenheim said. 'How I love them.'

'Pappi's in the rogues' gallery with the goth,' Müller said to Carey Bloomfield as he put the phone down. 'Something there he thinks we should see.'

'The goth,' she said. 'Hedi Meyer. Tall, ethereal. Fragile-looking . . . as if. Loves to dress in any colour, as long as it's black; paints her fingernails in a way that would make the Surrealists weep for joy; can disarm tiny electronically primed bombs attached to people . . . and has a fancy for you.'

'All correct . . . except that last part.'

'You wish,' she said.

He gave her a tolerant smile. 'Get your coat. After the gallery, we're going out. The weather does not look as if it wants to stop its end-of-the-world show today.'

'Too early for lunch, and I've had coffee and cake with Pappi. So, where to?'

'Hunting out another part of the mystery, to which the man who wanted to shoot you today belongs.'

'I'd like to shoot *him*. Lowlife bastard.'

'Did you bring your cannon?'

'You heard me, Müller. This is a strictly private trip.'

'Ah well. If you behave, I'll make certain you're not unarmed.'

'Gee, mister. Thanks!'

Müller gave her his tolerant look, as she got her coat.

Kaltendorf's beam had morphed into a benign smile as he entered his office. People he had passed in the corridors, more accustomed to his preoccupied scowl – which was just one down from the glaring scowl – had shot him darting, uncertain glances, as if doubting their own vision.

The phone began to ring almost before he had entered. He hurried to it, and picked it up.

'Ah, Heinz,' the person at the other end said, even before Kaltendorf had identified himself. 'Do you have any visitors?'

'I don't quite follow.'

'Simple enough question, Heinz.'

'We have visitors all the time. Colleagues from other units, prominent officials—'

'Yes, yes. I know. I mean special visitors.'

'We haven't had any . . .' Kaltendorf paused.

'Yes?' The voice sounded eager.

'I would not say special as such . . .'

'Let me be the judge of that.'

'Well . . .' Kaltendorf began uncertainly, 'a friend of ours has turned up . . .'

'A friend?'

'She's . . .'

'*She?*'

'Well, yes. That's why I didn't think you would mean . . .'

'You let me judge,' the voice repeated. 'So, who is she?'

'Miss Bloomfield. American. I'm sure you don't mean—'

'No, no. Alright, Heinz. Thank you. Sorry to disturb.'

The line went dead.

'How long were you really standing by the door while I was looking at the painting?' Carey Bloomfield asked.

They were on their way to the rogues' gallery.

Müller glanced at her with a slight frown. 'Why?'

36

'Were you looking at my butt?'

'Of course not!'

'Why not? My butt that bad?'

Müller shut his eyes briefly as they approached the solid, black, armoured-steel door of the documents room, with its keypad-operated locking system.

'You, Miss Bloomfield, are dangerous.'

Above the numbers on the keypad was a tiny green light; a clear indication that the room was occupied. This tell-tale sign could be disabled from within the room itself, if need be. Müller and Pappenheim frequently did so, when they did not want Kaltendorf to know they were in there.

'Believe it,' she said, the tiniest of smiles living briefly at the corners of her mouth.

Müller shook his head slowly, but said nothing as he tapped in the entry code. Titanium bolts slid back with a silky hiss and the door popped open, then swung wide. He stood aside for her to enter, and followed her in as the door began to swing back. He gave it a little push to help it on its way.

Bright lighting and the low hum of the air-conditioning greeted them, as the door hissed itself shut.

Three

Pappenheim and Hedi Meyer were waiting.

The windowless, large room was the most secure area in the entire building, and only three people had free access: Müller, Pappenheim, and Kaltendorf. Every wall save one, from floor to ceiling, was lined with wide, steel cabinets, each with its own keypad. A tall, wheeled ladder, which hung from a solid rail and had a two-ton breaking limit, could be slid to each cabinet in the room. The centrepiece of the room was a wide and solidly built central table, with a white top that also served as a photographic light box.

At the single wall without a cabinet was a big desk with a

computer on it. Already very powerful, it had been improved far beyond its original specifications by Hedi Meyer – a power junkie when it came to computers – who had seemingly locked herself into a continuing upgrade cycle. She was always tinkering with it. The goth had already made it the most powerful computer in the entire building, beating even those in her own department.

On either side of the keyboard were two items that had made Kaltendorf blow some fuses when he had first seen them: a joystick and throttle that seemed to have come out of an F-16 jet fighter, courtesy of the goth herself.

The computer, with its large plasma-screen monitor, was connected to a cinema-quality, multi-speaker sound system. Hedi Meyer was at the machine, sitting in the high-backed leather chair. Pappenheim stood close by.

Both looked round as Müller and Carey Bloomfield entered.

Hedi Meyer was the first to speak. 'Congratulations, Colonel,' she said to Carey Bloomfield. 'Nice to see you again.'

She had the ethereal paleness of complexion that Carey Bloomfield had described, a finely sculpted classic face, and rich dark hair that owed nothing to the hairdresser's skill with dyes. Her eyes were a vivid blue, and her paleness contrasted sharply with Carey Bloomfield's glow of health.

'Thank you,' Carey Bloomfield said, giving the goth a quizzical look.

'*Oberkommissar* Pappenheim told me,' the goth explained.
'Ah.'

'Miss Meyer,' Müller said, glancing at her hands, 'you've got green fingernails and blue eyeshadow today.'

'Back in my fertile period,' she said, displaying the bright-green nails for all to see.

'Your . . . fertile period. Doesn't that conflict with the –' he tapped at his right eyelid – 'blue?'

'Not at all. Blue stands for calmness and control. Can't get too carried away. And, besides, it matches my eyes.' She turned back to the computer.

'You've been warned,' Carey Bloomfield whispered to Müller.

'I heard that, Colonel,' Hedi Meyer said, not looking round. She paused. 'I enjoy working with you.'

'Now why does that sound like a warning?'

'I never warn,' Hedi Meyer said.

'Ladies,' Pappenheim soothed.

'But I—' Carey Bloomfield began.

'Ah-ah!' Müller interrupted, holding a finger briefly to his lips. He and Pappenheim glanced at each other with faint and very brief, surreptitious smiles, as he continued, 'For some time now, we have been building a database – low-level intelligence – gathered from, believe it or not, old newspapers and magazines. We all brought in the sort of things one never throws away, despite meaning to. Hedi Meyer beat us all with some quite incredible stuff she's had since childhood. Even Klemp, our resident gym addict, had valuable material. It is quite incredible what you can find in a newspaper or magazine, if you know where to look.'

Carey Bloomfield nodded. 'I know some people who've got whole departments dedicated to trawling through the world's news, print, and any other kind of media.'

'I can imagine. No prizes for guessing.'

'And I can imagine what you're hunting. No prizes for that, either.'

'Indeed. Miss Meyer,' he went on, 'what have you found?'

She was checking through the archives of a French newspaper. 'I'll bring it onscreen in a moment.'

He peered at the name of the paper. '*La Souris Atrichque*. The Naked *Mouse*? Is this a joke? A school rag?'

'No joke,' the goth said, continuing to tap furiously at the keyboard without pause. 'No rag, either, sir . . . as you'll see.'

'Did they know you went in there? Whoever they are?'

'Of course not.'

'Of course.' Müller glanced at Pappenheim, who had one of his most innocent of smiles tacked on.

The goth had stopped her tapping. 'There it is, sir,' she said to Müller.

He studied the page on the screen, and stared at the date. '1982,' he said, almost in a whisper. 'Grenoble. I was twelve. How did you get to this?'

'I don't think you want to know, sir. But read this.' She highlighted a section of the text, and increased the font size.

Müller began to read silently, then stopped, shocked. He continued to read, this time audibly.

'" . . . and why have we been given the wrong site of the crash? Witnesses we have spoken to confirm that the German private jet crashed elsewhere. They insist the real crash site is . . . "' Müller stopped again. 'My God!' he said, almost to himself. He moved away to stand by the lightbox table, then leaned against it. 'My God!' he repeated, staring at nothing, and at no one in particular.

The goth stared at the computer, unmoving.

Carey Bloomfield looked at Müller anxiously. She caught Pappenheim's eye. Pappenheim gave a barely perceptible shake of the head, advising her to leave Müller alone.

Then Müller took a deep breath, and returned to stand behind the goth.

'Alright, Hedi,' he began. 'Can you call up a map of the Grenoble area, and expand the site they mention?'

'No problem.' She had it onscreen in seconds.

Müller stared at the image. 'Can you give me a topographical view? I want to see what kind of terrain . . .'

She was doing it even as he spoke. 'There,' she said. 'Three-D.'

'Hmm,' he said. 'One can drive quite close to it . . . about a kilometre's walk away. Good. So, what is this *Naked Mouse*? How did you come by it?'

'You were right in one sense, sir. The paper began as a school rag. Two friends used it to poke fun at the school authorities. But they also began to do some serious investigating. They actually got a teacher sacked for creative accounting . . . with his budget.'

'Bet that made them popular,' Pappenheim said.

'It didn't,' Hedi Meyer confirmed. 'They nearly got thrown out, but their academic results were so good, it would have raised even more embarrassing questions.'

'So, they took their skills into the outside world, and annoyed the establishment instead,' Müller said.

'Exactly, sir. They got into plenty of trouble, but the paper got so successful, they had a big support base. Lawyers defended them for free.'

40

'Lawyers working for nothing,' Carey Bloomfield put in. 'That's something.'

'They're not American lawyers,' the goth remarked mildly.

'Oh wow!' Carey Bloomfield exclaimed. 'Did you see that arrow go by, Müller?'

'Goth?' Müller said to Hedi Meyer.

'Sir?'

'Behave.'

'Just joking.'

'Oh yeah,' Carey Bloomfield said.

'You too,' Müller told her. 'Go on, Hedi.'

'A friend of mine – he's a bit Left – collects old issues of the *Mouse*. I asked to borrow some 1982 issues. You'd think I was pulling his teeth with pliers. I almost had to insure my life, but he allowed me to take them on loan. I scanned them in, but couldn't find anything. So I . . . mmm . . . got into a database . . .'

'You "got into a database". That's the part I don't want to know about.'

She nodded. 'That's the part.'

'Alright, then. Fast forward.'

'It seems that the friends – despite being successful executives of the paper – decided to go back to what they loved doing best: investigating. They discovered discrepancies in the reports about the crash site.'

'Where are they now? Is the paper still running?'

'That's the strange thing, sir. Less than a year later, the paper went out of business . . .'

'It *folded*?'

'Yes, sir. But it gets stranger. One of them is dead. I can't find out exactly how it happened; nor what has happened to the other one. Can't say whether he's still alive, or dead too. Nothing I have dug into has come up with an answer. So far.'

'The paper had staff. What happened to them?'

'Working for other people, and not talking.'

Müller said nothing for some moments.

Pappenheim, hands in pockets, studied him watchfully.

Carey Bloomfield said, 'You're driving down to Grenoble.'

'Most definitely.'

41

'I'll come.'

'You don't have to . . .'

'I know I don't have to. It's an offer you won't refuse.'

Müller said nothing to that.

'What were the names of those schoolfriends?' he asked the goth.

'Roger Montville, and Jean-Marc Lavaliere.'

Müller repeated the names to himself, then nodded, as if in confirmation of something. 'That was excellent investigative work, Hedi. Thank you.'

She swivelled the chair round to look at him. 'No problem. Is there anything else you need? I've got to get back to my office. I'm upgrading one of our machines. Should get it done before the end of the day.'

'No. Nothing else for now. And thanks again.'

She gave him a warm smile, then turned back to the machine.

'I'll keep working on the stuff in here, of course,' she continued as she began to shut it down.

'Of course.'

'And I can fly my jet?' She pointed to the joystick.

'That was the deal.'

The computer gave a soft click, and shut down.

'That's it,' the goth said, rising to her feet. 'Better get back before *Kommissar* Spyros sends out a search party.'

'As ever, we'll defend you,' Pappenheim said.

'Then he hasn't a chance.' Hedi Meyer looked at Carey Bloomfield, startling blue eyes hiding everything. 'Nice working with you again, Colonel.'

'You too,' Carey Bloomfield said.

'Sirs,' the goth said to Müller and Pappenheim, and went out.

Carey Bloomfield looked on as the door sighed itself shut. 'Now, why did that sound like a challenge?'

'She's just being playful,' Pappenheim said. 'I'll take a leaf out of the goth's book and leave you children alone. You have plenty to discuss. And—'

'And you need your smoke,' Carey Bloomfield finished for him.

'And I do need my smoke. And you, sir, Boss?' Pappenheim

went on to Müller. 'As you're going to Grenoble, am I supposed to know?'

'For the moment, no.'

'Fine. I'll talk to a French colleague down there. He's very helpful. Keep unwanted people off your back.'

Carey Bloomfield looked at Pappenheim in wonder. 'Pappi, if I wanted to go to Vladivostok, would you have a contact there too?'

'Take a little time, but I could probably arrange it. Might not be strictly legal, though. Hard to tell, these days.'

'Pappi, with your kind of network, you could probably run a not strictly legal organization yourself.'

'Why do you think I'm a policeman? It's to avoid the temptation.'

'Yeah. Sure.'

'*Au 'voir*, children,' Pappenheim said. 'Have fun.'

'*French?*' Müller said.

'You're going to France,' Pappenheim responded, as if that explained it all. He went to the door, and paused. 'I'd disable the green light, if I were you. I'll keep in touch.'

Müller nodded. 'Alright. He means the one on the keypad outside,' he added to Carey Bloomfield after Pappenheim had gone. 'When it's on, it lets people know someone's inside.'

'People like Kaltendorf.'

'There's a needle going on,' Carey Bloomfield said.

'A needle?'

'Well, there's Miss Hawk Eyes . . .'

'Berger.'

'Berger. She—'

'Does not like you. You think.'

'I know,' Carey Bloomfield corrected. 'Then there's that partner of hers . . .'

'Reimer.'

'That's him. He called me a CIA princess . . . Are you smiling, Müller?'

'He called you that? To your face?'

'Not to my face. When Pappi and I came back, Pappi stopped by their office. They were going on about Reimer's girlfriend, I think . . .'

43

'They're always going on about Reimer's girlfriend. It's a standing joke around here.'

'Well, as we left, he said something like – "what's the CIA princess doing here?". He thought I hadn't heard.'

Müller was still smiling. 'It's territorial. They're afraid you might lead me astray.'

'Hah!' She paused. 'Well, Müller? Pappi's given me the background to your excitements in May. Do I get the details?'

'You get the details. How much did he give you?'

'Your glass palace was being bugged,' she began, 'by people who were supposedly official. Aunt Isolde's long-lost husband – the British officer – returned from the dead after thirty or so years. Only, he was doing things so secret, he played dead, and comes back with a genetic poison that accidentally infected him when he was prowling about in some laboratory, somewhere in the Middle East. The people in the darkness, who you've been hunting down, sent a hitman to get both of you. The hitman failed, and got himself killed for his pains – by them, not you. Greville, Aunt Isolde's long-lost, is still here. The hitman turned out to have been his own secret, adopted son, who didn't know it was Greville who had paid for his upkeep since boyhood. How am I doing?'

'You're doing very well. Go on.'

'You took Greville to the Eifel, suckering the hitman to follow. You ended up following *him*. In unfamiliar territory, he blundered on to the Nürburgring racetrack, which is where he ended up being splashed by his own controllers. They tried again, failed again. The two they sent this time were part of the group who were eavesdropping on this place. One dead, one captured. Your nemesis group bring down the police chopper that was taking the live one back to Berlin. All dead, including the police crew and escort.'

She paused once more.

'You discover that your father left some highly sensitive material for you. Pappi didn't say what; but the way he said what he did tell me, was enough to make me understand that your father was a very brave man. He worked undercover, out there in the east. He really was a spy, and you never suspected. It's also looking more and more like Rachko told you the truth last winter, on Rügen; and that your digging is bringing a lot of nasty things into the daylight. I include people in that. The mystery about the crash site all adds to it. They tried to kill Pappi, and today they sent one of their bastards to try and take me out. That's what I know.'

'Which is fairly comprehensive,' Müller said. 'I'll give you the rest, then we'll continue the hunt.'

'Grenoble?'

'Kreuzberg, then Baden-Württemberg, then Grenoble.'

'I always like to travel.'

'Perhaps you should reconsider. Being around me – as you have yourself seen today – is becoming very dangerous.'

'Are you kidding? These toads came at me today. It's personal now. I'm mad, and I'm going to get even.'

Müller went to the cabinet which held the sensitive information, and paused. 'Pappi and I wondered how come they knew so quickly that you were here.'

'It didn't come from my side of the ocean,' Carey Bloomfield said. 'I've told no one I was coming to Europe.'

'No one back at the Pentagon, or wherever it is you've got your office?'

'No one,' she repeated. 'And don't look at me like that.'

'Like what?'

'Like you don't believe me.'

Müller worked his way around the comment. 'Even if you've told no one . . . *someone* knows.'

'Well, I've no idea how that person found out. I've got my phone. But no one's been in touch.'

'Not even personal friends?'

'Not even.'

'The kind of people we're dealing with would have access to passenger lists . . .'

'They'd still first have to know I'd be coming over . . .'

'Not if they were doing a trawl, just in case.'

'You don't believe that.'

'No.'

'So, what have we got?' she asked.

'Betrayal . . . somewhere.'

'Great. So now my own people are suspect?'

45

'I'm not saying that.'

'No. *I* am. Damn it. Who would do this?'

'Perhaps,' Müller began, tapping in the code on the drawer keypad, 'you should see the rest. Make the picture a little clearer. Perhaps.' He paused again. 'I may be quite mad showing this to you.'

'You still don't trust me?'

'It isn't a question of trust anymore. It's a question of survival. Mine . . . and now yours. Their attempt to kill you was to get at me. And even though they have no real idea of the explosive potential of the information we now have in this cabinet, they are certainly beginning to suspect that I know rather too much. They see that I am meddling in areas where only specific knowledge would take me. However, if they really did know how far I've got . . .' Müller let his words fade and gave the cabinet a brief pat. 'Only Pappi, Greville, and I know the full, detonating force of what is in there. Kaltendorf has no inkling. Now that you are here, they will assume that I may have passed some knowledge to you . . .'

'Hung for a sheep, as well as a lamb.'

'Precisely.'

'Hey, I'm up to my neck. How much higher can the water go?'

Müller pulled open the deep drawer and took out a brown briefcase, well used, but in virtually pristine condition. It looked like a version of a doctor's bag.

'You judge,' he said, as Carey Bloomfield stared at it. 'My father left this for me with Aunt Isolde, when I was still a boy. The first time I knew of it was last May. Something Greville said made me ask Aunt Isolde. She had been instructed to give it to me only if I asked.'

'Meaning you'd be already looking.'

Müller nodded as he took the briefcase to the table. 'He gave it to her before he and my mother took that flight they were never to finish. They each wrote a letter to me. Both letters, in their own way, were goodbye notes. But my father's also carried some terrible information about what these people are planning. The individuals involved cover a wide spectrum and, in a few cases, different nationalities.' The corners of his mouth turned down briefly. 'You remember Neubauer.'

She nodded. 'That police director who was supposedly a pal of Kaltendorf's. He saw your parents the day before their last flight. The one who was shot by his own driver.'

Müller nodded. 'He was just one of the unexpected. Another person who regularly came to our house when I was a boy, was a bishop . . .'

'You're kidding.'

'If you're planning something like this, you need to contaminate the establishment. Think of the walks of life that make up the establishment of any nation, and you'll have an idea. They call themselves the Bretheren – spelt exactly as it sounds – but they know themselves more colloquially as the Semper . . .'

'"Always",' Carey Bloomfield remarked softly.

'They're saying they'll always be around.'

'An infection that won't go away.'

Müller snapped the catches on the briefcase, and prised it open as if working at the jaws of an animal.

'All in there,' he said to her. 'Help yourself.'

'Don't you have personal things among . . .'

'I've had time to adjust to it. Look at whatever you want.'

She gave him an uncertain look, then reached into the case with a hesitant hand. She took out some envelopes, clearly holding photographs. Then some files, and unbound documents.

She picked up a letter. 'No,' she remarked softly. 'That's to you.' She put it down, and picked up another. 'That's to you too.' Again, she put it down without reading it.

She picked up one of the envelopes, and gently shook the photographs out on to the table. She gasped when she saw the first. It was a photograph that had shocked Müller when he had first seen it in May.

'Your father!' she exclaimed in a voice barely above a whisper. 'You look like him.' She stared at the man in the uniform of a colonel of police in the DDR. 'What a handsome man. Even though I've seen the one in your apartment, this gives him an extra . . .'

'It's the uniform. Aren't all women supposed to like a man in uniform?'

47

'Speaking as someone who wears a uniform, and who has a father who wore one . . . it's more like what takes your fancy. I can show you two men in the same uniform, and one will look like a toad.' She studied the photograph closely. 'But not this one.'

'Romeo Six,' Müller said.

He had spoken so casually, she almost missed it.

'I know,' she said. 'It shook me when Pappi told me.'

'For me, it was an earthquake.'

'I can imagine. He put himself deep into danger.'

'For what he believed in.'

She nodded, and put the photograph down with something close to reverence. She continued to look at it, seeing much of Müller there.

Then, with seeming reluctance, she selected another. This time, it was a group photograph. She studied each face, then gave a sharp intake of breath.

'That's impossible!' she cried in a shocked whisper.

Müller came closer to peer down. 'What's impossible? Have you recognized a face?'

Instead of replying, she asked, 'Do you have a lupe?'

'We have many.'

Still staring at the photograph, she held out a hand.

Müller pulled out one of the drawers in the table, and took out a lupe. He shut the drawer as he handed it to her.

She grabbed it without a word, and placed it on a section of the photograph, then leaned down to put an eye against it.

She remained like that for some time, as if trying to prove beyond doubt that she had not been mistaken.

Abruptly, she straightened. Müller watched her curiously.

She placed the backs of her hands against each hip, and swung from side to side in a slow, yet clearly agitated motion. It was disturbing to watch.

'Carey?' Müller began. 'Are you alright?'

'Wow,' she said. 'You've actually said my name.' It was not bitterly spoken, but there was a sharp dryness to it.

Müller looked uncertain. 'Are you going to tell me what you have seen there?'

Carey Bloomfield tightened her lips, and wiped at her eye.

'You're *crying*?'

'Of course I'm not crying, damn it!' She did not turn to look at him. 'Would you cry if you discovered that the man with whom you've been trusting your life for years was dirty?'

'*What?*'

She jabbed a finger at the photograph. 'Toby Adams. Younger. But it's him.'

Müller looked at her steadily. 'Who is Toby Adams?'

'Long story, Müller.' She gave a short, bitter laugh, and still did not look at him. 'Short story . . . call him my controller. The man who's supposed to be my home-plate back-up. Toby Adams is my field controller. When I'm out there, he's the man with the cavalry if I get exposed. Toby Adams was there when I went – against orders – to rescue my brother, who was being peeled alive by that bastard cousin of yours, somewhere in the Middle East.'

'We killed the bastard cousin.'

'I know we killed him. I was there. Toby Adams was the controller when I first came here . . .'

'Posing as a journalist.'

'Posing as a journalist,' she admitted flatly. 'He was locked into the mission . . .'

Müller made a face. '"The mission." *I* was the mission?'

'Not you *per se* . . .'

'Fine distinction.'

'Don't roll the tape back, Müller. We're past that. We have something much more dangerous to deal with. If Toby Adams really is part of the Semper . . . this is major shit.'

'Perhaps, like my father, he has infiltrated. My father *was* Romeo Six . . .'

'Maybe. Maybe Toby has infiltrated them. Then again, as you would say . . .'

'What if he's the real thing?'

At last, she turned to face him as she nodded. There was a suspicion of moisture about her eyes.

'That bad, is it?' he asked.

'Not what you think. We weren't an item. He is . . . *was* like a father to me. I *trusted* him with my life . . . so many times. Yet, at any time, if it suited him, he could have

49

betrayed me. Maybe he sent that fake cop today. In the beginning, he may not have known I was here. But he knows the right people, and has all the connections. Toby's grade is equivalent to general rank. All he'd need is to do some checking . . .'

'Stop,' Müller said. 'You're running far ahead. You've seen a picture where you least expected to. That's it. All it means with any certainty, is that he is in the photograph . . . assuming it has not itself been faked. Everything else is conjecture at this stage.'

'I *trusted* him, goddammit!'

'Perhaps you may be able to trust him again.'

'And if not?'

'You are forewarned. He would never expect that and, certainly, not from this source. You have an edge. A big one.'

'I thought that fake cop had made me mad; but *this* . . . this really does.'

'Then if you later find you have reason to be . . . to use the anger profitably, and get good and even . . .' Müller gave a tiny smile. 'As *you* would say.'

'Throwing my words back at me, Müller?'

'No.'

Her smile was suddenly tired, and rueful. 'I think I'm beginning to understand, just slightly, how you feel. No one's killed my parents; but the sense of betrayal . . .'

'Wait, and see. How much have you told him since you and I first met?'

'Looking back . . . too damned much.'

'I see.'

'He was my main contact in the field, Müller: my source, my base, my rescue unit, my communications . . .' Carey Bloomfield paused. 'Get the picture?'

'Too clearly.'

'I got those oak leaves mainly because of what I was able to pass on since you and I met.'

'I see,' Müller repeated.

'It was a mission, Müller. It still is, I suppose . . .'

'Even now?'

'No! Not now. I came privately.'

50

'Have you told him about our mysterious, apparent Russian-American, or American-Russian – or possibly neither – contact who calls himself Grogan, and Vladimir, when it suits him?'

'No.'

'That's something, at least.'

'He does not know about this place, either.'

'That's a relief. Anything else I should know?'

She gave him a look. 'What's this, Müller? Third degree?'

'I am a policeman.'

'I won't forget.'

A silence descended between them.

'Look,' Müller said at last, 'let's not stand here facing each other like antagonists. We have an unexpected development. Let us attend to it calmly. We cannot change the circumstances under which we first met. Neither can we change what we are. You, intelligence officer . . . me, policeman. Right now, our interests converge: survival . . .'

'Truce?'

'As far as I am concerned,' Müller said, 'we were never at war.'

'Watchful wariness, then.'

'Quite possibly. And now,' Müller went on, 'where do you go from here?'

'To Toby Adams.'

'So, he is in Berlin. Is that wise?'

'He'd expect me to,' Carey Bloomfield replied. 'As this is a private visit, I did not plan to see him. But that photo changes everything . . .'

'Will you be able to face him without letting on . . . ?'

'Oh, I can do that. Believe you me.'

'Yes. I know you can.'

She shot him a look that carried more than a trace of guilt. 'I could see that arrow.'

'But you have also been very helpful to me,' Müller added, soothing the barb.

'That was diplomatic.'

'The truth.'

She nodded to herself, and began to replace the photographs. 'I don't need to see more, for now.' She began to put everything back into the briefcase, taking her time about it while she thought out her strategy. 'Do you remember seeing any document with his name on it?'

'I did wonder when you would ask,' he said, 'as soon as I heard you say the name. There is just the one mention. As I had nothing else to go on, I simply ringed it. Here. Let me . . .' Müller searched through the documents, then pulled out a single sheet. 'Here it is.' He passed it to her. 'Your German is excellent, so you don't need me to translate.'

She took the typed sheet, and began to read the paragraph bearing the name ringed by a yellow marker pen.

'"The American,"' she read, translating as she went, '"was introduced as Toby Adams. It may well not be his real name, as would be expected in these circumstances. He was looked upon as an important member . . ."'

She stopped, and returned the paper. 'I don't need to see more.'

Müller put it away, and shut the case.

'Do we have time for me to pay Toby a visit before we go off to Kreuzberg?' Carey Bloomfield asked, expression neutral.

He nodded, watching her closely.

'No tails, Müller. The last time you tried that, you sent Reimer. I lost him. He would not be any luckier this time round. Nor anyone else you sent.'

'I didn't know you then.'

'That remark can mean anything.'

'It can. But I assure you . . . no tail.'

'And if you try to find out where Toby is . . . Toby Adams, as you know, is not his real name.'

'I know. But I do have a positively identified photograph . . .'

'Old photograph,' she corrected. 'He does not look quite like that anymore.'

'Certain things about a person don't change, no matter how long ago a photograph was taken . . . unless – barring accidents, or illness – that person has undergone deliberate, radical surgery.'

'No surgery. That's for sure. So, Müller . . . do I go clean?'

'You have my word.'

'OK. Give me an hour.'

'You've got it.'

'I'll need my coat. I guess it's still pouring out there like it's the last day on Earth.'

'Quite possibly.'

The innocuous building near the Jannowitz Bridge overlooked the Spree.

Carey Bloomfield did not go there directly, despite Müller's assurance. She had found a parked taxi in the teeming rain, not far from Müller's glass palace, and instructed the driver to take her northwards, in the direction of Berlin-Wedding. She got out at the Amrumer Strasse underground station, near the University Clinic. She did not take the train. Instead, she walked for a while, despite the rain, turning into many side-streets along the way.

Her seemingly erratic route had a purpose. After many such turns, she was at last satisfied that she had not been followed. She ended up at the Pekinger Platz, on the edge of the Spandau Canal. There, she picked up another taxi, which took her to the Jannowitzbrücke. She was back in Berlin-Mitte and just two kilometres in a straight line from Müller's office.

She went up to the unobtrusive building, and pushed open the unlocked, solid wooden door. There was no lift. She made her way up a wide, classical winding staircase to the top floor of the three-storey building. Another solid wooden door, plain, with no legend to describe the business being practised within, was at the end of a wide landing. The inlaid floor gleamed from regular polishing.

She knocked.

'It's open!' came an American-accented voice, in English.

Carey Bloomfield entered.

The place was a travel bureau for people with lots of money to spend. No budget prices here. Glossy travel posters to all the expensive watering holes of the globe, it seemed, adorned every spare wall space. Racks of brochures were strategically dotted about the large, plant-decorated reception area. Comfortable chairs were placed at low tables. A coffee machine burbled in subdued politeness.

At the wide, curving desk, was a dyed blonde who had worked seriously at being thin. Her face was a paean to the art of make-up, so perfectly had it been applied.

She looked at Carey Bloomfield with a raking gaze that immediately decided that this visitor could not afford any of the holidays advertised. She did not turn up her nose at Carey Bloomfield's attire, but it was all there in the look.

Despite this, her welcoming smile was a searchlight of perfect teeth. 'Hi,' she said. 'And what can we do for you, madam?'

'Hi, yourself,' Carey Bloomfield said. She hated being addressed by people who used the royal we. It always gave the impression, she felt, of being spoken to by a schizophrenic. 'Toby in?'

The perfect blonde blinked. 'Excuse me?'

'Toby,' Carey Bloomfield repeated. 'Toby Adams,' she added for good measure.

The blonde blinked twice this time. 'I'm sorry. I think you've come to the wrong place. We are—'

Carey Bloomfield marched up to the desk and leaned over. 'Listen to me, you diet freak. If you give me any more bullshit, I'll squeeze that scrawny neck of yours so hard you'll want to spit out your larynx! And, while you're at it, do something about those zits.'

The blonde went a bright pink, and instinctively put a hand to a cheek, hiding what she thought was a pimple that had dared invade her perfect face.

Carey Bloomfield did not tell her there was nothing there. 'Well?' she demanded. 'Do you do your job and get me Toby?'

The blonde, one hand still hiding the non-existent pimple, pressed a button on her intercom with a delicate finger.

She cleared her throat. 'Mr Adams . . . there's . . . there's a Miss . . .' She looked warily at Carey Bloomfield, a question in her eyes.

'Bloomfield. Colonel Bloomfield.'

The blonde's eyes widened so much, they were in serious danger of popping out. 'C . . . *Colonel*? Bloomfield?'

'Which question do you want answered first?' Carey Bloomfield asked.

But the blonde was spared. Jacket missing from his summer-weight three-piece suit, a shirt-sleeved Toby Adams rushed out from the recesses of the office, beaming. He carried an expensive putter in one hand.

'Carey!' he greeted. 'This is a pleasant surprise.' He gave her a quick one-handed embrace, ignoring the dampness of her coat, then indicated the putter with a sheepish grin. 'Practising.' He looked at her clothes. 'Terrible weather, huh? Mary-Anne,' he went on to the blonde, who was now staring at Carey Bloomfield, transfixed. 'Two coffees, please? Milk and sugar both.'

'Ye–yes, sir.'

'Come on, Carey. My inner sanctum.' He put his free arm about her shoulders, and guided her back to his office.

The blonde gaped after them, then got up to prepare the coffee.

Toby Adams did not look like a man in his late fifties. But for the slight greying of his neck-length, naturally wavy hair, he seemed a good twenty years younger. Fit, with a flat stomach, he was a six-footer with greyish eyes that looked at Carey Bloomfield with the fondness of a father. He seemed for all the world like a genuine business executive.

They walked along a carpeted corridor full of closed doors.

'Eavesdropping going well?' Carey Bloomfield asked, studiedly casual as she glanced at the doors. Her coat dripped intermittently on to the carpet.

Adams smiled. 'You are a tease.'

'And where in God's name did you get that blonde?'

'Window dressing. She's what people expect to see when they wander in here.'

'She's well cast . . . or is she faking it?'

'The genuine stuff; but she thinks she's working for a VIP travel company. That's why everything's so . . . secret.'

'She believes that? She's dumber than she looks.'

'The pay's very good, and she gets to travel. She asks no questions. The best kind of front person. And here we are.'

Adams' office looked exactly like that of a CEO of any company. On the floor, beneath his pedestal desk, was a waste basket lying on its side. Within it were four golf balls. A lonely hatstand was in a corner.

'As you can see,' Adams explained as he shut the door behind them, 'practising my putt. Doing a few rounds tomorrow with some people . . .'

'This rain won't let up today and, anyway, the course will be soaked.'

'We've got wet-weather arrangements. Indoor.'

'I see. All nicely planned, then.'

'Yes.'

Adams did not seem to spot anything ironic in the remark. He slid the putter back into his high-tech golfing bag, and was about to lean on his desk, when there was a diffident knock on the door.

'That will be Mary-Anne,' he said, going to the door.

'That was quick.'

'She can be quick at some things, despite appearances.'

'I'll bet,' Carey Bloomfield remarked, looking about her. 'Somewhere I can hang my coat so it doesn't drip on something precious? On her, I wouldn't mind.'

He smiled at her. 'Same old Carey. Hang it on that hatstand. It hardly gets any use.' Adams opened the door. 'Thanks, Mary-Anne.'

Carey Bloomfield hung up her coat as a simpering 'You're welcome' came from outside.

Adams backed into the room carrying a small, black tray with two porcelain cups on saucers. The coffee in them was steaming. He swung the door shut with a heel, then came up to Carey Bloomfield, offering the tray.

'I have to admit it smells good,' she said, taking one. 'Thanks.'

'She's quite a coffee maker,' Adams said as he took the tray to his desk and set it down. He picked up his own, and leaned against the desk. He raised the cup in a brief salute. 'Didn't know you were in town, Carey. No one warned me.'

'No one was supposed to. This is private. I got in yesterday.'

'Private?'

'I'm on vacation, Toby.'

'So, you'd thought you'd come to Berlin.'

'Why not?' Carey Bloomfield took a sip of her coffee.

'Mmm. Good. I'm surprised. I thought she would be afraid of damaging her fingernails.'

'As I've said, Mary-Anne's good at some things.'

'Making coffee . . .'

'Among other things.'

'I won't ask.'

Adams smiled, and let it pass. 'So, you're in Berlin. No guesses about whom you've come to see.'

'Why?'

'Come on, Carey. You're not here to see me. Your favourite policeman is the likely candidate. You're soft on the guy.'

'I could take offence . . .'

'But you won't. I'm not wrong. In fact, that might be helpful to us.'

'Oh? I thought you didn't approve.'

'Times change. Things change.'

'Well, here's a change. Some people also seem to think they know why I'm here. They tried to shoot me today.'

Adams' eyes widened in astonishment. *'What?'* He slowly put down his cup. 'Are you kidding me here, Carey?'

'About this, I would not kid. Some guy in a fake cop uniform – or maybe a fake cop in a real uniform, or even a real cop – tried to splash me.'

'Jesus! What happened?'

'Pappi happened.'

'Pappi?'

'My "favourite" policeman's buddy . . .'

'So, you *were* seeing Müller.'

'What can I say? I cannot tell a lie.'

'That was a little sharp, Carey.'

'That's what it does to you when some fake cop tries to wipe you in broad, rainy daylight, in the middle of Berlin.'

'And you come to me for the answers?'

'I've come to you, Toby, because we go back years, and maybe you can tell me if there's something running concerning me, that I don't know about.'

Adams shook his head. 'If there is, this is the first I know about it; just as this is the first I know about your being in Berlin.'

57

'Whoever it is must have known I'd be here. Find out what you can, Toby.'

'You've got it. As you're here, anyway . . .' Adams went on.

'I knew it.'

'Well . . . you are on site, so to speak . . .'

Carey Bloomfield took a deliberate swallow of the blonde's coffee. 'You want me to keep an eye on Müller. Why?'

'Müller . . . has connections with the past which might be of use to us. Remember Dahlberg?'

'How could I forget?'

'We needed him alive . . .'

'I'm not the only one who killed him. Müller shot him too, to save his aunt.'

Adams nodded. 'I know. But there are those – and I'm not one of them – who think that this thing with your brother might have swayed your judgement a little.'

'As I said at the time, they were not there, Toby. And he would still have died, even if I hadn't been there. No way Müller was going to let him get away.'

'I understand that.'

'But you want me to shadow Müller.'

'As you're here . . .'

'I'll do a deal, Toby. I'll keep an eye on Müller . . .'

'And keep me informed . . .'

'And keep you informed. But you find out which asshole sanctioned a hit on me.'

'Deal.'

'I think I did that very well,' Carey Bloomfield said to herself as she walked away from the building. 'And I did not lose my temper. Not once. That thing with the blonde bimbo was a bagatelle. Why are you betraying me, Toby?' she went on, hunching herself against the rain as she looked for a taxi. 'Damned weather.'

A taxi came, and she gave the address of a big hotel on Friedrichstrasse.

Four

'This Toby Adams,' Pappenheim said, 'he's her *controller*?'

'According to her,' Müller replied.

They were in the rogues' gallery. Müller had called him there, some time after Carey Bloomfield had gone.

Müller had spent the intervening time poring over the documents his father had left, in the hope of seeing something else about Adams; but there had been no further mention, nor more photographs.

'Turn-up for the books, if he's now betraying her.'

'Seems like it. We must be getting too close, if we're beginning to touch deeply buried people like Adams.'

'I'd amend that to dangerously close. And it's a big web they're spinning. I'm not complaining, you understand. Feeling that chill at the back of your neck yet?'

'I've been feeling it for some time,' Müller said.

'That's alright, then. Just checking. If Miss Bloomfield admitted about Adams to you,' Pappenheim went on, 'it must have been quite a shock for her. By identifying him to you, she has blown the cover of a friendly agent, operating here under the deepest secrecy.'

'Not so friendly, if what little we know turns out to be true. She had little choice in the matter. Seeing that picture was a traumatic experience for her. Even I am still shaken by what this could mean; so God only knows what it's done to her. She trusted him with her life. They go back to the days when she went to the Middle East to try and rescue her brother – against orders – and found a living corpse having its skin peeled.'

'Despite knowing what happened,' Pappenheim said with a frisson of horror, 'it still gives me shivers to think about it.'

'Adams backed her up then,' Müller said. 'So, finding out he is with the Semper must be very tough for her. But it also tells us plenty about the kind of people who employed diseases like Dahlberg,' Müller went on, voice suddenly cold. 'The kind who had my parents killed.'

Pappenheim looked at him with some anxiety. 'You OK?'

'I'm fine. I'll get them, Pappi. One by one. I'll get them.'

'As long as they don't get you first. Or Miss Bloomfield . . .'

'Or you.'

'Or me,' Pappenheim agreed. He touched the back of his neck. 'The chill wind is doing a little dance there too.'

'I don't want you to take any chances.'

'You worry about your neck, and I'll worry about yours.' Pappenheim grinned. 'See? I'm smiling when I say that. And if Adams is also involved?'

'If Adams is involved . . .' Müller let his words fade.

Pappenheim understood, without needing to hear more. The iciness in Müller's eyes told him everything.

Adams was on the phone to someone.

'I've just had a visitor,' he said.

'Should that be of interest to me?'

'Oh, it should. It should.'

'And who is this person who should interest me?'

'Carey Bloomfield.'

'Ah. The lovely colonel.'

'She was quite upset. Understandably so. It would seem that someone tried, misguidedly – or was misguidedly instructed – to take her out. You would not know anything about that, would you?'

There was a pause. 'Are you questioning me?'

'I am asking a simple question, about a stupid decision.'

'Now listen . . .'

'No! *You* listen! If this was your doing, it was crass, stupid, *and* counterproductive. She is now aware that she is a target. She is forewarned, and will be extremely alert – as would be expected of someone of her calibre. I have told you on several occasions to leave her to me. I will attend to her when the time is right. *Not* before. You could have compromised us.'

There was more silence at the other end, as the person he

was speaking to considered this. Adams was also well aware he had offended the other's sensibilities; but he did not care.

'Does she suspect anything about you?' came the voice at long last.

'Of course not! There's not a chance in hell she'd know about me. I never act prematurely.' It was a deliberate barb. 'I want your assurance you'll rein in your dogs. This must *not* happen again.'

An even longer silence followed.

Adams waited.

'Very well,' came the answer at last, reluctantly.

The man Adams had been speaking to put down his phone, and looked at his companion.

'These Americans. They think they own the world.'

'They do,' the companion remarked with cheerful candour.

'That's surprising, coming from you, Vladimir.'

'Pragmatism,' the man called Vladimir said. 'But even the biggest of houses is vulnerable to burglars.' He smiled. 'The right kind of burglars.'

The other man smiled too. 'What I like about you, Vladimir, is your sense of humour.'

'What you like about me is my ability to get things done.'

'That too.'

'Adams was right, though. It was not a good idea to try it on the colonel. At least, not so soon.'

'You heard?'

'How could I not? He was shouting.'

They both laughed.

'And I must be going,' Vladimir said when the bout had subsided. 'I've been in this country long enough. Three days is a long time.'

'Another vodka, perhaps?'

'Most kind, but no. I've a long, tedious flight ahead.'

'You've said nothing about the genetic virus.'

'Because there's nothing to say. Success is as far away as ever. Whoever stole that sample all those years ago took the one and only original batch. And all documentation was destroyed with the lab. It's a start from scratch.'

61

'We thought we had a possible candidate, but the trail has gone cold. There was a vague rumour that the actual thief was shot, and that the vial might have been broken . . .'

'In which case, he would have been infected, and possibly dead by now.'

'Or infected, and alive.'

'His DNA would be interesting . . .'

'And a good source. We had many likely candidates whom we believed to be the thief. We are, of course, not the only ones looking.'

Vladimir nodded. 'I know. And your candidates?'

'All dead.'

'Naturally?'

'Unnaturally.'

The man called Vladimir pursed his lips briefly. 'I see a cul-de-sac. And the remaining candidate?'

'We mistakenly tried to eliminate him, for other reasons.'

'Which were?'

'He is related by marriage to Müller.'

'Ah! But are you certain he is the candidate?'

'No.'

'Then, if I may suggest, I would leave him be for now. Müller is no fool, as you have reason to know. In fact, I would also suggest leaving Müller alone for now. Let him relax. Let him lower his guard. There are indirect ways to get him. Work with Adams on this, instead of against him. We all owe our allegiance to the Semper. Never forget.'

'And if Müller continues to get too close?'

The man called Vladimir rose from the comfortable armchair. 'Then,' he said, 'like a moth to a flame, he will be burnt. Now, I really must go. Thanks for the vodka.'

'I do not like being countermanded.'

Vladimir paused. 'Is this addressed to me?'

'Certainly not. I am thinking of Adams.'

There was a diffident knock on Adams' door. He recognized it.

'Come in, Mary-Anne.'

She entered with uncertain steps. Adams was at his desk, staring at the golf bag with a thunderous expression.

'Everything . . . everything alright?' she asked as she approached him.

'Nothing I can't handle,' he remarked, looking at her. His expression softened.

She went round the back of the desk until she was behind him. With the ease of familiarity, she began to massage his shoulders.

'Mmmm,' he said, shutting his eyes in pleasure. 'You're so good at this.'

She pulled his chair slightly away from the desk, then, moving to his front, she hitched up her skirt, spread her legs, and straddled him.

'I'm good at this too,' she said, kissing him.

'The door,' he said against her lips.

'I locked it.'

It would be half an hour before she would leave the room.

One of the doors along the carpeted corridor was opened, and a man in shirtsleeves came out. He went to Adams' door, knocked, then tried to open the door. It did not move.

'What the hell . . . ?' he began. He knocked louder. 'Toby? Toby! Some news!'

There was no reply.

'Damn! Where the hell is he now that I need him?'

The man strode along the corridor to the reception area. The blonde swung her chair round to look, and gave him her searchlight smile.

'Mr Roberts! Can I help?'

'Mary-Anne, have you seen Mr Adams? Has he gone out?'

The eyes that looked back at Roberts were vacuous, betraying little brain activity. The voice did not help either.

'Haven't seen him, Mr Roberts . . . and if he went out, he didn't come this way. I've been here all the time.'

'I see.' Roberts appeared distracted. 'Alright. Thank you.'

'Oh, Mr Roberts.'

Roberts paused as he turned away.

'He had a visitor.'

Roberts frowned. 'A visitor?'

She nodded, pleased to have a secret to divulge. 'She said—'

'*She?*'

'Yes, Mr Roberts. She said she was Colonel Bloomfield . . .'

'A *colonel?*'

'I was surprised too. But Mr Adams treated her like an old friend. They went into his office. I made them coffee.'

'I see. Thank you, Mary-Anne.'

The searchlight smile was back on. 'You're welcome, Mr Roberts.'

Roberts went back along the corridor, a bemused expression on his face, and returned to the room he had come out of.

Carey Bloomfield knocked on Müller's door.

'In!'

She entered, carrying a travel bag. 'Sorry I'm a little late. Thought I'd check out . . . if the offer of a room still stands.'

Müller got up from behind his desk. 'It does. No escort?'

'If you mean Miss Hawk Eyes, no. But I did have an escort.'

'Oh?'

'One of your new sergeants. He was by the front desk. I met him before with Pappi. Hammer— Hammer— something.'

'Hammersfeldt.'

'That's it. Pappi had to tell him to stop staring at me.' She smiled. '"I know she's very pretty," I remember Pappi saying, "but it's rude to stare".'

'You've got a fan,' Müller said.

'Hammersfeldt is young,' she said deprecatingly, 'and it's summer.' She touched her wet coat. 'When it decides to make an appearance. Well? Are we ready to go?'

'We're ready. Your coach and four hundred and fifty horses await.' He went up to her and took the bag.

'I am grown-up, Müller,' she said. 'I can carry my own bag. I carried it all the way here. Well, no. Hammersfeldt carried it.' But she made no attempt to retrieve it.

'There you go,' Müller said.

They did not speak again until they were in the lift, descending to garage level.

'So?' Müller began. 'Is Toby Adams in town?'

'He is.'

'And?'

'I said nothing about the picture. But I did tell him someone tried to take a shot at me. He was horrified.'

'Genuine?'

She nodded. 'I'm certain of it.'

Müller studied her expression. 'Something in your voice tells me you're puzzled.'

'He sounded . . . kind of annoyed.'

'Annoyed? That's an odd reaction.'

'I thought he sounded annoyed by the timing . . . not by the act itself.'

'Are you suggesting it was no surprise to him that someone would try this?'

'Maybe I'm getting a little paranoid.'

'At the right time and place, a little paranoia can be good for the health. Does he suspect you know anything about him that you should not?'

She shook her head slowly, but said nothing. She seemed deep in thought.

The silence stayed with them as they got out of the lift and walked to Müller's parking bay. It stayed as Müller squeezed the remote to unlock the car, reached down by the driver's seat to press the switch on the door sill to open the luggage compartment at the front. It stayed with them when he put the bag into it and gently clicked the bonnet shut. It continued as they got into the car and Müller started the powerful engine.

It was still with them as he drove up the ramp, out of the garage and into the teeming rain, as the armoured door continued rolling upwards.

Then he broke it.

'Kreuzberg,' he said.

'This is it,' Müller said, peering through the rain-drenched windscreen at the ungated entrance of a courtyard.

A sign on the left wall proclaimed: *Anlieger frei*.

'Not being residents,' he continued, 'we're not supposed to drive in here. But . . . as we are going to see a resident . . .'

He drove through. The courtyard was bigger than expected;

a large square with low-visibility parking bays and seamlessly bordered by renovated buildings with large windows. Very few of the parking bays were occupied.

'Nice place to live,' Carey Bloomfield remarked, peering upwards. 'Looks almost Tuscan.'

'A gentrified quarter,' Müller said. 'Much of Berlin is still a building site, but some places are being nicely restored. The person I'm looking for used to be the editor of a newspaper.'

'He can afford it, then.'

'Not necessarily. He could have been living here for years, and the renovation came to him. Kreuzberg was a frontline district in the days of the DDR. It bordered the Wall . . . which, as it was in the American sector, I'm certain you already know. Imagine,' Müller went on before she could make comment. 'My father may well have met people here.'

'Spooky.'

'In both senses of the word.'

'Well. Your weird humour is still intact. That's a good sign. So, which one of these "gentrified" places is it?'

Müller pulled into an empty bay, before a house with a mahogany-coloured door. 'According to my information, this one. Hope he's home. He will have long retired. You wait. No point both of us getting wet.'

'Yes, sir.'

He gave her a tolerant look as he switched off the engine. But her attention was elsewhere. 'Someone's coming out.'

Müller turned to check. A middle-aged woman, in a dark raincoat with the hood up, was pulling the door shut behind her. Just in front of the house, three small squares, embedded in a neat row among the cobbles, gleamed in the rain.

Müller got out quickly and hunched against the rain, hurried towards the woman.

'Excuse me . . .'

'Oh!' The woman put a hand to her chest. 'You startled me.'

'Sorry.'

'No harm done.' She peered at Müller, glanced at the car, then back to Müller. She had a kind face and eyes. 'That's a pretty car. What can I do for you?'

'I'm looking for Herr Vogel.'

'Oh, I'm so sorry. He's not here. I look after the house for him. His wife died many years ago, you know, so he spends much of his time at his other place.'

'His other place? Where is that?'

'He has a small villa on Wannsee . . .'

'I don't believe it,' Müller said to himself.

The woman caught the murmur, but not the words. 'What was that?'

'Something I forgot.'

'Ah.' She peered at him from beneath her hood. 'You look so disappointed. I'll tell you what . . . I'll get you the address of the villa, shall I?'

'That would be very kind.'

She took out a key, and began to reopen the door. 'Come out of the rain while I get it. You look like a nice young man, and from what I can see, you've got a lovely young lady in your lovely car. I don't think you'll attack me, will you?' She turned her head briefly to smile at him over her shoulder.

'I don't think so,' he said, smiling back at her.

'He used to be in the newspaper business, you know,' the woman said as they entered a long, narrow hall whose walls were covered with news photographs that spanned many years.

'Yes,' Müller remarked softly. 'I can see that. May I look?'

'Help yourself. I'll go and get you an old envelope with the villa address. Many people write to him, and visit him too. It's to do with his old job.' She paused. 'Sometimes, I think he still does it in a part-time way.'

'Do they come here? Or the villa?'

'Here, and the villa. Only yesterday, a man came to see him. I sent him to the villa. American, I think. He spoke very good German, but the accent was definitely American. In the days of the Wall, we had many Americans here, of course. He sounded the same.'

'I see.'

'I'll get you that envelope.'

'Thank you.'

As she went off, Müller began to walk slowly along the hall, studying the photographs. He was about halfway when he stopped, heart beating.

67

He stared at a collage of black and white photographs, in a single frame. One was of his parents. Another was of their aircraft, intact, parked at an airport. The third was of the crash site, with wreckage strewn over a wide area. The fourth was of the rock face against which the aircraft had slammed.

Müller felt sick. In this house, belonging to a man he did not know, he had found a photo-montage of the last moments in the lives of his mother and father.

'Are you alright?'

The solicitous voice of the woman was suddenly there.

Müller gave a slight start. 'Yes. Yes, I'm fine.'

'You look a little pale. I saw you staring at the picture. Do you know those people?'

'My parents,' he said after a while.

She looked distressed. 'Oh. I'm so sorry. You poor boy. You must have been very young when it happened.'

'Twelve.'

'Terrible. Terrible. I remember when it happened. So very sad. Everybody was talking about it. Such a wonderful couple too. So, you must be the *Graf* now,' she added, a tone of respect coming into her voice.

Müller nodded, but said nothing. He was still looking at the photograph of his parents.

'Will you please do me a favour?' he said to her.

'Anything, Herr Graf.'

'I don't want anyone to know I've been here. Private, you know.'

'I understand perfectly, Herr Graf.'

'And as for Herr Vogel, as I'm going to see him anyway, no need to call him.'

'I understand, Herr Graf,' she said again. 'I hope he can help you.'

'So do I.'

'Here,' she said. 'The envelope with the address.' She handed the postcard-sized envelope to him.

'Once again, my thanks,' he said to her as he took it and slipped it into a jacket pocket. 'I'm most grateful.'

'My pleasure, Herr Graf. I am very sorry about your parents.'

'It was a long time ago. One gets over it.'

'But it still hurts.'

'Yes. It still hurts.'

She looked as if she wanted to give him a hug, to say it would be alright.

'Look after yourself,' she told him with sudden gentleness.

'Thank you. I will.'

He went out of the house, leaving her staring after him with a look of concern.

Outside, in the rain, he paused to study the three small squares. There were inscriptions upon them. He read each silently, then hurried back to the car.

'What is it with you and women, Müller?' Carey Bloomfield said as he got in. 'It doesn't matter what age. They fawn over you.' She paused. 'You OK? You look kind of strange.'

'I just saw a photograph of my parents in that house.'

Her eyes widened. 'You're kidding.'

He described what he had seen.

'Jesus,' she said.

'That man,' Müller went on, 'has had that picture of my parents on his wall like some trophy, for all these years. One of his great scoops,' he continued, a cold bitterness in his voice. 'He's the bastard who wrote an editorial about their having the morals of alleycats. According to that editorial, my mother deliberately crashed the plane, because she had found out about my father's supposed affairs. People still believe that was the reason for the crash. It was that editorial that started the smear campaign rolling. Even that woman in there, helpful though she was . . .'

'She knows?'

'She saw me staring at the photograph. Something like that, so unexpected, I could not have helped it.'

'And you *told* her?'

'Yes.'

'Was that smart?'

'Smart or not, to have denied it, after she asked me if I knew who they were, would have felt like betrayal.'

'I guess I can understand that. Sorry you had to see that photo, Müller.'

'One of those things. It was there, and I was led there. I was meant to see it.'

'Was the guy home?'

'No. He's in Wannsee. She gave me the address. Ironic. I was down there this morning. The person who gave me this address either did not know about Wannsee, or he knew and still chose not to tell me.'

'He wanted you to see that picture?'

'Possibly.'

'We might have got here later, and missed the woman. Then what?'

'But we didn't. And that, for me, is all that matters.'

'What are those things you were looking at?'

'*Stolpersteine.*'

'Stumbling stones? What's that supposed to mean?'

'They are small memorials. Those three out there have the names of the people who once lived in that house: two adults, and a child; their dates of birth, and of death, and their fate, are written there. Written in stone, if you like. They died in concentration camps.'

'Now he's living there.'

'Makes you think, doesn't it?' Müller said as he started the car. 'These stones are being laid all over Germany. I wonder if Herr Vogel sees the ghosts of those three people. I wonder if he sees the ghosts of my parents.'

'Back to Wannsee?' Carey Bloomfield said tentatively, noting the stillness of his expression.

'Back to Wannsee, and a slight change of plan.'

'Which is?'

'That room I offered . . .'

'Oh no, Müller. You're not going to say I've got to check back into the hotel.'

'Not that at all. But you'll have to wait for the organ recital. We'll not be going back to my place. But I promise you'll like your room. You've been there before.'

'Aunt Isolde's?'

He nodded. 'So, it's on to Thüringen, and Aunt Isolde's near Saalfeld. She'll be very pleased to see you.'

'I love that great mansion she calls a Schlosshotel. And I get to see the long-lost husband?'

'You get to see the long-lost husband.'

'How can I refuse?'

They drove slowly out of the courtyard, the exhausts rumbling in the rain, the powerful sound bouncing off the buildings like muted thunder.

Roberts, in his thirties, was at a console with a bank of monitors, topped by a bank of state-of-the-art speakers. Next to him was an older man with glasses, like him, in shirtsleeves. Conversations in several languages were coming through. Discs within the console were recording everything.

'What do you think?' the older man asked. 'Where could he have gone? And without telling us?'

Roberts shrugged. 'Maybe he went out with that colonel Mary-Anne talked about. Although she did say she never saw him leave.'

The older man made a dismissive noise. 'Mary-Anne. Brains in her fingernails. A good decorative plant.'

'Be nice, Joe,' Roberts said with a smile. 'She can't help it, and she's useful where she is.'

The man called Joe gave a world-weary sigh. 'The people who send us kids like that need their heads examined. She belongs on some beach where testosterone-rich boys can drool over her all day; not in an office like this.'

'Then talk to Adams. He chose her.'

'Maybe she's got a relative on Capitol Hill. Maybe she's just close to Adams, if you get me.'

Each gave a knowing smile.

'I've heard of Bloomfield,' the older one continued. 'Adams definitely knows her. They worked together in the Middle East. She's meant to be good.'

'Why didn't he warn us she was coming?'

Joe shrugged. 'Beats me. Maybe they're running something special.'

Roberts looked puzzled. 'It still feels strange. I'm going to check again.'

'If it'll make you feel better,' Joe Mahony said.

Roberts stood up and left the room once more. He went to Adams' door, tried it, and discovered it was still locked.

'Damn!' he swore. He went back into the room. 'Still locked,' he said to Mahony.

'What do you want to do?'

'I don't like it. I've got a bad feeling.'

'I repeat . . . what do you want to do?'

'We've got a master key. I'm going to open the office.'

'What do you expect to find? He's not in there having a little cosy with Mary-Anne, unless she can manage to be in two places at once. As she's hardly in one place at a time . . .'

'Have your fun, Joe.'

'Check the other rooms first. Maybe he's in there talking with the guys.'

Roberts nodded. 'Right.'

He went out again.

Mahony shook his head slowly.

The Porsche was racing along the A115 to Wannsee, trailing a high plume of spray.

Carey Bloomfield glanced at the speedometer, then thought better of it.

'What?' Müller said.

'Nothing.'

'Are you afraid?'

She looked at the ribbon of road ahead of them, made dark by the wetness of the day. She glanced in the wing mirror on the passenger side, and could see the rising spray. She listened to the fierce roar of the engine behind her.

'A speedboat on land. What's to be afraid of?'

'Part of this stretch of road,' he said, smiling at her comment, 'used to be a section of the Avus . . . the original racetrack.'

'No wonder,' she said.

'Is there something you're trying to tell me?'

'What makes you say that?'

'You're thoughtful. Your remark lacked its usual bite.'

'You're a mind-reader now?'

'Only when I need to be.'

When she made no comment on this, Müller glanced at her thoughtfully.

They drove on in silence.

Roberts came back into the room. 'That's it. I'm going to open the office. No one has seen him.'

He reached into a drawer and took out a small bunch of keys. He also took out an automatic pistol.

Mahony stared at him. 'A *gun*? Are you nuts?'

'Just being careful,' Roberts said, going out again.

Mahony stared at the closing door. 'Nuts,' he repeated.

Roberts went up to the door to Adams' office and unlocked it. Gun at the ready, he slowly pushed the door open. He entered, and stopped in shock.

'Oh Jesus!' he said.

Adams was in his chair, mouth open, head back at a strange angle.

Roberts went forward, made a quick check. 'Oh Jesus!' he repeated.

He left the office quickly, shut and locked it.

Mahony swung round as Roberts re-entered the room. He stared at Roberts' expression. 'What?'

'He's dead,' Roberts said flatly. 'Neck broken.'

Mahony's eyes seemed to grow behind his glasses. 'He *what*?'

'Dead,' Roberts repeated. 'Someone's snapped his goddamned neck.'

'But how . . . ?'

'Do I look like a wizard? How the hell should I know?' Roberts tightened his lips. 'I *knew* something was wrong . . .'

'Sounds like wizardry to me.'

'That's not funny.'

'Alright. What do you want to do?'

'What do *I* want to do? You're next in line, Joe. It's *your* ball game now.'

Mahony sighed. 'I guess it is.' He got to his feet. 'I've got a call to make. Looks like your Colonel Bloomfield might have some questions to answer.'

'*My* Colonel Bloomfield?'

'Manner of speaking. Relax. I'll make the call from Adams'
. . . *my* office.'

Mahony went out.

Pappenheim was leaning back in his chair blissfully polluting
his lungs, when one of his phones rang. He blew a stream of
smoke at the ceiling, and picked up the phone at its third ring.

'Pappenheim.'

'You've got trouble.'

'So, what's new?' Pappenheim retorted, recognizing the
voice at the other end. 'I've always got trouble.'

'Not like this, you haven't.'

'I'm all ears.'

'Then sit back. An American called Adams has just been
killed . . .'

'*What?*' Pappenheim sat bolt upright, and stubbed out the
cigarette he'd been enjoying.

'Is that the sound of a Gauloise dying?'

'If this is a joke . . .'

'I never make jokes.'

'Tell me about it,' Pappenheim remarked pointedly. 'So?
What's the full story?'

'Early days yet. Only just got the essentials, and it looks
like a certain Colonel Bloomfield – whom I'm certain you've
never heard of – is in the frame.'

'You have got to be joking.'

'I've just said—'

'Yes, yes, I know. You never joke. How certain are you
about this?'

'Don't insult me,' the person said. 'I'll call you later.' The
line went dead.

'Touchy as ever,' Pappenheim said as he slowly replaced
the receiver. 'With news like this, one needs corroboration.'
He picked up the other phone, and dialled an extension. 'Ah.
Miss Meyer. I need your expertise again, I'm afraid. I'll square
it with Hermann.'

'I'll be right there, sir.'

'Thank you.'

*   *   *

74

They left the A115 at the Zehlendorf junction and fed on to the B1, for Wannsee. The rain had stopped for a while and the road, though damp, was no longer wet enough for the fat wheels of the Porsche to generate much spray. Müller barely needed to use the wipers.

'Hey,' Carey Bloomfield began, peering upwards. 'Think the sun will make it?'

'It might,' Müller replied. 'On the other hand, it might not.'

'What kind of an answer is that?'

'The weather's.'

'You're something, Müller. You know that?'

'I know it.'

'Müller?'

'Yes?'

'The Wannsee Conference villa is near here, isn't it?'

'Yes. Once we cross the water, we'll be getting off at the next junction. That's Am Grosser Wannsee. The villa is along that road.'

'Can we have a look first, before we go check on Herr Vogel?'

'It's on the way. Why not? But are you certain you would like to? The pictures in there are not pretty.'

'I know what you're getting at. My dad's Jewish; but my mom isn't. And I'm as secular as it's possible to be. I can hack it.'

'You don't need to be Jewish to be moved.'

'I realize that. Have you been there?'

'No.'

She looked at him in surprise. 'Why not?'

'I don't need to. But I'll come with you.'

They came to the turning and Müller left the B1 to take the road which skirted the shore. He drove along it until they came to an area on a wide bend where they could stop.

'There's a car park further along,' he said, 'but, as we're not going to be long, might as well stop here. That's the place, over to the right. The Villa Marlier.'

The sun had actually begun to shine, and a strangely clear light had come upon the day. They walked along a tree- and hedge-lined driveway, towards a circular flower bed at the entrance. They went round it, then paused just before entering.

'What a beautiful building,' Carey Bloomfield said.

The sun, as if given an extra luminescence by the recent rain, appeared to light up the building.

She looked about her. 'And beautiful grounds too. Great place to have a villa.'

They entered the villa, with its dark, polished wooden floor, and pale walls covered with captioned photographs depicting humankind's notorious inhumanity to itself.

They went through to the concentration camp display. Carey Bloomfield's face was still, but she showed no emotion. They then went through to the actual room where the conference had been held. This room held a neat array of the photographs of the actual participants, with information on each individual.

She stared at them for some moments.

'I need some air,' she remarked suddenly.

'Of course.'

They went back outside and walked round the building until they came to a spot close to the water, with two benches facing each other. They stopped, and looked out across the lake, at a long stretch of beach. They remained silent for long moments, enjoying the sudden warmth of the sun.

'Gives a special meaning to *let's do lunch*,' she said, hugging herself. 'Christ. They had a buffet lunch while they did this. Such a beautiful place. I mean, who wouldn't have wanted to live here? All those ghosts. It's obscene.'

Müller said nothing, merely looking at her.

After a while, he said, 'Are you alright?'

She nodded. 'I'm fine. Let's get out of this beautiful, horrible place. Sorry I asked you to bring me.'

'Nothing to be sorry about.'

Pappenheim was already in the rogues' gallery, and opened up to Hedi Meyer's knock.

She went straight to the computer and powered it up. 'What are we looking for, sir?'

'The beacon our mysterious informant left as a calling card,

76

months ago,' Pappenheim told her. 'I want to see if he has sent us any recent updates.'

'Soon find out,' she said.

The computer settled down and an icon pulsed on the task bar.

'There!' she went on in some surprise. 'Something's waiting.' Her fingers fled across the keys. 'How did you know?'

'I'm clairvoyant.'

'Hmm,' she said, scepticism itself. A window of scrambled letters and figures came onscreen. 'We've got mail. I'll have that readable in a few moments.'

Again, her fingers did their magic. Section by section, the encrypted message began to reveal itself.

'Done,' she said.

It was in English, and not very long.

'"Bloomfield will be set up for Adams' death",' Pappenheim read aloud. 'What does that say to you, Miss Meyer?'

'It's a prediction.'

'Quite so. Sometimes, predictions come true rather quicker than expected.'

She looked up at him. 'It's happened? Is that why you asked me to check?'

'It's happened and, yes, that's why I asked. I had to be sure. Our friend either knew well before the event, or he found out just before it happened. Not much warning, but it's a help. Thank you, Hedi. No need to tell you to keep this strictly to yourself. No exceptions.'

'No need, sir.'

Five

Like the conference villa, Erwin Vogel's own, much smaller villa had a perfect location near the water.

On two storeys, with the high attic converted into a huge study with large, arched French windows that opened out on to a wide balcony, the villa was neatly spacious. French windows on the first floor also opened out on to a second balcony, from the master bedroom.

There was a boathouse, within which a fast speedboat was moored. A small jetty close to the boathouse protruded into the lake, from the gently sloping garden.

'Nice piece of real estate,' Carey Bloomfield observed as they walked across slightly unkempt grounds from the short driveway. 'He's not done badly for himself. But he needs a gardener.'

'Perhaps he's his own gardener.'

'I guess. Müller?'

'Mhmm.'

'I think you should know Toby asked me to keep an eye on you.'

Müller stopped, forcing her to come to a halt. He looked at her steadily. 'Thank you for telling me.'

'I . . . I thought you should know.'

'I appreciate it. Won't that get you into trouble?'

'After seeing that photo of him? What trouble could I get into? He's dirty.'

They walked on. The jetty came into view.

'Look,' she said. 'Someone by the water.'

'I see him.'

Vogel, in rough-weather clothing, was on the jetty, peering into the water at something. He looked round, and straightened when he saw his visitors. He was a small man, with a weather-beaten face. The hood of his jacket was thrown back, to reveal wispy grey hair. He looked more like a fisherman than a retired newspaper editor.

'Dead fish,' he said as they approached. 'God knows what's going into the water these days.' Despite his age, he looked far younger than expected.

They stopped at the water's edge, waiting for him to come off the jetty.

'Herr Vogel,' Müller began as Vogel approached. 'I'm—'

'Von Röhnen,' Vogel finished, astonishing Müller. 'Yes. I know. I've been expecting you for some time.' This was said with an air of resignation.

'You have?'

'Yes, young man. I have been following your career both with respect, and with apprehension. It was only a matter of time before you got to me.' Vogel gave the sign of someone who was glad to have come, at last, to the end of a hard race. 'Please come up to the house.' He looked at Carey Bloomfield. 'You are his wife?'

Taken aback, she said, 'Er . . .'

'This,' Müller interrupted, 'is Colonel—'

Vogel's reaction was totally unexpected. *'Colonel? A woman?* My God!'

Müller and Carey Bloomfield glanced at each other, puzzled.

'You've got something against women colonels?' she asked him.

'No, no. You don't understand. Your German is very good, but that's an American accent. My God. My God.' Vogel seemed very agitated.

'Herr Vogel,' Müller said firmly. 'Calm yourself. What are you talking about?'

But Vogel was not forthcoming. He also appeared to have forgotten his invitation to them to come into the house.

Müller decided to get directly to the point. 'I am here, Herr Vogel, to ask why you defamed my parents in your editorial, all those years ago.'

'They made me!' The agitation was suddenly back. 'They made me do it!'

'They? Who's "they", Herr Vogel?'

'You have no idea what you're dealing with . . .'

'I've heard that many times before.'

'You should have listened! Left the dogs alone!'

'The dogs?' Carey Bloomfield asked Müller.

'I think he means *let sleeping dogs lie.*'

'Bit late for the advice. They've been awake for some time.'

'So they have,' Müller agreed. 'Why do you have photographs of my parents, and their plane, and the crash site, on your wall?' he now asked Vogel.

Vogel stared at him. 'You've been to my house in Kreuzberg? Of course you have,' Vogel went on to himself. 'You are here. So you must have known the Kreuzberg address too. All these years. And here you are. My nemesis.'

'I told them,' Vogel went on, staring blankly into nowhere. It was as if Müller and Carey Bloomfield could no longer be seen. 'I told them you would start digging. They—'

'Who's "they", Herr Vogel? A bunch of aging men with murderous dreams?'

Vogel gave Müller a look that was not all there. '"*Aging* men"? How little you do know. They recruit all the time. Suitable candidates. They even thought *you* could be groomed, once. You fit the profile perfectly. Then when you became a policeman, they were disappointed. But then they had a rethink. As a policeman, and an intelligent one at that, you suited their plans perfectly. You had all the right connections. Noble family . . .' Vogel paused, seeming to ponder upon something only he could know.

'But then,' he went on suddenly, as if a switch had been thrown, 'you began investigating in areas they did not like. Worse, you began investigating the death of your parents. They knew then you might stumble across a can of worms. They could not understand how you managed to start in the first place. You know,' Vogel continued, wandering off again, 'I had this place built for my wife and . . . and I, so we could have a wonderful place to spend our winter years. But she died. No children. So I am alone here . . .' Vogel stopped, and changed tack again.

'I told them you would not give up. I'd studied your cases from the very beginning. You were unorthodox, I told them. Unpredictable, and good with it. All very bad news for them. I told them. I told them it had all been a mistake. But they would not, will not listen. Stakes too high. Now the colonel—'

'Herr Vogel. I must interrupt. You speak of "they" and "them". Do you mean the Semper?'

Vogel jerked as if hit by a bolt of lightning. If he had been agitated before, he was now terrified.

'You *know*?' It was a whisper of horror. 'To know this means you know even more than they dared suspect. It means you know people who . . .' Vogel stopped again. 'I'm finished,' he said quietly. It was almost with relief.

Suddenly, before they realized what was happening, Vogel

set off at a run for the villa. His speed was unexpected and, by the time they had begun to chase after him, he had already entered the building.

'*Herr Vogel!*' Müller called. 'The phone!' he added to Carey Bloomfield. 'He's going for a phone, damn it!'

But Vogel was not heading for a phone. By the time they had entered the villa, they heard a door slam somewhere above their heads. A short while later, a sharp bang followed. Both knew exactly what had happened.

'Shot!' they said together, and raced up the winding staircase.

'Touch nothing!' Müller cautioned.

'I won't.'

Müller pulled a pair of cotton gloves out of a pocket, and put them on.

They split to check the four bedrooms on the first floor. Müller also gave a sweeping glance in each room he searched, looking for cameras; but this was far too rudimentary to spot anything hidden, given the pressure of time.

'Nothing,' Carey Bloomfield said as they met up again on a central landing.

'Same here,' Müller said, looking upwards. 'Did you spot any security cameras?'

'Nothing in the open. Could be some hidden stuff around, though.'

'If so, we're on camera.'

A straight flight of stairs, built against a wall, led up to the attic floor. They went up cautiously and, just as cautiously, Müller turned the handle of the door at its end.

The door was not locked.

He pushed it open with care. He need not have bothered. In the vast study, lined with packed bookshelves, was a large desk that faced the French windows with a fantastic view of the lake. At the desk was a crazily slumped Vogel, body leaning to the left, in response to the single shot to the right side of what was left of the head. The gun he had used had fallen out of his hand and on to the floor near the desk.

Müller entered, followed by Carey Bloomfield. Again, there were no signs of any security cameras.

'You've got a great effect on people, Müller,' she said as they walked up to the desk.

Carey Bloomfield averted her eyes from the mess, and looked out of the French windows.

'At least he got a last look at a great view.'

Müller walked slowly round the desk, studying Vogel's body as he did so. 'I can't say I feel sorry,' he said.

'I'd be surprised if you did.'

'See if there's anything hidden in here.'

'Like bugs or cameras?'

Müller nodded.

'This could take some time to do properly,' she said.

'We don't have it. Do the best you can, but don't touch.'

'Hey, Müller. I'm no bimbo.'

'No offence meant.'

Obeying his own instructions, Müller touched nothing as he worked his way round the desk. 'I did not get as much out of him as I'd hoped,' he said. 'But perhaps more than was to be expected, under the circumstances.' He looked down at the gun. 'Makarov, DDR model. Interesting gun for a then West Berlin editor. We should leave,' he added. 'Now.'

'You've seen something?'

'No. But I don't have a good feeling.'

'Then you don't have to tell me twice,' Carey Bloomfield said, hurrying out of the study.

Müller followed, closing the door quietly. He removed the gloves on the way down, and put them back into his pocket.

'Did you touch anything?' he asked when they were again outside. 'A door, a bed. Anything.'

She shook her head. 'I made sure.'

'Good.'

He got out his mobile as they walked to the car. It rang.

'Bound to be Pappi,' he said to her. 'Nice timing, Pappi. I was just about to call you.'

'Great minds,' Pappenheim said. 'Tried the car. Assumed you were on walkabout. You first? Or me first?' Pappenheim paused and the sound of a long drag came down the connection. 'You first, I think. You'll need to be sitting down for what I've got to say.'

82

'That bad?'

'Not good.'

Müller took a few seconds before saying, 'Alright. Here's mine. We're just leaving the second home of the first person on my list . . .'

'As supplied today?'

'As supplied.'

'And?'

'He's dead.'

'You do have an effect on people.'

'Someone's already beaten you to that observation, Pappi.'

'I'll take three guesses. It will be the same person each time. So, how did person one get dead? You?'

'The body did it.'

'Now you frighten them to death. Shame on you.'

'I'll ignore that but, yes, he was indeed very frightened; but not of me specifically. More of what's behind my visit.'

'Well, I've got some scary stuff for you too. I take it you want the usual clean-up squad?'

'I do. Discreet. And nothing's been touched.'

'Are you still within Berlin jurisdiction?'

'Yes. It's Wannsee . . .'

'You must love that place.' Pappenheim began to sing, '*Nix wie raus . . .*'

'Pappi!'

'Just bringing a little cheer. You'll need it. I'll put our Tuscan German, Max Gatto's team on it.'

'Max the Cat. Good choice. He knows his stuff. Tell him to check the place for surveillance gear. I've got a feeling about this.'

'There are feelings, and then there are feelings. One thing . . . Max and his team can't get down right away.'

'Why not?'

'He's giving a talk on surveillance techniques to some VIPs.'

'You're joking.'

'Don't look at me. It was something planned by the Great White some time ago. One of his mad PR exercises. No one could have guessed you would need Max today.'

'God!' Müller said in frustration. 'How long is this "talk" supposed to last?'

'He won't be out of there for another hour. At the least.'

'This is just great. Alright. Get our local colleagues. Ask them to spare two people to watch the villa and ensure *no one* goes in till the team arrives. This includes the watchers. I don't want them wandering about in there. They are to remain outside and wait for the team.'

'Will do. I know someone down there who can set it up.'

'Of course you do, Pappi,' Müller said with one of his brief smiles. 'I'll only be surprised the day you tell me you didn't know someone, somewhere.'

'You know me too well. Details of the location?'

Müller told him, then went on, 'Now your news.'

'Are you sitting down now? And where's your companion?'

'I'm walking, and she's a little distance away.'

'She's in trouble.'

'What do you mean?'

'Adams is dead, and she's the number one suspect.'

'*What?* Dead? How?'

'I'll take the last question first, and work back. The how is still unknown. My contact only just got it. I didn't believe it, so ran a check with the beacon. You remember the beacon.'

'I remember the beacon. And?'

'And lo, there was a message waiting. Prophecy . . .'

'Prior knowledge?'

'Definitely. It seems that your friend was to be set up for the killing. Next answer . . . yes, he is really dead. As to the "what", my reaction too. Nice sequence of events, eh? Someone tries to give her an early send-off, now this. Plus your stiff in his villa. What a day, so far, eh?' The sound of Pappenheim's long drag came again. 'So, my fine friend, the hornets are buzzing. You're poking close to the centre of the nest, it seems.'

'Closer than I thought. You should have seen the fear on Vogel's face. Terror would be more appropriate. He made some strange comments that made no sense. About a colonel . . .'

'You've got her right next to you.'

'That's the point. He was talking of someone else. He was surprised it was a woman. He was thinking of a man.'

84

'Hmm,' Pappenheim said. 'She gets the blame for someone else's little undertaker job. So what happens? *Her* lot begin hunting her. Better than someone doing the job themselves. They get the result, without the blame. They must obviously have thought better of that clumsy episode this morning.'

'Someone, somewhere, stepped in with a smarter plan . . .'

'And tougher for you. Cunning. I like it.'

'Thanks, Pappi,' Müller remarked drily.

'Don't mention it. Where are you off to now? Or mustn't I know?'

Müller had reached the car, and looked round to see Carey Bloomfield hanging back to give him privacy. He made urging motions that she should get in, then moved slightly away to continue the conversation with Pappenheim.

'Off to my aunt's, but you don't know. Then it's on to do some Alpine work, which . . .'

'I don't know about, either. I know so little, it really hurts.'

'Let me know when more comes in on that Adams thing.'

'Will do. And Jens . . .'

'Yes?'

'It really is a set-up. I don't think she did it.'

'Neither do I.'

'That's a relief,' Pappenheim said.

'Of course, we could be wrong. She was not a happy person when she saw him with that crowd.'

'We're not wrong.'

'And you were so sceptical of her, once.'

'Things change. Times change. People change.'

'As always. Later, Pappi.'

Müller put his phone away, and got back into the car.

'That was a long one,' Carey Bloomfield said to him. 'Trouble?'

'I was arranging with Pappi to have Vogel's body taken care of. And, yes, we've got trouble.'

'We?'

'You, to be precise.'

She stared at him. '*Me?*'

'Adams is dead.'

She gave a shocked gasp, mouth hanging open for long moments.

'Oh Jesus!' she said after a while, echoing the comment made by Roberts when he'd found Adams' body. 'But . . . but *how*? He was alive when I left him!'

Müller started the car and began to drive off. 'Pappi got a call from one of his contacts. It's a set-up. Someone else did the killing, and you're being framed for it. Pappi decided to double-check. As you know, Grogan leaves little encrypted messages on the rogues' gallery computer, from time to time. One about you was already there when Pappi asked the goth to check.

'It was predictive. It said Adams *would* be killed, and you would be blamed. Someone's after your scalp . . . perhaps to get to me; perhaps not. Pappi believes it's a smarter variation of what they tried to do to you earlier. This way, they get your own people to do the job. I happen to agree. The baffling thing is Vogel's reaction to you. He talked about a colonel, but clearly he did not mean you.'

Carey Bloomfield was staring unseeingly at the road ahead. 'They killed Adams,' she said, after a long while. '*Why?* Why kill one of their own, even if to get me? He was important. It's so . . . wasteful.'

'Perhaps he annoyed someone.'

'Drastic response.'

'Who knows with people? The important thing right now is to hope that your people don't jump to the wrong conclusions, but think first. In the meantime, you stick with me.'

She gave a weak smile. 'Protective, Müller?'

'Ohh . . . you're quite capable of protecting yourself.'

'It's OK, Müller. I won't think you've gone soft all of a sudden. But thanks. And thanks for not believing I took Adams out.'

'You're welcome.'

She suddenly stiffened. 'That's *it*!'

He gave her a quick glance. 'What is?'

'What you just said.' She was genuinely exercised by whatever it was that had caused the reaction.

'Do you mean "you're welcome"?' Müller gave her another glance, this time of uncertainty.

'Yes! The bimbo.'

'What bimbo?'

'The diet freak of a blonde bimbo in Toby Adams' office.'

'I can tell you liked her.'

'She's a stinker. Take my word for it.'

'What's that sound?'

'What sound?'

'The unsheathing of claws.' Müller grinned.

'You should have seen her, Müller. I get there, she's at the reception desk, looking as if she's only slumming it until a film producer discovers her. Right now, the reception area is decked out like a luxury travel company; but it doesn't exist. It's just a front, and it's also changeable. I ask for Toby. She gives me this vacuous routine. "I'm sorry. I think you've come to the wrong place",' Carey Bloomfield mimicked the high-pitched, empty voice. 'I told her if she gave me any bullshit, I'd squeeze her scrawny neck until she felt she wanted to spit out her larynx.'

'Her *larynx*? That must have made you a friend.'

'It was the best I could think of. Finally, she buzzed Toby, and he came out. We went to his office. Simpering Mary-Anne – that's what Toby called her, and the "simpering" is my addition – brought us coffee. After talking with him, I left. He was very much alive and kicking. There are other doors in the place, all closed at the time I was there. But I know there are always people in the rooms. Any one of them could have done it, and Miss Diet Freak would have been only too glad to point one of her polished fingernails at me. I can imagine the question. Did anyone visit Mr Adams, Mary-Anne? "Oh yes!" came the mimicked voice again, "'A Colonel Bloomfield". Bingo. There you have it.'

Müller took out his phone and passed it to her. 'Here. Call Pappi. Ask him to get one of his contacts to check out this Mary-Anne.'

'Come on, Müller,' Carey Bloomfield said as she took the phone. 'You can't believe that bimbo—'

'No. But a background check might help. You never know. Pappi's number is the same one, from the time you last used this phone.'

'That was way back, Müller. The time of Dahlberg. But I remember it.'

She dialled Pappenheim.

'You again,' Pappenheim said, thinking it was Müller.

'It's me, Pappi.'

Pappenheim coughed in his surprise. 'Miss Bloomfield! Is he alright?'

'He's fine. He's driving.'

'Ah. Obeying the law, like a good policeman.'

'I won't even pass comment on that one, Pappi.'

'Good thing too. So, what does he want?'

'The contact who called you about me. See if he or she has heard the name Mary-Anne. No surname, I'm afraid. It's all I have.'

'Leave it to me. And Miss Bloomfield . . .'

'Yes, Pappi?'

'Hang in there. We're with you.'

'Thank you, Pappi.' She had a warm feeling as she ended the call and passed the phone back. 'He's sweet,' she said.

'*Sweet?* Don't let him hear that.'

'He won't, if you don't tell him. Müller?'

'Yes.'

'I'd love to drive your car. You don't have to look so pale,' Carey Bloomfield continued when Müller had said nothing to this unexpected request. 'I'm not trying to steal it.'

'You want to drive *this* car?'

'It's the only one we're sitting in. I'm familiar with stick shifts. Not all Americans drive automatics, you know. I've got me a Bimmer, with a stick shift. A small three-series, but it goes. Used to be my dad's. He treated it like a baby. It's in great condition . . .'

'This is not a three-series. This is four hundred and fifty horses of ceramic-braked Porsche Turbo. This, *never* gets driven by anyone else.'

'That tells me. But I seem to remember one time when you left me in it and said I could drive it away if—'

'That was an emergency situation. This isn't.'

'Like I said, that tells me.'

*   *   *

'Müller.'

'*What?*'

'Open your goddamned eyes. We're not moving yet.'

Müller had stopped to fill up at a service station on the A9 Autobahn, heading south towards Halle and Saalfeld.

He had then driven to a parking bay, called Aunt Isolde to warn of their arrival, and, in an unaccustomed fit of generosity regarding the car, had made the decision to switch seats. As if in sympathy, the rain had decided to hold off.

'I've taken leave of my senses,' he now said to himself.

'Are your eyes open?'

'They're open. I might as well see where my temporary insanity is leading me.' He made a show of checking that his seat belt was secure. 'Reverse is—'

'I can see it on the shift, Müller.' She started the engine. 'Oh. My. Oh . . . I can *feel* it.' She selected reverse.

'Go gently,' Müller advised. 'The clutch is—'

The car jerked rearwards, and stalled.

'—fierce,' Müller finished, then added, 'This is not the blonde bimbo's neck.'

'You going to be like this?'

'Like what?'

'A mother hen.' Carey Bloomfield put the gear into neutral, and started again. 'Well?' she challenged. 'Are you?'

'I've created a monster,' Müller said to himself.

The rain continued to hold off.

For once, Pappenheim was not smoking when the phone rang.

'Something to tickle your fancy,' the voice said as soon as he had picked it up. It was the same person who had phoned earlier.

'Try me.'

'I'll give you a direct quote.' The voice switched to American-accented English. '"I'm telling you the guy was unzipped, and there's semen all over his pants. He was doing it at the goddamned time." End of quote,' the voice finished in German.

Pappenheim sat in dumbfounded silence.

'Hello! You there?'

Pappenheim roused himself. 'I'm here.'

'It seems your colonel lady is a bit of hot stuff.'

'If you're right about her being framed, that wasn't her, either.'

'Look, I'm only giving you the bare facts . . .'

'A lot of people are lying.'

'There's lying, and then there are untruths.'

'There's a difference?'

'You're a policeman. You ought to know that. Untruths are variable. Lies are total fabrications . . . then there's all that grey area in between.'

'Is that what they teach at the fancy colleges these days? How to mangle language?'

'Language has been mangled well before the days of Plato; from the days your ancestors first uttered "ugh!".'

'*My* ancestors? What about yours?'

'Oh, they came with perfect linguistic skills. I'll be in touch. And try and get me a description of the mystery woman. It might help.' There was the distinct suspicion of a laugh when the caller hung up.

Pappenheim put the phone down. 'It's got a sense of humour. I don't know which is worse.'

He spent a full five minutes trying to decide whether to tell Müller. During that time, he did not light a single cigarette.

Then he sighed, and picked up the phone.

Müller got the mobile out as soon as it rang.

'Yes, Pappi.'

'You're using the mobile and *driving*? I can hear the car.'

'You can certainly hear the car, but I'm not driving.'

'I think I need a cigarette. You're letting *her* drive?'

'Right now she's at two hundred and twenty kilometres per hour, and I'm praying she won't go higher.'

'Hi, Pappi!' Carey Bloomfield shouted. This was followed by a cackle.

'An adrenalin junkie,' Müller said to Pappenheim. 'I've created a monster.'

'Serves you right.'

'Thank you, Pappi. I really needed that. So what's the news?'

'You won't like it.'

'There are many things I don't like. I get over them.'

'Adams was found with his flies open. There was semen.' Müller had fallen so silent, Pappenheim was forced to continue. 'Don't jump to conclusions, Jens. You know it could not have been her. What does that woman look like? Do you have a description?'

'Yes.'

'Well? What are you waiting for? Let's have it.'

Müller had again fallen silent.

Carey Bloomfield was darting him glances and slowing right down. 'Something wrong?'

'Pappi wants Mary-Anne's description.'

'You know as much as I do. Give it to him.'

Müller nodded. 'Miss Bloomfield describes her as a diet freak, Pappi. Dyed blonde, very thin, possibly an airhead. She calls her a bimbo.'

'There you go,' Pappenheim said with obvious relief. 'It's a certainty, if Adams was romping anyone, it was the bimbo. My contact is calling back. I'll let you know.'

'Alright, Pappi. Thanks.'

Carey Bloomfield was still in the slow lane, and giving Müller quick glances as he put the phone away.

'You look strange. Pappi had bad news?'

'Not really,' Müller replied.

He successfully killed the initial sense of betrayal he had felt when Pappenheim had given him the news about the way Adams had been found.

I have no right, he thought.

'It would seem,' he went on, 'that Adams was enjoying himself when it happened. With Mary-Anne.'

I don't know that for certain, he told himself.

'No kidding! Toby was playing around with *Mary-Anne*?' She laughed out loud. 'That stick insect? How bizarre.'

'He does not like stick insects?'

'I've no idea what he likes; but she's a surprise. Intellectually she's . . .' Carey Bloomfield let her words die.

'Some men prefer that.'

'With Toby, that would be a real surprise. But then, as I've found out, you never really know someone.'

'That is true enough.'

She gave him another glance, as if wondering whether there was more hiding within that remark.

An hour had passed before Pappenheim got the call he'd been waiting for. This time, he was idly blowing smoke rings at the nicotine-painted ceiling of his office. After speaking with Müller he had immediately called his contact with the information, not wanting to wait until the other got back to him.

He grabbed the phone at the first ring.

'Pay dirt, as the Amis would say,' the contact began. 'Your description was helpful.'

'She is known?'

'Oh yes. The name alone would have helped, of course, but not as conclusively. The description fits neatly, even though the hair does not.'

'Well, she is a dyed blonde.'

'But no bimbo. In certain circles, she is known as the Killer B.'

'A killer *bee*?'

'Not as in honey maker, but as in bitch.'

'Oh, very nice.'

'Not if you happen to be the object of her attentions, or desires. She's a hired gun, and psycho with it.'

Pappenheim puffed furiously at the ceiling. 'Tell me more.'

'Known by many names – Marie Valbon, Marianne Hirsch, Mary-Anne Norton, Mavis Böhm, Maria Chavez, and many more. She's half German, half Ami. The father is German. It is possible she belongs to the group you're hunting. Er . . . I've got to go.' The line went dead.

Pappenheim slowly replaced the receiver. 'Somebody must have walked in.' He squinted at the ceiling. 'Well, well, well. I wonder if our friend Grogan can shed more light,' he added.

He picked up the internal phone and punched in the goth's number. 'Another session at the computer, I'm afraid,' he said when she answered, 'if you can spare the time.'

'No trouble at all, sir,' she said.

'Thanks, Hedi. See you as soon as you can make it. Put Hermann on, will you, please?'

'He's right here.'

'Hermann,' Pappenheim began with bright cheeriness when Spyros came on the line.

'No need to grovel, Pappi,' came the long-suffering response. 'I have long accepted that I have lost this battle. What it is to have both the good fortune, and the misfortune, to have a genius on my staff.'

'Hard world, Hermann.'

'Tell me about it. She's already on her way, by the way.'

'Thanks, Hermann.'

'Nada.'

'That's not Greek.'

'It's not Latin, either. Well . . . it has Latin roots . . .'

''Bye, Hermann.'

The goth was waiting by the door when Pappenheim got to the rogues' gallery.

'I won't keep you longer than is absolutely necessary,' he said to her as they entered.

'No problem. No rush. *Kommissar* Spyros is fine with it.'

'Alright then. Power up.'

'What are we after this time?' she asked as she took her seat at the computer and turned it on.

The machine booted and raced to the desktop.

'We're going to send an encrypted message to the beacon.'

'And then?'

'We wait.'

'That could be a long time, sir. We may not hear for a week. He may not *see* it for a week.'

'True. But I have a feeling this may get a far quicker response. Ready?'

'Ready.'

Pappenheim decided to choose one of the aliases he'd been given for Mary-Anne.

'Here's the message: who is Maria Chavez?'

The goth encrypted it, placed it in the beacon, and went online.

'You might as well surf while we wait,' Pappenheim suggested.

'I could do some online flying with my friend, if she wants to. She's a researcher, and works from home most days.'

'I know you're dying to take your jet up,' Pappenheim said with a smile. 'Go ahead.'

The goth needed no second bidding. She put on her spider – a headphone and mike set she had designed – and launched the incredibly detailed F-16 simulation. She made contact with the person who usually alternated as her online wingman and, within seconds, a very lifelike jet appeared on her left wing.

They talked to each other and flew air-to-air combat missions against artificial intelligence adversaries who were remarkably dangerous.

Pappenheim, always astonished by the fidelity of the game, watched with amused interest as the goth and her friend became totally immersed in it. At times, when engaged in dogfights, their language rivalled anything that could be heard in a crowded pub, or beer hall.

This went on for nearly an hour, then the goth called, 'Knock it off! Knock it off!'

'Knocking off,' came the reponse.

The second F-16 vanished, as did all the other aircraft. Only the goth's cockpit and the simulated world, a coastal landscape beneath a cirrus sky, remained.

'You've got something?' Pappenheim asked with eager anticipation.

She pointed to the F-16's left-hand, multi-function display. 'The left MFD.'

Pappenheim looked. Instead of the normal air-to-air radar display, a bright message had appeared.

'"Very dangerous,"' Pappenheim read aloud.

That was all. Bare seconds later, the message blinked once, and vanished. The radar display went back to normal.

'Now we know,' Pappenheim remarked softly. 'That was all I needed, Hedi. Stay longer if you wish. Just make certain you shut the door properly when you leave. The security system will arm itself, as usual.'

'I think I might have another flight.'

'Help yourself.'

Pappenheim was turning to leave, when Hedi Meyer stopped him with a soft exclamation.

'Look! Something else is on the display.'

Another message had appeared. 'IF HUNTING, EXTREME CAUTION ADVISED.'

As before, the message blinked once, and was gone.

'And we'll take that advice,' Pappenheim said. 'Anything else comes in, let me know immediately.'

'Yes, sir.'

'Thanks, Hedi.'

'No problem.'

Pappenheim returned to his office and called Müller, who picked up instantly.

'That was quick,' Pappenheim said. 'She must still be driving.'

'She is.'

'Where are you now?'

'Almost there.'

Pappenheim was amazed. 'You let her drive *all* the way? Greater love hath no man . . .'

'Don't push it.'

Pappenheim chuckled. 'Well, here's a little something to ease the pain. The bimbo, is no bimbo.'

'What's that without the code?'

'She is, my young Graf, a killer. A pro. Hired gun. Confirmed by my contact, *and* by our man with the beacon. Many aliases. There is also strong evidence that she may be a group member . . . but most certainly an employee. Father German, mother American. The beacon advises extreme caution. He should know, if anyone does.'

There was a silence interrupted by the background growl of the car as Müller pondered upon this.

Then he was back. 'Great work, Pappi. Thanks.'

'Feel better about Miss Bloomfield now?'

'It puts things into perspective.'

'It does,' Pappenheim said, unashamedly relieved. 'Some would say Adams died a happy man,' he went on with ghoulish humour. 'But you've got your peace of mind at a price. You've got to worry about a psycho killer now . . .'

'With a grudge,' Müller added.

'Against whom?'

'The lady in question. When they first met, she threatened to squeeze the bimbo's scrawny neck until the bimbo felt she wanted to spit out her larynx. I paraphrase her very words.'

'Uh-oh. Not good.'

'As if we needed more.'

Pappenheim gave another chuckle. 'Enjoy the flames.'

'You can go right off some people.'

'I heard that,' Pappenheim said. 'I'll keep you posted.'

'Do that. Any news on Max?'

'I was hoping you wouldn't ask. At the end of the talk, he did the usual any questions . . .'

'Don't tell me. I can guess the rest. Couldn't they just have got up and left? That's usually what happens. People tend to remain firmly silent and head for the buffet with relief.'

'You know how it is. If you didn't want him, there'd be no Q and A. But you need him, so of course, today of all days, they want to ask all the tedious questions. But he shouldn't be much longer. He knows we need him down there. As soon as he and the team can get away, they will. It's only fourteen kilometres and they'll do that at speed. If it's any consolation, our local colleagues have been in place. No alarms.'

'At least that's something. Thanks, Pappi.'

'So, what's the story?' Carey Bloomfield asked, as Müller put his phone away. 'And what was that about me and the diet-freak bimbo?'

They were now close to the *Schlosshotel*, and the Porsche cruised along the tree-lined country lane that led to it. Carey Bloomfield had settled down nicely with the car.

'No bimbo, she,' Müller replied.

'What do you mean?'

'Your "bimbo", Miss Bloomfield, is a many-aliased professional killer.'

'*What?* No way!'

'Eyes on the road, please. Both Pappi's contact, and Grogan, have confirmed it. Separately.'

'Sweet . . . Jesus. That stick insect?'

'She may look like one, but her instincts are those of a praying mantis. It certainly looks as if she sent Adams on his way, after first enjoying him.'

She shook her head in astonishment. 'Toby Adams gets taken like this? A killer is planted on him, and he didn't know? Adams is . . . *was* a top veteran.'

'We all have our blind side. Adams was clearly no exception, and he got taken. It happens.'

'He *fell* for her?'

'It seems like it.'

'But she's not his type.'

'Does that upset you?'

'What a dumb question, Müller . . .'

'Watch the road!'

'What a dumb question,' she repeated. 'Of course it doesn't upset me. I'm just surprised. So unprofessional.'

'As I've just said, we all have our blind spots. It's possible he did find himself sexually attracted to her, even though he might have had no real feelings for her.'

'Are you like that, Müller?'

'Watch the road! *Please*. It narrows from here, and it's two-way traffic. There are many bends. A car can be on you before you realize it. And don't switch this to me.'

She gave a brief little chuckle. 'We're arguing like an old couple, Müller. You know that?'

'We're not arguing,' he said, scanning the lane for oncoming traffic.

'Sure. So, Adams couldn't keep his zip closed, and gets killed for his pains?'

'It's rather more than that. The bimbo has dual nationality – German and American. She is also a member of the Semper, or is its employee, at the very least. And *don't* look at me. Look at the road. The *road!*'

'Jesus, Müller. Ease up. I'm not going to ding your car . . .'

'*Car!*' Müller shouted.

Carey Bloomfield hit the brakes harder than she had intended. The Porsche came to an abrupt halt with a sharp squeal, and felt as if it was trying to stand on its nose.

97

'Oops!' she said. 'Sorry.'

The other car was still some distance away and there was plenty of time for the two to pass without incident.

'Do you want to change seats?' she offered tentatively.

'No.'

'Glutton for punishment?'

'I must be.'

'So, skinny Mary-Anne – or whatever her name is,' Carey Bloomfield went on, hiding a smile, 'turns out to be a pro killer. Why set one of their own on one of their own?'

'Perhaps he upset someone. Whatever the reason, you are being framed for the deed. And, with the zip thing, you're the praying mantis your people will be hunting.'

'Great. I always wanted to be a praying mantis in my next life.'

'She may not be the only Semper in there. If so, they will ensure that the bimbo never comes under suspicion. And she may come after you too.'

'Oh, it just gets better and better.'

The classic lines of the *Schlosshotel* came into view.

'And here we are,' Carey Bloomfield went on. 'Safe and sound.'

'Safe for now, perhaps,' Müller said. He looked about the car, as if searching out blemishes. 'Sound, I'd leave for later.'

'Lighten up, Müller. I drove well.'

He gave a brief smile. 'You drove well.'

'There you go. Do I get another try?'

'Don't push it.'

Six

Schlosshotel Derrenberg. The fat wheels of the Porsche crunched along the drive which curved its way through the magnificent grounds of the beautifully restored mansion. Carey Bloomfield brought the car to a sedate halt, a short distance from the entrance to the hotel wing of the building.

'Mmm,' she said. 'I hate to leave this seat.'

'So do I,' Müller said.

'I get the message,' she said. 'You're never going to let me touch this wheel again.'

'I did not say that.'

'You said don't push it.'

'I certainly did.'

'That sounds like a no to me.'

'You're a professional. Don't read into a comment what isn't there.'

'Word games, Müller.'

'Fact. Now, smile as you get out. Here are Aunt Isolde and Greville.'

'Yes, sir.'

They climbed out as Aunt Isolde, tall and elegant, reached them, accompanied by Greville. Greville, complexion made dark by decades of Middle-Eastern sun, in his inevitable white suit and wide-brimmed hat, smiled when he saw Carey Bloomfield.

Aunt Isolde greeted her with a warm embrace. 'So good to see you again, my dear,' she said in English. 'Your old room is ready and waiting.'

'Hi, Aunt Isolde. Good to see you too.'

Greville doffed his hat. 'Miss Bloomfield. I have heard so much about you.' He offered his hand.

'All good, I hope,' she said as she took it.

'All absolutely good. Jens has nothing but praise.'

'Has he? That's news.'

'Ah. I detect a slight barb.' Greville smiled. 'Only to be expected, and confirms my initial prognosis.'

'Which is?'

'Now, that would be telling.'

Müller stood a little to one side, watching all this with some amusement. 'You can let go of her hand now, Greville,' he said.

'My dear Jens,' Greville said. 'Good to see you again, old

boy.' He grabbed Müller by an arm, and led him slightly away. 'My word,' he continued, voice lowered, 'she is a beauty! Done all right there, what? Gratifying to see, at last, the face to that name.'

'Greville,' Müller said, 'you're an old rogue.'

'Of course, old boy. Shameless about it. A pretty face like that. Reminds me of what it was like with Isolde. Fell like a ton of bricks. Still falling.' Greville's smile was full of wonder. 'All these years, and she's as fresh to me as that first day. Same with you, I suspect. Though you won't admit it.' Greville lowered his voice still further. 'Word to the wise, old boy. Learn from my experience. We don't all get a second chance. I was very lucky.'

'Lucky? With what you're carrying?'

'Small price. I got to see her again. Never thought I would.'

Müller looked at him, searching for evidence of the onset of his DNA nemesis. 'And how is it doing?'

'My own, bespoke DNA poison? Working its way through as usual, but no alarms. Assume it's still biding its time. Fiendish thing. Meanwhile, I make the most of my own time with Isolde. So, how goes it in the big bad world?'

'As bad as ever.'

'The Semper?'

'Among others, yes.'

'So, things have hotted up since our little jaunt in May?'

Greville, perhaps because of his decades-long absence from England, tended to speak in a blend of fifties accents, interwoven with expat slang and more modern rhythms that had worked their way up the last century.

'They have,' Müller told him. 'I'm getting closer to those responsible for what happened to my parents.'

'Good show!'

'But, there's a price . . . which seems to be getting higher.'

'There always is, old boy. Always is. What, precisely?'

'They made an attempt on Miss Bloomfield this morning.'

'Good . . . Lord!' Greville shot a quick glance in Carey Bloomfield's direction.

Engrossed in conversation with Aunt Isolde, she did not spot it. Both were laughing at something Carey Bloomfield had said.

100

'So, after what happened with your chum Pappenheim, they're raising the stakes.'

'Or getting desperate.'

'A wounded tiger is always the worst. It won't get better, old son.'

'I don't expect it to.'

'Realistic. Good.'

'I found the man who wrote that scurrilous editorial,' Müller went on.

'And?'

'He killed himself.'

'Before? Or after you found him?'

'After.'

'You must have terrified him.'

'He terrified himself. When he first saw me, an air of resignation came over him. He'd been expecting me for years.'

'Guilt. The bugger. Serves him right.'

'From what we learned before he blew his brains out, it seems he had been instructed by the Semper. He even said they had hoped to recruit me.' Müller spoke with disgust. 'They had the gall to consider it, after what they had done.'

'New blood, old boy. You can only keep a thing like that going with new blood. They have planned for a long future.'

'Not if I can help it. Do you remember your saying something to me about an American during your time in the Middle East?'

'I do remember. I believe I was recounting an odd tale of convenient allies. I think I said something in the order of: "Once teamed up with an East German who previously had been my mortal enemy. We allied ourselves with an American, to eliminate some privateers. People who did it for the money." Something like that.'

'That's exactly how I remember it. Good memory, Greville.'

Greville's smile was fleeting, and carried memories with it. 'Saved my bacon on more than one occasion, I can tell you. And what about this American? He was very young at the time, mark you.'

'Then it fits. I believe he was the same man who was Miss Bloomfield's controller in the field.'

Greville had eyes that looked into a great distance. They studied Müller with an unnerving directness. 'I know there's more coming.'

'It would seem that this man, Adams, was also with the Semper.'

'He compromised her?'

'I believe he planned to either betray her one day or, in time, have her killed.'

'And you believe he tried today?'

Müller shook his head. 'For some reason, I think not. I have the strangest feeling this morning's incident was a screw-up. She went to see him—'

'She *went*?'

'She was not a very pleased woman.'

'I can imagine.'

'But she told me,' Müller said, 'he seemed genuinely surprised. It does not mean he wasn't planning to.'

'How did you find out he was with the Semper?'

'In a way, it was she who found out. We were looking at the photographs my father left. She spotted Adams in one.'

'Well, I'll be damned,' Greville said in wonder. 'On such small things. Your father did sterling service, old boy. He gave you a potent weapon. If they ever found out . . .'

'They won't. And I'll use it against them in ways they will not expect. There's one other thing that editor, Vogel, mentioned. He talked of a colonel. At first I thought he meant Miss Bloomfield—'

'She outranks me?'

'She outranks you, Major, retired. She's a lieutenant-colonel.'

'Ah. They make them so young these days. Do go on, old chum.'

'He was not talking about her. In fact, he was quite astonished to see a woman. I had the feeling that perhaps they got the rank wrong, and really meant you.'

'We both know they tried to get me last May, but—'

'You two!' came Aunt Isolde's voice. 'Stop gossiping. Let's go in.'

'I don't think . . . Vogel, was it?'

Müller nodded.

'I don't think Vogel meant my good self,' Greville finished in a hurried whisper.

'Then we'll just have to see.'

'Forewarned, eh?'

'Exactly.'

They halted their conversation. Aunt Isolde and Carey Bloomfield were approaching.

'It's rude to whisper among yourselves, in company,' Aunt Isolde scolded them with a smile.

'You two were laughing about something,' Müller countered.

'Ah yes. Carey was telling me all about her little drive in your car. Panicked you, did she?'

Müller gave Carey Bloomfield a neutral stare. 'I was *not* panicked.'

'You were hanging on to the door handle.'

'I was . . .'

Whatever he had been about to say was interrupted by the arrival of a luxury minibus, with the hotel logo on its flanks.

'We've got a convention booked in,' Aunt Isolde explained as they turned to look. 'Japanese. They've taken the entire hotel wing. Some of them have booked the bus for a trip into the Thüringer Wald. They'll be gone for a couple of days.'

'What kind of convention?' Müller asked.

'They're scientists.'

'And their field?'

It was Greville who answered. 'Genetics.' He sounded amused.

Müller was about to turn to Greville when the guests for the minibus began to come out. They milled around for a second or so, then one of them spotted the Porsche. He turned to a colleague, spoke excitedly and, within moments, a group of them had surrounded the car, eagerly studying it. This went on for several minutes.

'Anyone spot something unusual?' Carey Bloomfield asked.

'Like what?' Müller demanded.

'Cameras. No cameras. Shouldn't they be snapping away at your Porsche, Müller?'

'Surely you don't go in for that old cliché about the Japanese and their cameras when abroad? Besides, these are not tourists.'

The admiring group reluctantly left the car and boarded their bus.

'Seems I wasn't so wrong, after all,' Carey Bloomfield said, as the bus left. 'Someone just took a picture.'

Müller turned to follow its progress down the drive. 'Of the car?'

'No. Of us.'

Müller stared after the bus until it had disappeared. 'Are you certain?'

'Positive,' she replied. 'I would not make a mistake like that.'

'Why us?' Aunt Isolde asked. 'There's nothing special about us.'

Müller glanced at Greville, whose eyes telegraphed a message Müller quickly understood.

'Tell you what, Aunt Isolde, why don't you and Greville take the Mercedes up to Berlin tomorrow? Stay at the apartment for a few days. We'll be gone some days ourselves, so it's all yours. What do you say, Greville?'

'Not a bad idea . . .'

'But we can't,' Aunt Isolde began to protest. 'The hotel . . .'

'Practically runs itself,' Müller cut in. 'You've got such good staff, they can virtually do everything in their sleep. Tell her, Greville.'

'He does have a point, my dear,' Greville said to Aunt Isolde. 'And you know – if anybody does – what he's like when he has a point. The hotel can run by itself.'

'Sounds like a conspiracy to me,' she said.

Both looked at her innocently. 'Conspiracy?' they said together.

Carey Bloomfield took her own cue. 'Aunt Isolde, why don't you reacquaint me with that beautiful room overlooking the stream?'

The stream, a tributary of the river Saale that could, in heavy rainfall, turn into a raging torrent, meandered its way across the huge grounds and passed directly beneath the window of the room in question. The stream was a much admired feature of the Derrenberg.

Arm in arm, she led Aunt Isolde away.

The Derrenberg's central section and its right wing housed the hotel. The left wing was used exclusively as the owner's residence.

Greville watched as they walked towards the small gate at the side of the large, sliding steel-panelled double gate that allowed vehicle entry to the courtyard.

'Quick on the uptake, your Miss Bloomfield,' he said to Müller.

'She's no slouch.'

'You say that with pride, old man. Betraying your true feelings, what?'

'Greville.'

'Yes, old man?'

'Shut up.'

Greville allowed himself a huge grin. 'Of course.'

'Look after Aunt Isolde. She's all the family I've got.'

'Goes without saying, old boy. Any . . . weaponry at your place?'

'My bedroom. Aunt Isolde will show you which one. Bedside cabinet, left. Top drawer. A Beretta 92R. Three magazines, 15-shot.'

'You do like that gun. It's a cannon.'

'It's perfect for my uses. The weight, the balance, the firepower. I prefer not to use a gun . . .'

'But if you have to, you want one that is reliable, and hits hard.'

'One way of putting it.'

'I understand perfectly, old boy. And I'll see Isolde's alright. No fear. I won't let the buggers take her from me; not after all these years. Go in and see how she is, shall I?'

Müller nodded. 'I'll be along.'

In the luxurious bedroom suite overlooking the stream, Carey Bloomfield peered down from her window at the water. Its gentle rush was soporific. She took a deep breath of air that had the freshness of recent rain, though the grounds were not even damp.

'It's like coming home,' she said to Aunt Isolde, who was standing behind her, looking on with a gentle, speculative smile.

'Then treat it as such. You know you are welcome here at any time.'

'Thank you, Aunt Isolde.'

'And how are things with Jens? I see you still address each other rather formally. Müller. Miss Bloomfield.'

Carey Bloomfield turned round. 'In a funny way, it's not really formal at all. It just seems that way. Actually, I am sort of quite comfortable with it. I've waited so long now for him to call me Carey, I think I'd die of shock if he did. Does that make sense?'

'I think it reveals rather more than either of you are prepared to admit.'

'I can't just throw myself at him, Aunt Isolde. He'd run a mile.'

'Perhaps not as far as you think.'

'Just look at you and Greville,' Carey Bloomfield said. 'Müller told me the major fell for you in a heartbeat.'

'And do you think he did that all by himself?'

Carey Bloomfield stared at her. 'You *suckered* him?'

'My dear,' Aunt Isolde said, smile widening, 'all men like to think they made the running. It's nice to leave them with their illusions, but not to the detriment of our own capability for taking the initiative when it suits us. Now I'll leave you to unpack, and freshen up.' She paused at the door. 'And don't worry, we shall go up to Berlin tomorrow. I fully realize Jens would not have suggested it without very good reason.'

'You're the only close family he has, Aunt Isolde. He worries about you.'

'I know he does. But it's good to know he's got you too.'

Aunt Isolde left before Carey Bloomfield could respond.

Müller, still outside, was on the phone to Pappenheim.

'They'll be staying at my place. Can you have two people keep an eye on it for me?'

'Berger and Reimer would be my first choice, but they've drawn some diplomatic duty from tomorrow, for the next week.

106

Whoever it was actually asked for Berger and Reimer. Seems they were remembered for a similar duty they pulled ages ago. They've got to dress up.'

'Bet they liked that.'

'Bet they didn't, is more like it. Berger was cursing, and Reimer moaned about standing his girlfriend up.'

'I think he needs that girlfriend of his just for the pleasure of moaning about his love life,' Müller said.

'And driving us crazy. But he is an excellent cop. This came in only about half an hour ago,' Pappenheim went on. 'One of Kaltendorf's cronies made a request, and of course the Great White jumped. Couldn't deflect him, even when I tried to convince him I needed them both.'

'And do you?'

'I always need them. But I was forcibly overridden.'

'*You?*'

'Me.'

'Were you asleep?'

'I must have been.'

'Alright, Pappi. I've tagged along with the game. Why did you allow the GW to "forcibly" override you?'

'Could be because the person they're supposed to be babysitting has turned out to be one of the names we have.'

Müller digested this piece of news. 'Then by all means let them dress up.'

'Thought you'd say that. So, I'll talk with *Kommissarin* Fohlmeister, she of the Ready Group, to see if I can temporarily poach a team from her.'

'And can Ilona help?'

'She will.'

'I like your certainties, Pappi.'

'Certain. That's me.'

'They're all coming out of the woodwork,' Müller said.

'Some of them seem to be. But they don't know we know. That's the beauty of it.'

'And we'll keep it that way.'

'Are you quite sure Miss Bloomfield saw what she thought she saw?' Pappenheim asked.

'I've no doubt she did see it,' Müller said, 'though I didn't.

107

I was not looking in the right direction at the time; but, in the present circumstances, I'm taking nothing for granted. I'd rather be wrong and prepared, than unprepared and vulnerable. They were all around the car, Pappi. Like excited children. But no one took the expected photograph.'

'They're scientists, not click-happy tourists.'

'Exactly my thoughts. But a sneak shot of the four of us, from the bus, was definitely out of the ordinary.'

'Well, don't you worry about Wilmersdorf,' Pappenheim said. 'I'll make sure they're looked after.'

'I appreciate it. And I have to ask. Any news from Max?'

'He and his team have left, and should be there any time now.'

'Thank God for that. And thanks, Pappi.'

'Nada.'

'*Nada?*'

'Something Hermann Spyros said earlier.'

'Now you've lost me.'

Pappenheim's chuckle sounded in Müller's ear as they ended the conversation.

Carey Bloomfield looked down at the stream from the wide window of her room. Slightly to the left was the small, arched wooden bridge. Both brought back several memories, some of which she would have preferred to forget.

To avoid flooding of the grounds during heavy rain, the banks of the stream had been substantially raised all along the section where it crossed the property. Today, it was flowing peacefully and was so clear she could see the bottom. But the day she and Müller had faced Dahlberg, the stream had been a torrent in pouring rain; and she had been in it, at night, trying to make her way across to the hotel.

Under fire.

She had been crawling across the bridge when a bullet had whacked into it, very close. She now wondered whether the bullet were still there, or had been dug out, and the gouge smoothed over. She assumed it had been.

Müller had left her in the car with strict instructions to call Pappenheim, and then leave. But, unknown to Müller, she had been after Dahlberg herself, the man who had tortured her brother by peeling him alive; and, also unknown to Müller, she had brought her own gun.

She shut her eyes briefly in an effort to blot out the vision of the bloody, mutilated thing her brother had become, in that hellhole in the Middle East. But the vision was etched upon her mind.

Dahlberg, despite using Aunt Isolde as a shield in a last, desperate attempt to escape, had not made it.

'We got you, you bastard,' she now said, barely audibly.

Both she and Müller had shot at the same time.

She looked down at the stream once more. Dahlberg, dying, had fallen in, to be swept away.

She was still staring down at the stream when a knock sounded on her door.

'It's open!' she called, turning to look.

Müller opened the door a crack. 'May I?'

'Of course. I was just admiring the stream . . . and remembering. Seems a long time ago.'

'It does, at times,' Müller agreed, entering. He left the door slightly open, as if not sure that he should be in the room with her, with the door fully closed.

'But it feels good to be back. I love this room.'

'It's yours any time you want it.'

She nodded. 'Aunt Isolde said. It's very kind of her.'

'She did not say it to be kind. She said it because she wants you to know you can look upon this place as a home.'

'Keep this up and I'll be embarrassed by the generosity.'

'Don't be.' He joined her at the window, and looked down. 'You were very brave that night.'

'Scared,' she corrected. 'I thought there were snakes in there. During a vacation in Florida when I was a kid, I got bitten by a cottonmouth in a creek. It's a memory that stuck. My brother saved my life that day. He did everything right. That's why I went after Dahlberg, to get the bastard for what he did to him.'

'Although your orders were to take him alive.'

She nodded. 'I've no regrets.'

'Neither do I,' Müller said. 'Given the slightest chance, he

109

would have killed Aunt Isolde. Do you believe,' he went on, 'that this incident could have been the trigger for Adams?'

'You mean the moment he decided to betray me one day?'

'Yes. After all, Dahlberg was part of the Semper, or worked for them.'

'I don't think so. I think Adams had his own agenda and that moment would have come anyway, whenever he was ready to do it; whether I had killed Dahlberg or not.'

Müller nodded slowly, still looking down at the stream. 'That is my reading of the situation. I've been thinking about Vogel's place in Wannsee,' he continued. 'I have been searching my memory to check whether I might have seen something, but had not consciously registered it.'

She looked at him. 'You're really bothered about hidden cameras, aren't you?'

Müller was thoughtful. 'Something's nagging at me.'

'You mean they bugged him?'

'In their position, wouldn't you? Years of guilt was taking its toll. They would expect him to crack one day. These people are adept at long-term planning. Easy enough to plant devices in a wide-open building like that, with a sole occupant.'

Carey Bloomfield was tracking Müller's thoughts. 'So, if there were bugs, or cameras, in there . . . or both . . .'

'We've been seen and/or heard.'

'As Pappi would say, not good.'

He turned from the stream to look at her. 'Not good at all. I've asked Pappi to send in a clean-up team. They'll scour the place.'

'But you're still worried.'

'Pappi won't waste time getting people in there.'

'But the others might be faster.'

'There is that possibility. We don't know where they are. The information we have so far, pinpoints some of the top people; but their . . . drones . . . if you like, can be anywhere. They may well have had people watching him for years.'

'Then they would have seen us arrive. They could have shot him to stop him talking.'

Müller shook his head. 'Too crude. They want as little attention as possible drawn to them.'

'What about that fake cop who tried to take me?'

'If it hadn't been for Pappi, he would have got away with it. For the brief period necessary to do the job, he would have been well within the time frame. The gun would have been silenced. No one would have paid much attention to a policeman leaning into a car to talk to the occupant; especially as it was raining. Before anyone suspected anything was amiss, he would have been long gone, and no probable witnesses would have been able to say more than that they saw a policeman. People tend to avoid looking at uniformed police. They're the "invisibles" of society. There, but not there. A uniform is a uniform is a uniform.'

'Well, that's true enough. It's the same anywhere, I guess. You don't look at cops, in case they look back at you with interest.'

'Exactly.'

Carey Bloomfield gave a slight shiver as Müller again turned to look down at the stream. 'I could have been dead right there in that rain. I was caught flat-footed. Like a damned rookie.'

'Pappi is no rookie,' he said to her, 'and see what happened to him.'

'Trying to make me feel better?'

'No. Just emphasizing how dangerous these people are.'

'I'm convinced,' she said. 'And I haven't forgotten about the guy in the bus who took our picture.'

'It could have been a simple tourist shot, of course.'

'But you don't think so.'

'No.'

'Nor that a bunch of genetic scientists coming here was coincidence.'

'Aunt Isolde gets all sorts of people here.'

'But you think they came to observe Greville.'

'I did not say that. I'm simply keeping all options open. If there's nothing to their presence, fine. If there is . . .' Müller left the rest unsaid.

She gave him a surreptitious glance. *Why don't you just take hold of me?* she said in her mind.

But he made no such move.

'I'll leave you to get on with settling in,' he said, turning again from the stream. 'Off to my room. Then we're expected in the breakfast room. Aunt Isolde is preparing something. I'm sure you're hungry.'

'Are you saying I like stuffing my face, Müller?'

He smiled. 'It's a pretty face.'

He went out, leaving her staring at the closed door.

'A compliment!' she said to the door. 'Do I faint now? Or later?'

Pappenheim had received a surprising phone call.

'What do you mean there's *no* body?' he barked at Max Gatto.

'Sir, there's nothing. No body. No blood. No gun.'

Pappenheim thought about that for half a second. 'And our local colleagues? What were they doing? Sleeping?'

Gatto's cough was apologetic. 'As a matter of fact . . . yes.'

'*What?*'

'Not of their own volition. Someone put them under. Some kind of knockout drug. We found them in their car.'

'Shit!' Pappenheim said. 'Are they OK?'

'They're still asleep, but otherwise fine.'

Pappenheim took a drag of his cigarette, exhaled a twin stream of smoke through his nostrils, then blew out the residue as a single, perfect smoke ring.

'I assume you have checked through the villa.'

'Completely,' Gatto, a *Kommissar*, replied.

'Any surveillance equipment?'

'Nothing.'

'*Nothing?*'

'Not even a hole to show where anything had been removed.'

'Very curious. Max, is there anything about the place that does not feel right to you?'

'Apart from a body that seems to walk?'

'Don't try the jokes with me, sonny.'

'Sorry, sir,' the other said quickly. 'Just being—'

'Forget it. Now think about that villa. What doesn't seem right?'

'Everything's as it should . . . be . . .'

'Yes?' Pappenheim said in anticipation, straightening in his chair.

112

'Television.'

'What about it?'

'No television in the house. Not in any room. No radio either. No CD player, no CDs; no video, no tapes, no satellite receiver. I can't believe anyone living by himself in a place like this would not have a single item of home entertainment.'

'As would no one who had been a professional newsman. Now we know how they did it.'

'They hid them in the systems. No telltale signs. Now they no longer need them, all they had to do was unplug everything and take them away. Easy.'

'As you should know, having done it yourself on occasion. ISDN through the phone system, a local, secure network, and you've got sound and vision twenty-four hours a day.'

'Phones are gone too.'

'What a surprise. They're thorough, if nothing . . . Anything else in the area?'

'There's a boathouse, and a small pier . . .'

'Do you have anyone near that boathouse?' Pappenheim asked sharply.

Startled by the tone of voice, Gatto replied, 'Er . . . no, sir. We were just about to—'

'Be very careful. They could have put everything in there . . . body, all the equipment and phones . . .'

'And booby-trapped them.'

'Exactly.'

'Paul Zimmer is with us. He's our explosives man. He's got all his gear. I'll ask him to have a look, shall I?'

'Alright. But the back of my neck's itching. Tell him to be extra careful. No heroes, Max.'

'Paul is one of the most careful people I know. He takes his time. A snail is a racing car by comparison.'

'Even so. I don't want another dead body.'

'I'll make certain he understands that.'

'Thanks, Max.'

'I still don't like it,' Pappenheim said to himself as he replaced the phone.

He blew another smoke ring at the ceiling. This time, it was not one of his better efforts. The ring staggered upwards, collapsing upon itself as it went.

'I don't like it,' he repeated.

He knew if anything went wrong out there, it could damage Müller. Despite the fact that a serious crime had been committed, Kaltendorf would see the deployment of the clean-up team as an unauthorized use of a special unit for private reasons. Kaltendorf would attempt to show that Müller had been working on a personal case. Vogel had died because Müller had gone to see him.

'*Ergo*,' Pappenheim remarked softly, 'if something happens to the team out there, it will be seen as Jens' fault, and the GW would be only too happy to nail him. Thin ice, Jens.'

Pappenheim blew another smoke ring upwards. It was a perfect example, and floated majestically.

'I still don't like it,' he said a third time.

Wannsee. Max Gatto secured his headset and spoke to Paul Zimmer. 'Alright, Paul. How do you hear?'

'Loud and clear,' Zimmer replied. Fully suited up in protective clothing from head to toe, he looked at Gatto through the visor of his secured helmet. 'And stop looking so worried. This is not my first job, you know.'

'All jobs are the first, Paul. You know that.'

Zimmer reached forward to touch Gatto's shoulder briefly. 'Yes, Papa. Can I go now?'

Gatto nodded.

Zimmer began walking towards the boathouse. The rain had stopped, save for a thin, ephemeral drizzle. The damp ground marked out his footsteps, the grass lying in serried ranks within each footprint.

The remaining four members of the team, Gatto included, fanned out a safe distance from the boathouse. They would all mention those footprints in their individual reports.

Zimmer reached the boathouse, and stopped. He lowered himself carefully, squatting on his heels. A cautious hand probed the ground. He moved sideways, doing the same thing, until he had covered several metres. He looked to his right, and left. The whole thing took several agonizing minutes.

'No tripwires. Moving forward.'

He sounded perfectly at ease. Not even his breathing, clearly heard on the headphones, had changed its rhythm.

He repeated his performance three times before he actually reached the boathouse. Each time, his report was negative. His entire progress had taken half an hour.

'That's it, Paul,' Gatto whispered. 'Take all the time you need. Don't rush.'

'What?' came Zimmer's voice. 'You said something?'

'I said no need to hurry.'

'Who's hurrying?' was Zimmer's cheerful riposte. 'Checking the door,' he continued.

Zimmer took a long time about it.

'I'm not going to use a sensor,' he went on, 'in case they've got something in there that would respond as a trigger.'

More minutes passed.

'Clean,' he said at last. 'Trying the handle . . . now.'

All held their breaths. Nothing happened.

'Opening the door.'

This took a few more minutes as Zimmer checked all possibilities. Again, nothing happened. The door was now wide open, and Zimmer could see in. He remained where he was.

'No boobies at the door, but everything we're looking for is in here. All the TVs and stuff . . . and the body. A speed-boat's in there, and he's sitting in it. Some sense of humour they've got.'

'Paul!'

'Yes?'

'Wait.'

'Waiting.'

Zimmer stood still, but did not turn round.

Gatto passed a hand across his forehead. The others watched him tensely.

'Apart from the things you've mentioned,' he went on to Zimmer, 'what else do you see?'

'Usual boating stuff, as expected. The TV gear is chucked all over the place. The body's hands are tied to the wheel of the boat. There's a red baseball cap on his head. There's an

115

emblem on it, but I can't see properly in the light in here, without going closer. Usual light switch . . .'

'Don't touch it!'

'Of course I won't, Max. What do you think I am? A first-day probationary?'

'Just be careful. It's a trap.'

'Of course it's a trap. Doorway clear, though. No wires –' Zimmer paused, turning his head slowly as he scanned the interior of the boathouse – 'no infrared, or laser trip. I've got to go in, Max. I can't do much just standing here.'

'Alright,' Gatto said reluctantly. 'But *slowly*.'

'The word fast is not in my vocabulary.'

Zimmer began to make his way inside. 'So far so good.'

'What was that?' Gatto asked.

A garbled response came back.

'Paul! What the hell's going on? You're breaking up!'

In the boathouse, Paul Zimmer had raised his voice above the sudden static in his ears.

'I can't hear you, Max! You've got interference!'

He was standing in a relatively clear part of the boathouse. There was nothing particularly close to him, and no trip devices of any kind that he could see.

'Paul!' Gatto was yelling. 'Get out! *Get out now!*'

The explosion, when it came, was massive.

The entire boathouse lifted into the air. The speedboat rose through the fireball and exploded in a violent sunburst that spread blazing fuel in all directions. Something dark and heavy detached itself from the cauldron, rose to apogee, then hurtled earthwards to land on the jetty, breaking the structures's back. Whatever it was, it disappeared into the water. Both ends of the jetty rose in a broken V, their supports looking for all the world like the dental stumps of a prehistoric animal.

Then the entire, raging fireball collapsed upon itself. Shards of hot metal and burning wood hissed in sharp bursts into the water, loud enough for the four men to hear quite clearly. A huge pall of dense, black smoke boiled upwards.

Gatto was running towards the flames, shouting. 'Paul! Paul! *Paul!*'

He did not get far. Two burly members of his team flung

116

themselves upon him and brought him down. Despite the fierceness of his struggles, they held him fast.

'Sir!' one of them bawled at him. 'You can't do anything! He's gone! No one could have lived through that!'

'Let me go, you bastards! *Let me go!*'

They were immovable.

'No, sir,' the second one said.

The other two stood by, faces grim, ready to add their own weight on top of their still-resisting commander, if need be.

After long moments, Gatto stopped fighting.

'Alright,' he said with unnatural calm. 'You can get off me.'

They released him and got to their feet warily.

Gatto stood up. A large swathe of his clothes was a huge damp mark, with bits of grass upon it. It looked funny, but no one was laughing.

He turned to stare at the billowing of flame and smoke that had become Paul Zimmer's pyre.

'Sound,' he said tightly, face stretched in a mask of sorrow and anger. 'Something in there caused enough interference to force us to shout at each other to be heard. It was voice-activated. Paul triggered the bomb himself. They could have put it anywhere. No wonder everything looked nice and clear. No wonder there were no tripwires. They didn't need them. Bastards. *Bastards!*'

Wannsee Station, Brücke C, the white lettering on the blue background declared.

The bastards in question were two men across the water. They had been standing near one of the boarding piers for the lake shipping lines. On spotting the rising cloud of the explosion in the distance, they hurried along the stretch of waterfront to the right of the pier, until they came to what seemed like a deserted rescue station, behind a wire fence. They could go no further without vaulting the fence.

Just beyond it was a large, square box with a red cross within a blue circle, fixed to a post. Atop the box was a big clock with black figures on a white dial. It had stopped at 10.35, and seemed to have been like that for a very long time. The whole structure looked very much the worse for wear.

117

One of the men leaned against the fence and raised a pair of binoculars that was hung about his neck. He paused to stare across the grey of the water, then brought them to his eyes. He focused on the location of the explosion.

'Curiosity killed the cat,' he said.

He passed the binoculars to his companion, who put them to his own eyes.

'Boom,' the second man said, and gave a silent laugh.

Both men, in deck shoes and yachting gear, attracted no curious glances from the few people who had decided to brave the weather. Those few were now staring in puzzlement at the distant pall of smoke.

The voice of one of the onlookers came drifting upon the light breeze. 'Some accident somewhere.'

Those who had even bothered to look at the two men had worn expressions that had clearly betrayed their thoughts. The two, they assumed, were fanatical sailors who had been crazy enough to take to the water on such a day.

Neither of the men had been on the water, nor had they any intention of doing so.

The second man returned the binoculars. 'Let's see how Müller likes this.'

The other grinned and said nothing.

They turned and retraced their steps for a short distance, before crossing a patch of green to take a surfaced path that zigzagged up to where they had parked their car.

Seven

Pappenheim sat at his desk, head in his hands. Ten minutes before, he had received a distraught call from Max Gatto, and had not touched a cigarette since.

Wearily, he passed his hands through his hair. 'Paul Zimmer. Wife, two kids under five.'

Finally, he took out a cigarette from the pack on his desk,

lit it, then drew loudly upon it. He did not look as if he found it enjoyable. He gave a sigh of foreboding.

'The shit,' he said, 'is about to hit the fan.'

He picked up a phone and called Müller.

Müller was just about to leave his room to go downstairs. He got out his phone at the first ring.

'Yes, Pappi.'

'Paul Zimmer is dead,' Pappenheim said without preamble.

Müller shut his eyes briefly, said nothing, went across to the large four-poster, and sat down at its edge.

'How?' he asked at last.

Pappenheim gave Müller the full details, as had been related to him by Gatto. 'It was a sucker job,' he added in a hard voice. 'I want those bastards.'

'That makes two of us.'

'We're in a queue. You should have heard Max. He sounded as if he was chewing his phone.'

'I can well understand.'

'They did everything right,' Pappenheim said. 'Not their fault.'

'From what you've just told me, he certainly can't be faulted. He could not have known they would have had a set-up like that. Not even Paul could have expected it. What about the local colleagues?'

'They're OK. Sleeping drug. That was all. Two men in sailing gear came up to them asking some stupid questions. Deliberately so, of course. Our colleagues reacted as would be expected. Idiot tourists. They did not take them seriously. Then wham . . . two needles in the neck.'

'Smart. Can they identify them?'

'Nothing we can use. Only one really spoke. The other positioned himself in such a way that the attack, when it came, was so quick and co-ordinated, our colleagues had no chance. Both "sailors" had their rain hoods up, and screwed up their faces as if against the light drizzle that was falling at the time.'

'They considered everything.'

'Hopefully not everything. Max and the others are scouring the place for clues. But we've got a big problem.'

119

'The Great White.'

'The man himself. I'll have to report to him before he gets to know from other sources. You know he'll do everything to nail you for this.'

'The surprise would be if he didn't try,' Müller said in a voice born of experience.

'So, what do you plan to do?'

'Coming back to Berlin won't bring Paul back, nor help the case. Far better that I continue with my investigations, whatever the GW thinks. This is not just a personal case. These people are inimical to the country. They have killed a colleague today. They had a good try at killing you, and they nearly got Miss Bloomfield this morning. They once kidnapped the GW's own daughter. Even he can't be stupid enough to miss all these connections. If he hadn't set up his ludicrous PR exercise of a talk for his pet VIPs, Max and his team would have got down in time, and Paul Zimmer would not have left a widow and two little kids behind.'

'Now you've got that off your chest, I can see the line of attack if Kaltendorf starts to flame from every orifice. Just so you know, I concur.'

'OK, Pappi. Will you be calling Paul's wife? Or are you leaving that to Max?'

'I think it is appropriate for Max to do the initials. I'll call her afterwards.'

'When you do, give her my condolences and sincerest regrets. And let her know we'll get the bastards.'

'You can be sure of that. Now I'd better run off like a good boy to Kaltendorf.'

'Thanks, Pappi. Terrible news.'

'Not good. I'll keep you posted.'

But Pappenheim had already been eclipsed.

In his own office, Kaltendorf picked up one of his phones at the second ring. 'Kaltendorf.'

'Ah, Heinz,' a familiar voice said. 'What's this I hear about one of your men going down?'

'*What?* None of my people are down. Where did you hear that?'

The smooth voice ignored the question. 'It appears this happened at Wannsee . . .'

'I have no special teams out at the moment. Anywhere. What would they be doing in Wannsee?'

'Don't you know where your own people are, Heinz?' The question had been deliberately framed to cause embarrassment. 'Now, I wonder who would authorize *Kommissar* Gatto's team—'

'*Gatto?* Gatto was giving a talk – on my authority – to some dignitaries. His people were in attendance. What the devil are they doing in Wannsee?'

Again, a direct reply was avoided. 'All I can tell you is that there was an explosion. *Hauptmeister* Zimmer is down.'

Kaltendorf's mouth opened and closed like a fish out of water, as he took in the news of the death of the senior sergeant.

'Down?' he said after a while, shocked voice so low it was almost inaudible.

'If you did not authorize this,' the voice went on, totally devoid of mercy, 'who did?'

Kaltendorf gripped his phone. '*Müller!*' he snarled.

But the other person had already hung up.

Kaltendorf slammed down the phone, then picked up another. He dialled Müller's extension. When he got no reply, he slammed it down, then picked it up again.

Pappenheim was just about to leave for Kaltendorf's office when one of the phones rang. He picked it up almost before the first ring had stopped.

'*Pappenheim!*' came the roar in his ear. '*My office!*'

'I was already on my way . . . sir . . .'

The sharp click told him that Kaltendorf had already hung up on him.

Pappenheim sighed. 'And the condemned man had a last smoke.'

With great deliberation, he took a cigarette from the pack, and lit it. He leaned back in his chair and smoked the weed slowly, taking it out every so often to look at it, before putting it back into his mouth. He continued like this until it had burned right down, then he took it out for a last look, before stubbing it out with deliberation.

He stood up, and brushed the specks of ash off his clothes. They showered on to his chair, the desk and the floor. The phone began to ring as he moved from behind the desk. There was something about its insistence that led him to believe it was Kaltendorf.

He let it ring and went out.

Kaltendorf was on his feet and glowering when Pappenheim entered.

'You're late!' Kaltendorf barked.

'I came as quickly as I could, sir,' Pappenheim said calmly.

'I want an explanation, Pappenheim!' Kaltendorf raged. 'One of my officers is down! I want to know what *Kommissar* Gatto's team are doing in Wannsee! I want to know why they were called out without *my* authority . . . *Don't* . . . interrupt me! *I* am in command here! *Not* Müller! *How many times do I have to say it?*'

Pappenheim held on to his calm. 'May I speak now, sir?'

'Make it good! I want to hear you justify the death of *Hauptmeister* Zimmer!'

'*Hauptkommissar* Müller, sir, is investigating a group of people whose activities are inimical to the state . . .'

'Who gave him permission?'

'Sir,' Pappenheim began, grimly maintaining his careful calm as he went for the jugular, 'these are the same people who kidnapped your daughter last summer; and the same people who tried to kill me last May.'

Mention of his daughter caused an involuntary twitch to flit across Kaltendorf's right cheek.

You poor bastard, Pappenheim thought with short-lived sympathy. You're still on the hook. They're still yanking your chain.

He pressed home his advantage. '*Hauptkommissar* Müller was following a lead which took him to Wannsee, where he discovered a body . . .'

Kaltendorf stared at him. 'A *body*? Whose?'

'I've no idea, sir,' Pappenheim lied. 'He called me and

122

asked that I send down Gatto's team. He wanted the place immediately made secure, and a thorough check made . . .'

'Why not a normal forensics team . . .'

'With respect, sir, if I may finish.'

Still shaken by the reference to his daughter's kidnapping, Kaltendorf nodded.

'A normal forensics team might have inadvertently destroyed clues that Müller would recognize, given his experience with the case. The explosion proves he was right. Gatto's team are highly expert. Had it been an average forensics team, we might have been looking at the deaths of several colleagues, instead of one.'

Even Kaltendorf could not have argued with that logic, so he allowed Pappenheim to continue.

'Müller ordered that we ask our local colleagues to put two officers to guard the scene until Gatto's people arrived. The officers were instructed not to enter the building, to avoid unwitting obliteration of vital evidence.'

'So, what killed Zimmer?'

'Lateness, sir.'

Kaltendorf gave Pappenheim a baleful look. 'Lateness?'

'Yes, sir,' Pappenheim replied, face expressionless. 'I wanted Gatto and his team to get down there immediately. Müller thought people might try to get into the house to take away incriminating evidence. Unfortunately, they were held up.'

'How?'

'They were, sir, at a talk being given to—'

Kaltendorf paled with outrage. 'Are you trying to lay the blame on *me*, Pappenheim?'

'Not at all, sir. I am stating facts regarding timings. Because of the delay, persons unknown had time to do the very thing Müller feared. Our local colleagues were assaulted by two men posing as sailing enthusiasts, and injected with a drug that put them to sleep. The men then entered the house and removed the body. They then cleared the building of incriminating evidence, placed most of it in the boathouse with the body, and rigged a booby trap.

'Despite all the normal precautions – and we all know how

123

careful Paul Zimmer was – an explosion occurred, killing Zimmer and destroying the evidence that had been left. The body from the house has been torn to pieces. Most of it is gone. The trigger was voice-activated. I will have a full report from Gatto and the surviving members of the team on their return. They are currently sifting through the place for anything that might lead us to the perpetrators.'

Pappenheim stopped and waited.

'Where is Müller now?' Kaltendorf asked, after a long stare at Pappenheim.

'I'm not sure, sir,' Pappenheim again lied without batting an eyelid. 'You know how he works, sir . . .'

'I *know* how he works!' It was a curse. 'You tell him I want him here, in my office, as soon as he returns!'

'Yes, sir.'

'A colleague down. This is . . . this . . .'

'Yes, sir,' Pappenheim said again.

Kaltendorf kept staring at his subordinate, as if trying to find something hidden behind the neutral expression presented to him by Pappenheim, then he turned away.

'May I go now, sir?' Pappenheim asked with studied politeness.

Without turning round, Kaltendorf nodded.

'Thank you, sir,' Pappenheim said, and left.

While Pappenheim was walking back to his office, a man in another part of Berlin picked up his phone.

'Time for the colonel, I think,' he said to the person at the other end.

'When?'

'In your own time . . . but not too long.'

'Understood.'

Müller stood at one of the two large windows of his room. Like Carey Bloomfield's, this also looked down upon the stream, and the small wooden bridge.

After Pappenheim's call, he had decided to remain a while longer, in case the *Oberkommissar* called again. His instincts proved correct.

'Well, I've just had my audience with the man,' Pappenheim began.

'And?'

'I think I won the argument.'

'If you "think" it, it means you have.'

'He did fire a parting shot.'

'Let me guess. Me, in his office.'

'Clairvoyant, you are. When is he likely to see you?'

'When I'm finished.'

'Thought so. Right now, I don't know where you are.'

'Thanks, Pappi. So, how did it really go with him?'

Pappenheim gave a detailed, blow-by-blow account of his meeting with Kaltendorf.

'That was good, linking the lateness of the team with what happened,' Müller said when Pappenheim had finished. 'It might make him stop those stupid PR exercises.'

'I have my doubts.'

'So do I,' Müller agreed with some gloom.

'Interesting about the mention of his daughter,' Pappenheim went on. 'Whoever's pulling his chain still has a firm grip. Raising the subject also gave him an opportunity to refresh his dislike for you. You went after the kidnappers and saved her. You saw him with his guard down, pleading. His gratitude at the time has transformed into something close to hatred, because he feels indebted to you . . .'

'Are you quite finished?'

'No. There's more. What really drives him insane is the fact that his lovely, precious, darling daughter has a crush on you; so she tells him. Out of the mouths of babes . . .'

'She *tells* him? Oh, I really do need that. And anyway, how do you . . . ?' Müller paused. 'Why do I even ask?'

'Why indeed? I am assuming,' Pappenheim continued, 'that when you leave where you are, you will be seeing the second candidate, then wandering further afield.'

'You assume correctly.'

'As long as I know. And, just so you know, Max and his crew are going over the scene, almost blade by blade of grass. Max has asked for a sniffer dog, and it's on its way with its handler. The two bastards who did this may have been pros, but they must have left something. If it's there, Max and his people will find it.'

'Let's hope so. What state was Paul in when they found him?'

'Not pretty. The explosion and the shrapnel ripped into him. But here's a very strange thing . . . his entire head was virtually intact. Not a mark on his face. His suit obviously helped limit the effect of the blast.'

'But not enough.'

'Not nearly enough,' Pappenheim said with a sigh. 'He was much too close. It's amazing they found much at all. Max believes, even at that late stage, he tried to either get away, or dropped low to somehow minimize the force he would be facing. He might have shielded his face in his arms. Could be why it's untouched.'

'Either way, it's very bad news. Tell Max to try and get as much as he can from our local colleagues about those two sailor boys.'

'Max will keep on it. You can bet on that. He feels guilty about Paul.'

'He should not. It was not his fault.'

'I've told him, and I'm certain the team have told him. That won't help much.'

'Understandable.'

'One last thing. About your place. Ilona has let me have Hammersfeldt . . .'

'Staring boy?'

Pappenheim gave his first chuckle since the news about Zimmer. 'Not jealous, are you?'

'Wash your mouth with soap.'

'Just did. Hammersfeldt is keen, and he is partnered with Hans Schörma. Good man. He'll keep Hammersfeldt in check.'

'Schörma, our ex-*Bundeswehr* vet and ex-Legionnaire. If I know him, he'll take an armoury with him. Explain to him this is not an assault. If anything does happen, which I doubt, I don't want bullet pockmarks all over my building.'

Pappenheim seemed to be grinning. 'I'll tell him. Not sure he'll listen. Perhaps he'll wear gloves.'

Werneck, Northern Bavaria. The dark-blue Volvo estate pulled into the side of the road on Schönbornstrasse, and came to a stop. The woman at the wheel was a petite, genuine blonde with bright-green eyes, and a calmly beautiful face that belied her real age. A mother with a ten-year-old daughter, and a boy of twelve, she seemed far too young. On this day, only her son was with her. He was strapped in the back seat, engrossed in a game on his mobile phone.

'Just going to the bank, sweetheart,' she said as she unclipped her seatbelt. 'Won't be long.' She spoke flawless English with an American accent, but her roots did not come from America. 'Will you be OK?'

The boy nodded without looking up. He was finished with school for the day, and had come along for the ride. His sister was with friends.

'And keep your seat belt on,' she ordered.

Again, he nodded without looking up.

He was a handsome child with neck-length, well-cut hair that was darker than his mother's but which also carried much of her blonde colouring. His eyes, like hers, were green, with the slightest muting of the brightness. His complexion was a slightly darker version of hers, his features bearing much of the strong planes of his father's.

He still did not look up when she got out of the car and so was unaware of the black Mercedes saloon, with its darkened windows, pulling up a short distance behind. Like his mother, he was equally unaware of the two heavy-set men in the car, and of their deep interest in the Volvo.

Minutes later, she was back. She got into the car and drove off. The boy was still wrapped up in his game.

The rainbelt from the east had reached Bavaria and gone on; but its passing was still marked by damp roads and a gloom that seemed out of place for both the time of year and of the day.

Lights on, she drove along Schönbornstrasse towards the castle that dominated the little town, into Neumarkt then left, skirting the castle, continuing into Würzburger Strasse, which was the B19 to Essleben. The B19 went through Essleben and on to Opferbaum. She continued along it. She was heading for Würzburg.

'Do you know, Josh, I first met your dad in Würzburg.'

'Yes, Mom,' the boy said with the air of someone who had heard it all before. 'And every time we go to Würzburg, you tell me.' He looked up briefly to smile at the back of her head. 'It's OK.' Then it was back into the game.

She smiled as she drove. 'How come you never get carsick playing that game on such a small—'

'Mom!' Joshua Jackson cried. 'I'm concentrating!' But there was no real irritation in his voice.

Neither of them noticed that the Mercedes was following.

They were on an open stretch of road; no buildings were immediately nearby. Traffic, for the moment, was virtually non-existent; save for the following Mercedes, and the second one that had taken up station behind it.

Then life for the boy and his mother, was changed forever.

'What are these people *doing*?' she said in annoyance as the first Mercedes raced past to cut in sharply and slow down, forcing her to brake hard. The car skidded briefly. 'There are such stupid drivers on the road these days!'

She was slowing right down.

The boy had looked up and instinctively looked back to check on following traffic, in case someone was in danger of hitting them. What he saw alarmed him.

'*Mom!* There's another car right behind us! It's stopped!'

The Volvo had also now stopped completely, because the Mercedes in front was not moving.

She threw an anxious glance behind her and saw that her son was right. She looked forward again, in time to see the two men, now in black balaclava masks, get out of their car. They carried what looked like short batons.

'*Josh!*' she yelled as she pressed the switches to lock all four windows of the Volvo. '*Call your father!*'

Josh forgot all about his game and hurriedly began to dial his father's mobile.

The men had reached the car and had begun to strike at the windows, which, for the time being, failed to break.

Josh had made his connection, when he saw a third man, gun in hand, pointing at him. The man wagged an admonishing finger.

Josh did something smart. He dropped the phone, as any scared boy would have done. The man nodded slowly in approval; but, unknown to him, the connection was active.

'*Mom!*' Josh yelled as loudly as he could. '*There's another man here! He's got a gun!*'

'Oh my God!' she said, voice rising with dread, jumping each time the blows were struck at the windows.

Colonel William T. Jackson was an imposing man, and as tall as Müller.

His smart uniform was smarter than any of his personnel; which was saying something. Commander of Combined Attack Force Alpha (CAFA), he demanded, and got, smartness from his entire force; from the officers down to the lowest rank, male or female. His full complement appeared to mirror the entire ethnic spectrum of his country.

He did not suffer fools gladly; yet he was no martinet. His force was loyal down to each man and woman; and he was one of those commanders who believed in leading from the front. Highly decorated, he was also a qualified combat helicopter pilot and, in his mixed force, two squadrons of Apaches were under his command.

The sombre look of the day was matched by the thunder of the Apaches in a rigorous training programme, as the colonel kept his crews up to speed. It was an open secret that Colonel Bill, as his people called him, would soon be gaining a general's star. One of those who knew the secret was the commanding general, eager to bestow it upon one of his favourite officers.

The colonel was an unexpected surprise to those who met him for the first time. A native of Mississippi, he was a man whose genetic mix owed much to African and Apache heritage, within which were also various European strains, including more than a bit of Saxon. His potent grey eyes could sometimes appear intimidating to the unknowing. As one of the youngest colonels around, his cropped hair, almost white, belied his real youth.

Today, Colonel Bill, general-in-waiting, was listening to the worst nightmare of his life come true.

He had quickly understood what his son had done, and had

been wise enough not to speak, in case whoever was out there heard. He also knew that Josh's yell had been as much for his own benefit, as for his wife's. So, he listened to his wife and child being attacked, reasoning that, as he could not immediately go to their aid, knowing as much as he could about the situation would be of help later.

He continued to listen, face tightening with a growing anger, a chill descending upon his heart. An explosive smash told him that the Volvo's strong windows had at last given way.

'*What are you doing?*' he heard his wife shout. She had spoken in German, in which he was also fluent.

'Elisabeth,' he said softly, closing his eyes.

'Out! Nigger-loving whore!' he heard a rough voice say in the same language. 'Or I'll drag you out!'

Jackson's eyes popped open. A *racist* attack?

'Mom!' he heard Josh shout again. 'Let her go, you bastards!'

'Josh?' Jackson murmured. 'You swear? Of course you do. Your buddies do.'

Josh was clearly preparing to go on to the attack.

'No!' Jackson heard his wife say. 'No, Josh! Don't! They'll hurt you!'

But Josh did not care. His mother was under attack, and he was the only man around to help.

Jackson heard his son open his door.

'*You leave her alone!*' he heard the child shout. '*My father's a colonel and he'll kill you all!*'

Then came the sound of Josh clearly striking out.

It was, inevitably, an unequal contest. Jackson heard a cry of pain, and knew the boy had been hit.

Jackson's steel-grey eyes burned with a cold fire.

'*Josh!*' came his wife's anguished cry. Then in German, '*He's only a child, you monsters!*'

There seemed to be an argument going on among the men. Jackson could not catch what was being said.

'*Americans?*' one then shouted. 'What is this? We attack the family of an *American colonel*? Are you *crazy*? No one said—'

'You will do as you're told!' another voice snarled. 'Now

130

shut up and take her to the car! And as for you, little hero, see how you like *this*.'

Then Josh was screaming. '*Aaaagh! Dad! Daaaad!*'

'He can't help you,' came the hard voice.

Jackson gripped his desk tightly, jaws clenched as he listened to his son's cries of pain. Faintly, he could hear his wife screaming the boy's name.

Then there was the sound of doors slamming, and of cars driving away.

Jackson waited, a fear in his heart. After a while, he thought he could hear, very faintly, a low whimpering. If Josh could still move, Jackson thought, the boy would go to the phone.

He forced himself to wait.

Then, 'Dad?'

'Josh! Are you alright?'

'They cut me . . . Dad.' The boy was weeping. 'I . . . I tried to stop them. But . . . they were . . . too strong.'

'I know you did, son,' Jackson said, heart heavy. 'You were very brave.'

'They took Mom away!' Then, as if being brave were suddenly too much for him, the boy broke down. 'They . . . they took her, Dad!'

'And I'll get them for it, son,' Jackson vowed. 'I'll get her back, and I'll make them sorry they ever did this. Now you must be brave again. Can you tell me where you are?'

'We . . . we were on our way to Würzburg. Mom was telling me – *again* – how special it is for the two of you . . .'

Despite himself, Jackson forced out a grim smile at the boy's emphasis. 'It is.'

'But she doesn't have to tell me *all* the time.'

Jackson felt his eyes go hot at the sound of the child breaking through the boy who was trying to be brave.

'I know,' he said. 'Grown-ups are like that sometimes. Never know when to stop. Now tell me . . . where exactly are you?'

'We're on a different road than usual, because we're coming from Werneck. The B19. I was playing my game, but looked out once. I saw a sign . . .'

'That's very good. I'm coming to get you. Stay on the phone. We'll keep talking. You got that?'

131

'Yes, sir.'

'And Josh?'

'Yes, Dad?'

'That was very brave of you, but you must promise me something: you *never* again go up against a man with a gun, with your bare hands. Do you hear?'

'But *you* would . . .'

'Do you hear, Josh?'

'Ye–es, sir. But Mom was in danger . . .'

'I know, son. I know. You did fine. Now I'm coming to get you.'

CAFA Base was not a great distance from Werneck itself. The colonel, now in civilian clothes, slowly drove his black Audi four-door saloon towards the solid-iron, sliding gates – which were open, but the barrier was down. Two smartly turned-out and armed military policemen were on guard at the lowered barrier. A sentry hut was on each side of the entrance.

Approaching from the outside, a visitor would be greeted by a large sign with, emblazoned upon it, an attacking bald eagle carrying a rotary cannon in its claws, and beneath that, the legend:

WELCOME TO
COMBINED ATTACK FORCE ALPHA
Col. WILLIAM T. JACKSON Commanding

Beyond the barrier was a long, low building to the right.

Jackson stopped the car. The policemen, on either side of the road at the entrance, had drawn themselves to attention, and were about to raise the barrier to let him through. A tall, black officer – a lieutenant, older than expected for the rank – came out of the building and approached the car.

The lieutenant saluted.

The colonel briefly raised a snappy hand in the direction of his head.

'Lieutenant Henderson,' Jackson began, 'Colonel Dales has the base. I'm going out for a short while. Back soon.'

Henderson looked at him closely. 'Permission to speak, sir.'

132

'Granted.'

'Is the colonel OK, sir? Can I help?'

Jackson gave a tired smile. 'No, Cody. You can't. But thank you.'

'Sir!' Cody Henderson said, and saluted once more.

Jackson nodded, and drove on as the barrier was raised. The guards gave him sharp salutes as he passed.

Henderson, with a thoughtful expression, watched his boss depart. Then he went back into the building and into his office. He picked up his phone, and dialled the deputy commander, Lieutenant-Colonel John Dales.

Dales was a New Yorker, and slightly older than Jackson. 'Dales.'

'Sir,' Henderson began. 'Lieutenant Henderson. May I speak freely?'

'You may.'

'I just saw the colonel leaving. He seemed worried about something . . .'

'And you wondered whether I knew anything about it.'

'Well . . . yes, sir.'

'I know you two go back a long way, Cody, and if I knew, I'd tell you. All I can say is that he has ordered the doc to wait for him at his home.'

'Kind of strange, sir.'

'Yes. But I don't know any more, and he did not expand on that. Let's just say, if he needs us, we'll be right there.'

'You got it, sir.'

'Alright, Cody.'

'Sir.'

Henderson put down his phone, and did not feel any better.

It didn't take Jackson long to find the Volvo.

The lights were still on, and the broken windows gaped like crystalline, eyeless sockets. Two cars were parked close by, and their occupants were trying to persuade Josh to come out. It was clear he had not let them come near him. Jackson pulled up behind the Volvo and got out.

'It's OK,' he said to the people in German. 'I'm his father. I'll handle this. Thank you for trying to help.'

One of them, a man in his sixties, looked him up and down. 'American?'

Jackson nodded as he opened one of the rear doors of the Volvo.

'There is blood on his face,' the man continued. 'We tried to get him out but he would not let us get near. He screamed each time. Someone has called the police, I think.'

'No need,' Jackson said. 'I'll take it from here.'

As soon as he put his head inside, Josh, bleeding from a strange wound on his forehead, flung his arms about him.

'Dad, Dad, Dad, Dad!' Josh repeated this over and over again, weeping

'But where is the driver?' he heard the man say.

Jackson did not reply. 'It's OK, son,' he said to Josh. 'It's OK. Dad's here. Let's look at that cut. I've brought field dressings. They'll do till the doc takes a look. OK?'

The head nodded against him, smearing blood on his shirt.

'OK. Now let's have a look.'

Sensing the people were themselves crowding to look, Jackson glanced back and said, 'Please. A little room.'

They moved back, but not very far.

'Alright, Josh. You've been very brave. Can you be brave just one more time?'

The boy again nodded, and raised his head for Jackson to have a look. 'He just wouldn't stop cutting me! He wouldn't stop!'

'It's OK, Josh. It's OK. I'm going to clean it now, then bandage it. Be brave. OK?'

'OK,' the boy whimpered.

Jackson cleaned the wound as gently as he could, then stared. 'Oh my God,' he said quietly, a great anger rising within him. 'Bastards,' he muttered under his breath. A perfect, tiny swastika had been carved upon the boy's forehead.

Jackson bandaged it quickly, so that the people around the car would not have a chance to see it. Then he got Josh out of the Volvo, carrying him in his arms.

The people gasped when they saw the smeared blood on Jackson's shirt.

'Is he badly hurt?' the same man asked.

'A small cut,' Jackson said, hiding his anger at the men who had done this. 'It bled a lot. He'll be fine. Thank you again.'

'We tried to help.'

'I know. He was just scared.'

'But the police . . .'

'Will be informed.'

Jackson quickly went back to his car, put Josh in the back, and secured his seat belt. Then he got in behind the wheel and drove off, wanting to be well away from there, before the police put in an appearance.

Wannsee. The dog had become excited about something it had found. It was pivoting about a spot just in front of its nose, and making snuffling sounds punctuated by short barks that had a come-and-see-what-I've-found command about them.

'Max!' the handler called. 'Gigi's found something!' To the dog, she added, 'Good girl. Good girl!'

The dog answered with a high-pitched whine of acknowledgement, and continued its pivoting.

Gatto hurried to the spot, which was some distance from the destroyed boathouse.

'What is it?' he asked as he arrived.

'I don't know,' she said, looking down at a small tuft of grass in Vogel's unkempt garden. 'I can't see anything.'

'OK, Trudi,' Gatto said. 'Call her off. I'll have a look.'

'Alright, Gigi,' Trudi Lohtal said to the dog. She gave the lead a gentle pull.

The dog stopped instantly, gave another little whine, and squatted.

Gatto took a measuring glance at the ruin of the boathouse. 'If it came from there, that was quite a flight.'

He got to his knees, and began to search with a cautious hand through the tuft of grass. After a while, the hand came up against something small, hard and cold to the touch.

He pulled it out, and stared at it as he got to his feet. It just about covered the length of his palm, and was a gleaming black. There were a few spots of the tiniest of scorch marks but, apart from those, the object was virtually intact. On one side was a strange design.

'It looks like a knife without a blade,' he remarked thoughtfully.

As he was probing it with exploratory fingers, a section was depressed, and a gleaming blade shot out with a soft, metallic hiss.

The startled Gatto swore. 'Shit! That nearly pierced my finger! A retractable dagger. Sharp as hell. Nice toy,' he added with grim disgust.

He got down on his heels and placed the dagger on the grass, in front of the dog.

Gigi sprang to all fours, barking furiously.

Gatto took the weapon away. 'Now we know. Perhaps it's got some traces.'

The dog quietened down once more, and went back to its squatting. It looked from Gatto to Lohtal, as if wanting to join in the conversation, before lowering its head on to its paws.

'This looks like a very special dagger,' Trudi Lohtal said. 'Would someone not search for it if they dropped it?'

'If one of them did drop it, he probably hasn't realized it as yet. He might have put it down after cutting something and, in a hurry to get away before we got here, probably thought he had put it back into his pocket. It happens. This could be a piece of luck for us. If it helps us get the bastards who killed Paul, I'll be a very happy man.'

He stooped to pat the dog. 'Well done, Gigi.'

The dog made a sound that could easily have been interpreted as *you're welcome*.

Gatto called Pappenheim. 'We've got something.'

'Ah! What is it?'

'It's a sort of . . . knife,' Gatto said, uncertain about the object. 'More like a dagger. Retractable. Black handle. The blade looks made of strong metal. Probably titanium. Gigi found it. She went crazy.'

'Traces?'

'Could be. But, before full lab tests, it's hard to tell what exactly. We'll do a preliminary with the sensors. They will at least confirm explosive material, if any. Gigi definitely picked up something. And one other thing . . . it's got a strange design on the handle. More like *inside* the handle . . .'

'What's the design look like? On second thoughts,' Pappenheim went on quickly, 'don't tell me. Just bring it directly to me when you get back. *No* one else. To me.'

Clearly puzzled, Gatto said, 'I will.'

'I can't explain, Max.'

'No need to,' Gatto said. 'I'll hang on to it until I see you.'

CAFA Base, near Schweinfurt. At roughly the same time, one of the military police guards spotted Jackson's Audi returning. The guard went into his sentry box, picked up the phone and called Henderson.

'The colonel's returning, sir.'

'On my way,' Henderson said.

'Yes, sir.'

The guard replaced the receiver just as the Audi turned the corner to enter the short straight to the barrier, which his opposite number was getting ready to raise.

As the car drew closer, both guards snapped their salutes, and the barrier began to rise. The guard who had phoned Henderson leaned forward slightly, eyes popping when he saw the bandaged Josh in the back.

Jackson's hand snapped towards his right temple in brief response, then the Audi was through.

'What the fuck?' the gate guard said to himself as the barrier was again lowered. He looked at his colleague. 'Did you see that?' he asked in a loud whisper.

The other nodded, but said nothing as he saw Henderson getting ready to meet the car.

But the car did not stop.

They saw Jackson's hand again rise in its brief answering salute to Henderson, then the Audi sped away at the sort of speed reserved for emergency situations on the base, which had a normal blanket speed limit of 20mph.

Henderson, hand slowly falling to his side, stared in puzzled astonishment after the Audi, then hurried to the guards.

They came towards the centre of the barrier as they saw him approach.

Henderson waited for an Apache helicopter to throb past above their heads before speaking.

'Has the colonel's lady returned?'

Both shook their heads.

'No, sir,' the guard who had phoned answered. 'I thought I saw some blood on the kid's bandage, sir . . .'

Henderson fixed him with a level stare. 'Brons.'

'Yes, sir?'

'You forget you saw anything, until you know something.'

'Yes, sir.'

'That goes for you too, Ryan.'

'Yes, sir!'

Henderson softened. 'If I get to know anything, I'll tell you.'

'He's our colonel, sir,' Brons said. 'Something happens to him, we want to know.'

'Likewise here, sir,' Ryan agreed.

Henderson looked at each in turn. 'As I said. I'll let you know.'

'Sir!' they said together.

Henderson returned to his office, and curbed his impulse to call Dales. Lieutenants did not call lieutenant-colonels for updates.

Half an hour later, he got the call he'd hoped for, though the news that came with it was not so welcome.

'Bad news, Cody,' Dales said, getting straight to the point. 'The colonel's lady has been kidnapped, and his boy attacked.'

Henderson's jaw dropped in shock.

'Cody! You there?'

'Sir . . . er . . . yes. Sir. What . . . what happened?'

'According to the boy, two cars blocked them on the open road. Then masked men attacked the Volvo, breaking its windows. They dragged Mrs Jackson out of the car and took her away. Then one of the sadistic bastards carved the boy's forehead.'

Henderson felt an anger rising within him.

'Cody,' Dales pressed on. 'I can guess how you're feeling

right now, if it's anything like my own response. But I need you to keep a tight lid on that when the news spreads. Next to the colonel, the soldiers on this base respect you more than any other officer—'

'Sir, I—'

'Don't interrupt me, Lieutenant, and take your bouquet.'

'Yes, sir.'

'I want you to ensure that none of the soldiers get it into their heads to go looking for some kind of revenge. That includes the NCOs. You got that?'

'Yes, sir. I do.'

'Even if it means we've got to keep them all in barracks. You were once their top sergeant. Can you handle it?'

'I can, sir.'

'Alright, Cody. I'll get back to you.'

'Yes, sir.'

Eight

In the commander's residence, Jackson sat at the desk in his ground-floor study, writing. He did so with a measured deliberation. When finished, he neatly folded what he had written, and put it into the plain, white envelope he had placed close by.

He sealed the envelope, and left it on the desk.

Footfalls on the stairs made him leave the desk to check. The senior base doctor, bag in hand, was on his way down. Jackson closed the door to the study, and went to meet him.

'How's he doing, Doc?' Jackson asked.

'Given his traumatic experience,' the doctor replied, as he came down the last step, 'remarkably well. I've sealed the wound. He'll be OK. I've given him something to make him drowsy. It's very weak, so don't worry. He may not go down for a while, but when he does, he'll have a calm sleep.'

The doctor shook his head slowly as they went into the living room. 'What kind of animals did this? Whoever used that knife had skill approaching that of a surgeon. They were precise cuts, and that blade must have been extremely sharp. The sort of thing that could peel the skin off someone so finely, pain would hardly be felt, at the start. I believe Josh screamed more in fear than in pain. The real pain came later, long after those bastards had gone. Ironically, that's when he was bravest.'

'But he really will be OK?'

'Oh yes,' the doctor replied. 'The cut will heal well.'

'And that sick thing they put on him? I'm not happy about my son walking around with a goddamned swastika on his forehead.'

'It should fade. If it does not do so completely, minor cosmetic surgery will obliterate it.'

'And in the meantime?'

'While it's healing, the bandage will of course keep it hidden.' The doctor gave a tiny smile of wonder. 'Know what he said to me? "Doc? Can I have a special bandage? You know . . . like the Ninja Turtles. It will be my headband. Think Dad will say it's OK?" I told him you would.'

Despite the way he felt, Jackson allowed himself a brief smile in return. 'He can have his headband. I'm glad his sister's with friends. I would not have wanted her to see this. Gives me some time.'

'Smart boy you've got there. Very clever move with his cellphone.'

'It was. Good presence of mind.'

The doctor, a bespectacled lieutenant-colonel called Melville, now asked, 'What's your next move?'

'Get the people who did this.'

'How?'

'I have some ideas.'

Melville gave Jackson close scrutiny. 'If I may speak as a friend, Bill, and not as a lieutenant-colonel, be very careful how you handle this. Watch your step. There are those who would like to see you fall.'

'Aren't there always such people wherever you go?'

Melville nodded. 'Yes. But I don't want them to get a man I look upon as a friend.'

'I'll watch my step.'

'And, as your doctor, I'd suggest you take a rest before doing whatever it is you're planning.'

'I'll listen to your advice as both my friend, and my doctor.'

'But you may not necessarily take it.'

'I did not say that.'

Melville's smile was rueful. 'I know you too well, Bill. Now I'd better be going. Mmm . . . I suppose you want me to hold fire on my report.'

'Only for a short while. What's more, I don't want the news going round the base. I don't want anyone getting ideas of going off base to kick some ass. We don't need that kind of trouble.'

Melville nodded. 'I'll see to it.'

'Can I talk to Josh? Or should I leave him for now?'

'You can talk with him. He'll probably pop off in the middle of your conversation, though. If he switches moods, don't read too much into it. He's got plenty to assimilate emotionally. He may also avoid talking about Elisabeth.'

'I understand.' Jackson held out a hand. 'Thanks for coming, Pete.'

'What for?' Melville said as he shook the hand. 'You watch yourself, Bill. You hear?'

Jackson nodded as he showed Melville out.

'If there's any ass to be kicked,' he said to himself as he heard Melville's car leaving, 'I'll be the one doing it.'

He went up the stairs to the boy's room. Josh was awake, playing the same game on his mobile.

'Hey, soldier. Winning that game yet?'

The boy looked up from his game with a huge smile as Jackson sat down next to him on the bed.

'Dad! Ahh!' he went on in some annoyance. 'It's tough . . . but I won't give up.' Then he brightened. 'Did the doc tell you? I'm going to get a cool headband.'

'He told me. Ninjas?'

'Well, not exactly. More like rapper stuff. I know you don't think rap is cool . . .'

'Some rap. Not all.'

'So? Can I have one?'

'You can.'

'Cool! I might change my mind, though.'

'That's OK. Josh,' Jackson, tentative, continued, 'can we talk some more about what happened? Not a long talk. Just a few things I'd like to clear up.'

The green eyes looked at him with unnerving directness. 'You want to know if I spotted anything.'

'Yes. Anything that might help. Anything you might have noticed about the men who did this.'

'Their cars. They were driving dark Mercedes cars.'

'Sports cars? Sedans? Coupes?'

'The one that blocked us in front was a sedan. The one at the back a coupe.'

'That's good. Anything else?'

'They all had masks, but when I was on the ground, I saw that the men from the car in front had jeans and trainers . . .'

'Trainers. You're sure? Not paratroop-type boots?'

Josh shook his head, clear about what he had seen. 'Trainers.'

'And the other man?'

'He's the one that hit me, and cut me. He had normal pants on, and shoes. Good shoes.'

'Two goons and their boss,' Jackson said, almost to himself.

'And . . . and there's the knife,' Josh said, voice rising in a quavering excitement. 'I was so afraid, I was looking at it to see what he was going to do with it. It was a small knife with a black handle. He pressed it, and the blade came out.' Josh shivered as memory of the experience came rushing back.

Jackson put an arm about the boy's shoulders. 'It's OK, son. We'll leave it for now.'

But Josh wanted to talk. 'There . . . there was a strange . . . marking on the handle. It seemed to be *inside*. And the men with the trainers . . . one of them talked about something called *semper*. He didn't sound very happy. The man with the shoes shut him up. I think the man said something that was important. I pretended I had not heard.'

'That was very smart. The man who said "semper" . . . a *Marine*?'

'I know about the Marines, Dad.' Josh was almost scornful. 'That's *semper fidelis*. That's not what the man was talking about. Anyway, it was all in German.'

'Alright, Josh. That was very good. Now get some rest.'

142

Suddenly, the boy's eyes filled with tears. 'She's not coming back, is she, Dad? Mom's not coming back!'

Jackson held his son tightly. 'I'm going to get her back for us, Josh. I swear to you. Do you hear? Josh?'

Jackson looked down.

The boy was fast asleep, the mobile still in his hand, the game still on.

Gently, the colonel settled his son into the bed, took the mobile away, and put it on the bedside table. He left it on. The display asked whether the game should be saved at its present level, or deleted. Jackson saved it.

He went on silent feet to the door, and looked back.

'I promise, Josh,' he vowed quietly.

Jackson was back in his study, this time recording a video message.

As he had been when writing, he was deliberate in his choice of words. When he had finished, he made an extra copy. He put each video into a padded envelope, and addressed them.

Just as he had finished, the doorbell rang.

He put the padded envelopes into a drawer, and locked it. Picking up the white envelope, he left the study to go to the door.

He opened the door to Dales.

'Thanks for coming, Jack.' He stood back for Dales – who gave him a wary look – to enter.

As they went into the living room, Dales glanced at the envelope. 'Is that what I think it is, sir?'

'What do you think it is, Jack?'

'I'm guessing. You're going after those people, and that's the explanation.'

'You're right . . . in part.'

'Sir, if I may . . .'

'You may, Jack. Forget the ranks. This is Bill, and Jack. And this –' Jackson held up the envelope – 'is for you. Don't open it until the right moment.'

'Which will be?'

'You'll know when. This envelope also gives you the base, in my absence. Take the envelope, Jack.'

Dales stared at him. 'Are you *nuts*? I can't stand by and watch you sink your career . . .'

'And I can't stand by and leave my wife in the hands of some sick bastards, especially after I promised my son I would get her back. I promised myself too.'

'Jesus, Bill. I know I cannot possibly understand what you're going through. But think! We've got channels for this kind of thing . . .'

'Channels that will take forever, while Elisabeth is out there in the hands of some maniacs, scared, and wondering what they might do to her. Do you want a picture?'

'Christ, no. But you're doing what you would stamp on any other soldier for.'

Jackson's smile was grim. 'The penalties and privileges of command. You can make your own decisions – within certain limits – and be hanged by them. Do you remember that time in the desert? We were standing by a humvee. Do you remember what you said to me?'

'I remember. "Bill, I think you should duck." Then we both hit the deck.'

'And a bullet hit the humvee, exactly where I'd been standing. Now, the crazy thing about that bullet was that it was fired from nearly two miles away. No way could you have known there was a sniper's bullet with my name on it, at that very moment.'

'It was a feeling,' Dales said. 'Couldn't explain it then, can't explain it now.'

'I have that same kind of feeling right now,' Jackson said. 'The people who took my wife and assaulted my son tried to make it look like a racist attack. Now I ask myself, why would anyone want that? Answer, to cause some very nasty trouble. But *why*? And that's what's been exercising me. That's why it's scaring the shit out me, because they've got Elisabeth. It's also scaring me that there have been no attempts at contact. Nothing. It's as if she has disappeared off the damned planet. The kind of people who would go to all that trouble, including cold-bloodedly doing what they did to Josh, are not your average lowlife no-brains.

'We are dealing with something far more sinister. They are

so sure of themselves, they can't even be bothered to make a single call, like any normal sicko kidnapper. They are making no demands. They're saying to me, we'll be in touch when we're good and ready. Meanwhile, you sweat. I overheard an argument between them, through Josh's cellphone. One man was worried. He never thought his orders meant he was to attack an American colonel's family. He mentioned a name, and was immediately told to shut up. Josh heard that name. Josh also saw something else, which I hope will help nail them.'

'I still say use our channels . . .'

Jackson shook his head. 'No way. I can't risk it. I may be blocked by those same channels, or it may take too long while people argue; and, meanwhile, Elisabeth runs out of time. My way will get results much faster.'

'And perhaps your head and career handed to you on a plate.'

'Jack, as far as my wife and kids are concerned, if I can't protect them, to hell with my career. Would you risk your career for Phoebe?'

'That's a low blow.'

'I got two low blows today.'

Dales gave a sigh of resignation. 'I can see there's no arguing.'

'None at all.'

Dales made a last effort. 'If you won't use channels, how about the German cops?'

'I have a cop in mind; from Berlin, but I don't know how to reach him . . .'

'Use the cops. They will know.'

'No. I don't want whoever is behind this to even know what I plan, until I want them to. For all I know, they've got access to the cops as well.'

'How can you tell? You could be way off-beam on this . . .'

'Sure I could.'

'So?'

'I'll do it my way.'

'Jesus, Bill. You're heading for a fall.'

'If I don't do this, Jack, I'm not fit to hold a command. I'm not fit to be a husband, or a father. I'm not being emotional. I think you know me well enough to understand that.'

Dales gave a reluctant nod.

'I need a favour. Two favours.'

'Whatever I may feel about this, you know you don't have to ask.'

'Thanks, Jack. First, you say nothing about what I have told you regarding what I think I know. No exceptions, Jack.'

'You got it.'

'Second, I want you and Phoebe to look after the kids for me.'

'That goes without question.'

Jackson nodded. 'Then that's it. When Elene gets back, I'll let her know what happened as gently as I can, then I'll let her and Josh know they'll be staying with you for a few days.'

'When should we pick them up?'

'Sometime this evening, if that's OK.'

'No problem.'

Jackson was still holding out the envelope. 'You'll need this.'

With some reluctance, Dales took it.

'The base is now yours, Colonel,' Jackson said. 'Officially, I'm now on a few days' vacation.'

'Yes, sir. Let's hope it isn't permanent.'

'We'll see. And Jack . . .'

'Sir?'

'Keep a tight lid on things. *No* one must even *think* of going hunting for these people, when the news gets out about Elisabeth and Josh. I'll have no vigilantes in my command, as long as I've still got it.'

'I've already started. I've given Cody Henderson a heads-up.'

'That's good. Cody will sit on them.'

'And I'll instruct all the other officers.'

Jackson nodded in approval.

'That cop you mentioned,' Dales said. 'Do I get the name?'

'Sorry, Jack. I'm keeping this one very close. I have to, for Elisabeth's sake. If I can reach him the way I believe I might be able to, you'll be hearing from him.'

'And where will you be?'

'You'll know when the time comes, just as you'll know when to open the envelope.' Jackson paused. 'I'm going to get those bastards to come looking for me, Jack.'

CAFA Base 19.00, Commander's residence. Elene and Josh were in the hall, the personal things they would need for their short stay in their small backpacks. The childless Phoebe and John Dales, concern upon their faces, stood to one side, waiting for the children to take leave of their father. Above their heads, the throbbing of the Apache helicopters continued.

Elene Jackson seemed a perfect, smaller replica of her mother. There was more blonde in her hair, which had more curls than Josh's. Her eyes, a dark green that was almost black, were brimming with tears as she hugged a squatting Jackson tightly.

'OK, baby.' He cleared his throat. 'Just a few days with Auntie Phoebe and Uncle Jack. You already spend as much time there as here, so it will be just like going to your other bedroom.' He took her by the shoulders to look at her with a smile. 'Won't it?'

She nodded, wiping at the tears. 'Mm hmm.'

'There you go.' Jackson straightened to look at Josh, who had put on a brave face, and was not crying. 'Look after your sister, Josh.'

'Yes, sir.'

He gave Josh a hug. 'OK, son. Off you go.' He nodded at his friends, who took the children's hands and led them out.

Just before he went outside, Dales glanced back.

Jackson had the distinct feeling that the look in Dales' eyes suggested that the lieutenant-colonel thought he was seeing his commander for the last time.

Jackson returned to his study.

There were two backpacks on the floor. In one was everything he felt he needed for his purposes. This included a micro Uzi sub-machine gun, and a Sig Sauer P226 automatic pistol, a large-calibre special-duties pump shotgun with folding stock, plenty of ammunition, and a combat knife. The second pack held a change of clothing for when he got to the destination he had in mind, and the padded envelopes.

He picked up his mobile from the desk, held it contempla-
tively for some moments, wondering whether he should leave
it behind. He decided to take it.

He closed the packs. He checked through the house to
ensure that all was secure, then, returning to the study to pick
up the packs, went out to place them into the boot of the Audi.
He then went back to lock the door, trying hard not to think
of his wife in the hands of the people who had taken her. Face
grim, he got into the car and drove towards the main gate.

Henderson was still there when Jackson arrived. The lieutenant aproached the car and saluted.

Jackson looked up at him. 'I'm taking a few days vacation,
Cody.'

'Yes, sir.' Henderson's eyes were lively with questions he
refrained from asking.

'Colonel Dales has the base.'

'Yes, sir.'

'I believe he's given you a heads-up.'

'Yes, sir. He has.'

'I'm relying on you, Cody.'

'You can, sir.'

Jackson nodded, and began to drive off.

'Sir?'

Jackson stopped. The gate barrier had already been raised
in anticipation.

'Just be careful out there.'

'I consider that serious advice, Cody. I'll take it.'

'Yes, sir.' Henderson saluted.

Jackson acknowledged in his usual way, and drove off
CAFA Base.

He drove towards Würzburg, taking his time. Just under an
hour later, he arrived at his first destination: a large house on
the outskirts of the city. He parked the Audi in front of it,
leaving the entrance to the double garage clear.

He got out, went to the boot to get the two envelopes, locked
the car, and went up to the house. The door was answered by
a man about his own age with blond, neck-length hair. There
was a distinct resemblance to Jackson's wife.

'Bill!' Klaus Neusser beamed in welcome. He extended a

hand as he peered past Jackson. 'My little cousin with you?' He spoke English.

Shaking the hand, Jackson said, 'No. That's why I'm here.'

Neusser frowned uncertainly. 'Trouble? I can't imagine any trouble between you two.'

'Not what you think, Klaus. Something else entirely.'

'Come in. Come in,' Neusser said. 'I am on my own at the moment. Martha's away on one of her teacher's courses and Markus is, of course, at his college in the north; so, we can talk in absolute privacy, if that's what you want.'

'That's exactly what I want. Markus is about seventeen now, isn't he?'

'Nearer eighteen.'

'They do grow fast.'

'Oh yes. Before you know it, yours will be eating you out of house and home.'

Jackson gave a fleeting smile that was tinged with sadness. 'I think they've already started.'

Neusser gave him a searching look. 'Your voice tells me this is serious.'

'That, Klaus, is an understatement.'

'You're beginning to make me worried.' Neusser glanced down at the envelopes Jackson held. 'To do with these?'

Jackson nodded. 'I have something to show you, then we can both worry together. I have a video I'd like you to see.'

'We can play it in the living room,' an increasingly puzzled Neusser said, 'or my study.'

'Your study. Best place.'

'OK. Drink?'

'No. You might need one afterwards.'

'You are not worrying me,' Neusser commented. 'You're scaring me.'

They entered Neusser's large study, which accurately reflected the nature of his profession. It was set up like a mini television studio, with several monitors and different recording systems on a console bank that took up an entire wall.

Jackson opened the first of the envelopes and handed the video over. 'Play this.'

With another puzzled glance, Neusser took the cassette and slid it into one of the players.

Neusser gave a startled gasp when a stern-faced Jackson appeared.

He again glanced at Jackson, who said, 'Watch, and listen.'

'My name is Jackson,' the image began in German. 'William T., Colonel, United States Army. To the people who today kidnapped my wife on the B19, and brutalized my son—'

Neusser paused the tape. *'What? Elisa is kidnapped?'*

Face stiff, Jackson nodded.

'My God!' Neusser said in shock. *'My God!'*

'Let the tape run, Klaus.'

Silently, Neusser did so.

'—I have this to say: release my wife, unharmed and unmolested, immediately. Should you have other ideas, let me tell you this: the three of you tried to make it look like a racist act. You were not dressed for it. I am certain you know what I mean. The man who pointed the gun at my son when he was making the phone call to me should know that my son was smarter than you. He dropped the phone, but he left it on. I heard *most* of it. I heard your argument when one of your men did not realize the kidnap victim was my wife. He was worried. He should be. You should *all* be. He mentioned a name, and was told to shut up. I heard that name. And to the man with the knife who carved that foul swastika on my son's forehead: he clearly saw the very special knife you used, and gave me a very accurate description of it. He mentioned the emblem it carries.

'And finally, to the people who employed these animals: your problem now is to wonder how much I do know, and what you can do to prevent me from revealing it and blowing you out of the water. I will choose my own time to do this. *You*, will return my wife – and, I repeat, unharmed, and unmolested. You will not enjoy what will happen if you do not.'

The message ended.

Neusser stopped the tape, open-mouthed. He remained like this for long seconds, while Jackson watched him.

Finally, Neusser swallowed, and turned to Jackson. 'The bastards carved a *swastika* on Josh's forehead?'

Jackson nodded.

'You realize, Bill, if you broadcast this message – and I am certain that is what you want me to do – you will have issued a challenge. They will come after you.'

'That is exactly my intention.'

'And the shit will also hit the fan in all sorts of places.'

'That is not my problem. My wife is in danger. Everything else is fly manure. Will you do it? Will you have that released for me?'

'Of course I'll do it! Elisa is my cousin.'

'You could get into trouble.'

'I am a CEO,' Neusser said. 'I make executive decisions.'

'The police may not like it.'

'Once it's out, it's out.'

'There is one policeman who may come knocking on your door. He will be an ally.'

'Do I know of him?'

'Maybe,' Jackson replied. 'Maybe not. But you'll recognize which side he's on – if, and when, you do meet him.'

Neusser gave a slow nod. 'And when should I broadcast the tape?'

'I'll call your cellphone. I'll say one word. "Release".'

'OK. What about the second envelope?'

'That's meant to be for radio. I thought that perhaps you could talk to that friend of yours we met at dinner here . . .'

'Michael Brün.'

'That's him.'

'No problem. I'll talk with him.'

'OK. Thanks.' Jackson passed the second envelope over to Neusser. 'If you were not here, I would have put them through your letter box, and hoped you would do what I requested. There are letters in each, explaining. I have one other thing to ask.'

'Ask it.'

'I need an extra cellphone, but one that uses a card. I'll need you to get one for me tomorrow, but in your name—'

'I can do better. No need to wait for tomorrow. Markus left his old handy here. He does not use it anymore. It's in perfect order, and has plenty on the card. You can have it.'

151

'Thanks again, Klaus.'

'No problem. You said tomorrow. What are you going to do now?'

'Find a hotel . . .'

'Don't be mad. You will stay here. There is plenty of room. You will stay and we will talk about getting Elisa back, and how to get the bastards who did this.'

'Then I must take my car off the street.'

'No problem,' Neusser repeated. 'Plenty of room in the garage. And you were right. I need a drink. A big one.'

In Berlin, the man who had ordered the kidnapping of Elisabeth Jackson received a phone call.

'Did you receive the upload?' The speaker spoke German with a foreign accent.

'Yes. I am looking at a print at this very moment.'

'Is he the candidate?'

'We thought he could have been. As you know, we were wrong about all the others . . .'

'He could be taken, and tested.'

'If you will look at your own photograph, you will see a younger man. That is Müller, *Hauptkommissar*. An extremely dangerous individual who has been causing us considerable trouble. The young woman next to him is Lieutenant-Colonel Bloomfield. Those two work together. They killed one of our best men and his entire team, at that very place where you took the picture. I know you want to share our research, but I advise caution.'

'There is a rumour that caution was sorely lacking earlier today. There was a clumsy attempt on Colonel Bloomfield . . .'

The man reacted furiously. 'Have you been eaves-dropping—?'

The line clicked. The conversation had ended.

The man slammed his phone down, enraged.

Elisabeth Jackson came slowly awake in a bedroom in a house that was a long way from where she had been kidnapped. As she did so, she discovered that she was bound hand and foot, blindfolded, and tape was over her mouth. She felt groggy, but her faculties were all there.

'Ah,' a voice said. 'Awake, are we, Mrs Jackson? Don't roll about too much. You're on a bed. You might fall off.'

The person who had spoken was the same man who had carved the swastika on Josh's head. He used English.

He had been standing at the foot of the bed in the small room. Now, he moved forward until he was near her head, leaned slightly over, and ripped off the tape.

'Ow!' she cried.

'Sorry.' He did not sound sorry.

'Take . . . take that thing away from my eyes.'

'I'm afraid I cannot. Be glad I've removed the gag.'

'Why . . . why have you done this? And what did you put into me?'

'The second question first. We gave you something to put you to sleep. It will wear off soon.'

'And the first question?' she asked. 'Was it for money?'

The man gave a smile she could not see. It would have terrified her. 'How little you do know, Mrs Jackson.'

'My husband will come after you.'

'I very much doubt it. Like you, your war hero has no idea what is going on.'

'You've talked with him?'

'No. He will be contacted in due course. We're letting him stew.'

'You know nothing about my husband.'

'More than you may think, Mrs Jackson.'

'Your men didn't know. They were surprised. They . . . they argued . . .'

'They do as they are told,' the man said harshly. 'And, as for the colonel, he is a snare; bait, if you like.'

'*Bait?* For what?'

The man did not reply. Instead, he took out the knife that Josh had seen, and shot the blade out.

'What was that?' Elisabeth Jackson cried anxiously. 'What was that sound?'

The man looked down at her, studying her bound body. 'Why would a woman like you, a *German* woman, marry such a man? You like those kind of men, do you?'

'So, you're one of those,' she said with contempt. Despite being worried about what might happen to her, she was determined not to show it.

'I have in my hand,' he said, ignoring the remark, 'the knife I used to carve your boy's forehead. It is very sharp.'

'Is that how you feel strong? Cutting little boys? Preening over a helpless woman?'

'Don't try to appeal to my sense of self worth, honour, or decency, Mrs Jackson. As far as you are concerned, I have none whatsoever. You are not even a bargaining chip. I can do with you as I please.'

There was a sudden, quiet sibilance, and she felt a slight cooling on her right thigh. Then she felt two sections of her skirt slide down.

'Beautiful thigh,' he said in a voice that seemed to come from deep within his throat. He swallowed loudly. 'All that wasted on a man like the one you married, and with whom you bred two mongrels.'

Then the door slammed, and a key turned in the lock.

She waited fearfully, listening. Was he still in the room? Was he now getting ready to attack her? She knew he had used the knife to slice her skirt open, and was in no doubt that this was a prelude to what he planned for her.

She lay there, listening as hard as she could, for the slightest sound or movement within the room; but, after a long while, she began to realize that he had gone.

She allowed herself a small sense of relief.

'Oh God, Bill,' she whispered in a heartfelt prayer. 'Please come and get me.'

Schlosshotel Derrenberg, Saaletal. Blissfully unaware of these developments, Müller strolled through the gardens with Carey Bloomfield and Greville. The rain still held off, and the day appeared to have got brighter, the later it became. The evening was pleasantly warm.

His phone rang.

'Excuse me,' he said to the others, stopping as they went on. 'Yes, Pappi.'

'Max's team is back,' Pappenheim said.

'And?'

'They've brought a lot of stuff with them that will take the forensics people some time to sort out, but . . . I am looking at a little gem. It's a knife. Retractable blade, handle black, fits nicely into the hand. It's really a small dagger.'

'Why is that ringing bells?'

'Well, it *is* reminiscent of its bigger sisters of yore, and it's got an embedded emblem . . .'

'With which we are both familiar.'

'You are so sharp, you would cut this knife that I'm holding.'

'One of these days, Pappi . . .'

'You'll get your first gold star and be elevated in rank, whereas I . . .'

'Hate to spoil that lyricism, but do go on.'

'Ah. Yes. I told Max to bring it directly to me, not to forensics. It's got some singe marks, but is otherwise pristine.'

'Bit careless, their losing it.'

'Max believes that the piece of crud who did, put it down in the boathouse and in the hurry to get away, forgot it was there, believing it to be wherever he usually kept it on his person. Probably does not even know it's missing.'

'That won't please his masters.'

'Oh, I do feel sorry for him,' Pappenheim said with a merciless savagery.

'My feelings exactly. Any descriptions from our local colleagues?'

'Nothing. Their recollections are very unreliable. Probably something to do with the drug that was pumped into them. They seem a bit scrambled, according to Max. They're under medical observation. The stuff is probably more potent than first thought.'

'Can't have everything, but good about that knife. We may find a tie-in later, and it adds another piece to the jigsaw. A candidate for the gallery, then.'

'Great minds,' Pappenheim said.

'Has the GW been screaming for me?'

'He's been as quiet as a mouse on a full tummy. Mind you, all that could change as soon as he recovers and finds something else to blame on you. I sometimes think he has a dartboard in a secret room at his house, with your picture on the bullseye, and he—'

'Goodbye, Pappi.'

Pappenheim chuckled. 'I'll be in touch.'

Müller put his phone away and hurried to catch up with the others.

'News of note?' Greville asked.

'News of some note. A small dagger with scorch marks was found quite a distance from the site of the explosion. Interesting little item. There's a familiar design embedded within its handle.'

'The Semper,' Greville immediately said.

Müller nodded. 'Max Gatto, the team leader, believes it was left by mistake. A dagger like that could be more than just a weapon. Possibly, a symbol of rank within the group. If so, it's not something that would willingly be left anywhere. If it is indeed as important as I believe it to be, the person who left it will have an unpleasant time with his masters.'

'Does anything in the documents your father left make any mention of that kind of dagger?' Carey Bloomfield asked.

'I've seen nothing so far. But I haven't looked at all of it. So, possibly there's something in there, somewhere.'

They had reached the stream, and were looking down at it.

'Memories,' she said in a soft voice.

Greville put a fatherly arm about her shoulders. 'Let them go, old girl. Let them go.'

She nodded. 'Yes. I should.'

'But it's difficult. I know how that feels.'

'Yes,' she agreed. 'It is. I'm amazed you can stay so calm, Greville,' she went on, 'knowing that thing's working away inside of you, messing with your DNA.'

'My dear, I came to the conclusion years ago that I had two options: get the screaming abdabs, a certain shortcut to the funny farm, where all sorts of experiments would have been carried out upon me, or hang on to my sanity and play this thing out for as long as I've got. I chose the second option. So that no one gets to play with my remains, young Jens here has instructions what to do when the inevitable occurs.'

Greville took his arm away from her shoulders, and looked at Müller. 'Give the gel a hug. She needs one.'

Before either of them could react, he turned and went back up the garden towards the *Schlosshotel*, a tiny smile pasted upon his face.

Nine

Schlosshotel Derrenberg, 08.00 hours the next day. The Mercedes coupe and the Porsche were in the residential court-yard, ready to leave. Aunt Isolde and Greville were in the Mercedes, Aunt Isolde at the wheel. Carey Bloomfield waited in the Porsche.

Müller leaned on the passenger side of the Mercedes, and looked down at Greville. 'You've got the entry codes for the apartment and the garage, and Pappenheim's direct number, if any trouble comes your way. Pappi will have officers on watch. Stay there till I return. There's plenty of food and—'

'Jens,' Aunt Isolde interrupted from behind the wheel.

Müller peered in at her. 'Yes, Aunt Isolde?'

'It's alright. We'll be fine. And I do know my way around your apartment.'

'Of course you do.' He straightened. 'Well. Greville. You look after her, and after yourself.'

'Will do, old boy. Have no fear.'

Aunt Isolde started her car, pressed the remote-control button to slide the gate open and, with a little wave, drove through.

Müller hurried to his own car, started it, and went through before the gate had begun to close.

'Do I get a chance to drive later?' Carey Bloomfield asked, giving him a look that was amused, as well as challenging.

'No.'

'That was short and sweet.'

'Nothing to do with being short and sweet. You're a maniac at the wheel of this car.'

'Scared you, huh?'

Müller, eyes on the Mercedes ahead of them, said, 'Are you trying to needle me? If so, it's a bit early in the day. Weather seems good so far,' he went on before she could respond. 'No rain.'

'Give it time.'

He glanced at her. 'Why are you so . . . sharp-edged this morning? What am I supposed to have done?'

She chose to ignore the question. 'Anyway, where are we going?'

'To Baden-Württemberg, to see the second newsman. But you knew that.'

She remained silent, staring straight ahead, as they followed Aunt Isolde's car away from the Derrenberg.

'Nice start,' he said.

She did not respond.

Müller turned on the CD player, and made a selection. Taken from his 2001 live tour, the famous thirty-four-year-old opening riff to Clapton's 'Layla' slammed out of the speakers.

'That riff,' Müller said above the sound of the searing guitar and the rumble of the engine, 'is as old as I am! And it's still great.'

She continued to take refuge in silence.

Müller smiled to himself as they trailed after Aunt Isolde and Greville, enjoying the music. After a while, he noticed that she had relaxed in her seat, head back, eyes closed.

She was clearly listening, though her expression gave nothing away.

Jackson was also on the road, heading for Baden-Württemberg and already on the A81 Autobahn, on his way towards Stuttgart. But he would not be going to Stuttgart.

Elisabeth Jackson had been awake for some time. She had spent most of the uncomfortable night awake, expecting that the man would return at any time, to carry out his implied threat. But, to her great relief, nothing had happened. No one had entered the room at all. She fully realized he was playing

158

a sick game with her, aimed at keeping her in constant fear of being attacked.

Though she had not eaten since the kidnap, she did not feel hungry; but she felt unclean, and the inside of her mouth was less than pleasant. Then there was the call of nature.

Strangely enough, the bare mattress felt clean; so perhaps, she allowed herself to hope, she was not being held in some derelict place in the middle of nowhere. But she could not hear any sounds that might tell her what was nearby.

'Hey!' she began to shout in English. 'Anybody home?'

There was no response. Had they left her alone and gone off?

She tried again, in German.

Silence greeted her.

'*Hey!*' she shouted again, going back to English, and louder this time. '*Hey! Anybody home?*'

There was still no response. She felt a surge of hope. If they had simply left her, she could try to work herself free.

She was just beginning to enjoy that thought when the sound of footsteps killed all hope with a cruelty that almost brought tears of frustration to her eyes.

She heard the key turn in the lock, then the same man spoke. 'What's your problem?'

'I need to go to the bathroom. I haven't been since you and your pals dragged me out of my car. So, unless you'd enjoy watching me wet this bed . . .'

She felt rather than heard him cut the bonds at her feet.

'Get up!' he commanded roughly.

With great uncertainty, she tried to do so, and stifled a cry as feeling returned to her legs. She stumbled, and was grabbed roughly by the shoulder. A hand brushed a breast as this happened.

She said nothing, and allowed herself to be led unresisting to the door. The bathroom she was being taken to was not far. The man shoved her through.

'My hands,' she said. 'How do you expect me to . . .'

He said nothing.

'Planning to do it yourself, are you?'

'Don't piss around with me, Mrs Jackson,' he snarled. 'You're in no position to do so.'

'Then tell me . . . how do you expect me to attend to myself with my hands tied behind my back?'

She was roughly turned round and the bonds cut.

'Don't try anything stupid,' he warned. 'There's no one close enough to hear you if you try to yell. And if you did, that would piss me off. You would definitely not like what would happen next. And leave the blindfold alone. It is secured with tape at the back. I'll know if you try to loosen it. You will be tied again when you're finished. Now get it over with!'

He went out, and locked the door.

Half an hour later, he was banging on the door. 'Don't take all day! Come on! Come on!'

'*Alright!*' she shouted, annoyed. 'I'm done!'

The door was unlocked and opened. 'Don't try my patience!' he warned in a harsh voice.

'What do you expect?' she retorted. 'I can't see what I'm doing.'

'You don't need to see where your ass is. Or your—'

'I get the damned point!' She paused, sniffing. 'Is that coffee I smell?'

'That is coffee you smell. A cup, and a bread roll with ham in it, are being brought to you. Your feet will be tied, but your hands will remain free until you are finished. Then they will be tied again.'

'Thank you for the food.'

'I've told you before . . . don't appeal to my better nature. I haven't got one. The food was not my idea. And don't feel too good about the people who said you should be fed. You have no idea what they have in mind for you.'

'If that's meant to make me scared, don't worry. I'm scared already.'

'That's very smart. You should be.'

The man led her back, none too gently, to the room, and again tied her feet.

'Don't move off the bed,' he commanded. Then he went out again, locking the door behind him.

She remained where she was, feet off the bed, listening hard once more for any outside noise that might be some sort of clue to the type of location where she was being held. But all that greeted her was a strange lack of anything, even of traffic. No aircraft passed overhead. Some considerable distance from an airport, she reasoned.

Then the lock was once more being turned.

'Here you are, Mrs Jackson,' a new, kinder voice said in German. He guided her hands to the cup and the bread roll.

'Thank you,' she said. 'Why are you doing this?' She had recognized the voice as belonging to one of the men who had argued over the kidnapping.

His response was brusque. 'Don't ask questions.'

She heard him leave, and again the door was locked.

She began to eat. The coffee was surprisingly good. There was milk in it, and it had been sugared. She did not normally have sugar in coffee, but, given the situation, she thought it tasted good. The bread roll was fresh. So, they must be close enough to a bakery at least, she thought; perhaps only a kilometre or so away. She doubted they would have bought frozen, part-baked bread, to complete the baking process in the house. She had smelled the coffee, but no baking.

She finished off the coffee and the roll, then sat waiting with the empty cup on her lap, held between her hands.

She considered her options. All were bad. The blindfold had been efficiently put in place. The first layer was pads which had been put upon her eyes, so that she could not open them. Then the blindfold itself on top, tightly secured by the tape. Without removing the blindfold, she had no way of knowing whether the room was flooded with light, or was in total darkness; or whether its windows – if it had any – looked out upon anything that was recognizable.

She was locked in. Even if she broke the cup to give herself some kind of a weapon, it would be useless against her captors. And the man with the knife would take great pleasure in making her pay for such folly.

'And if I take off the blindfold,' she now said to herself, 'they'll know, even if I put it back on.'

She thought of her children, and of her husband.

'Bill will get me out of this,' she said.

*   *   *

161

As the Porsche and the Mercedes approached the Triptis junction on the A9 Autobahn, Müller passed his mobile to Carey Bloomfield.

'Would you please call Pappi? Tell him they're on their way.'

She nodded, and called Pappenheim as, up ahead, the Mercedes flashed its blinkers once and headed off to take the access for Berlin.

'It's me again, Pappi,' she said when Pappenheim answered.

'Always a pleasure to hear from you,' he said with smooth gallantry. 'So, he's not letting you drive this time?'

'I tried earlier, and got a sharp no.'

'He can be mean at times.'

'Tell me about it. I'm calling to let you know they're on their way.'

'Then tell Jens I'll see that everything's under control.'

'OK, Pappi. I'll do that.'

'And keep trying. You may wear him down.'

'That will be the day,' she said.

Pappenheim gave a suspiciously evil chuckle.

'And Pappi,' Carey Bloomfield went on, 'sorry about your colleague yesterday.'

'Yesterday,' Pappenheim said, all levity gone from his voice, 'was not one of our better days. Thank you for the sentiment. Much appreciated.'

'Hang in there.'

'You too.'

She passed the phone back to Müller.

'Thank you,' he said.

'You're welcome. Can I put "Layla" back on?'

'You like it?' he asked in some surprise.

'I've always liked it.'

'Then put it on.'

As Müller joined the A9 to head for Baden-Württemberg, he gave the car its head. The Turbo surged along the Autobahn, the fat sound of the riff charging through the speakers.

Pappenheim got a phone call from one of his contacts.

'Check your colleagues' reports of yesterday,' the voice suggested.

'I have colleagues all over the country,' Pappenheim said, watching two smoke rings race each other to the ceiling. 'I cannot even begin to think of the thousands of reports . . .'

'Specifically . . . on the B19 in the Schweinfurt, Werneck, and Würzburg area. That should narrow it down nicely.'

The line went dead.

Pappenheim put the phone down. 'Schweinfurt? Werneck? Why does that ring a faint bell?' He picked up his internal phone and dialled an extension. 'Miss Meyer,' he said when the goth had answered. 'I need you.'

'You're starting early, sir.'

'*Early?* The day's already old.'

'On my way,' she said.

'I'll be waiting.'

He was already in the rogues' gallery when she arrived, dressed in white. She seemed to gleam. She went straight to the computer and powered it up.

'What are we looking for?'

'You're going to hack some colleagues.'

'And here I was thinking you wanted something difficult.'

'I didn't hear that, did I?'

'No, sir. You didn't. If I might ask a question . . . why don't we just ask them?'

'Do you really want an answer to that?'

'Now that you've put it that way . . . no, sir. I don't. Ready when you are.'

'I want to see any reports centred on the B19, within an area bounded by Schweinfurt, Würzburg, and Werneck.'

The goth's fingers swept across the keyboard. Within seconds, it seemed, a page concerning the B19 was onscreen.

'That was very hard, I see,' Pappenheim commented. 'If you ever leave us, Miss Meyer, please don't hack into us.'

'I don't plan to leave.'

'Small mercies, for which we are ever grateful,' Pappenheim intoned as if in prayer. 'And what have we got?'

'I've highlighted everything to do with the B19.'

Pappenheim ran his eyes down the list. 'Motorcycle accident, someone throwing a bottle on to the road, two kids playing chicken with the traffic, no, no, no . . . What the hell was she

163

talking about? Wait a minute. Wait . . . a . . . minute . . .' he added softly. 'There. That one about the Volvo. Open it.'

Hedi Meyer clicked on it, and the full report opened out.

Pappenheim read it silently.

'Alright,' he said to the goth. 'You can close it, and get out of there before they find out.'

She made a scoffing noise. 'That would take them a few million years.'

'Oh, I do like the confidence of the very young,' Pappenheim said. 'Thanks, Hedi,' he went on. 'That's it.'

She shut down the computer, and stood up. 'Can I come in towards the end of the day to have a flight, before I leave for home? If you're still in your office, that is.'

'I'll be in my office. And yes, you can.'

'Thank you, sir.'

'Don't mention it.' Pappenheim seemed distracted, and vaguely lifted a hand in farewell as the goth went out.

'Military-looking man,' he murmured to himself, 'pulls injured boy out of Volvo combi with smashed windows. No driver to be seen anywhere. Passing motorists try to help the boy but, obviously very scared, he refuses their help. Then his father – the military-looking man, *American* – arrives in a black Audi. American license plate. Leaves before the police turn up. No attempt to contact the police so far, despite saying he would. One witness describes him as imposing. Not an ordinary soldier. Someone accustomed to command. Schweinfurt, Werneck . . .' Pappenheim's voice faded. 'My God . . .' He paused again. 'Jens once met an American officer down there. Could this be . . . *the* colonel? Surely not . . .'

He hurried out of the rogues' gallery.

They were approaching the A70 Autobahn sign for Bamberg, Schweinfurt, and Würzburg, 115 kilometres into their journey, when Pappenheim's call came.

'Can you take it, please?' Müller said, passing the phone to Carey Bloomfield.

'Sure. Hi, Pappi,' she went on to Pappenheim, 'it's the secretary again, I'm afraid.'

'I'm very happy to talk to the secretary,' he said. 'Still won't let you drive, eh?'

'Lost cause, Pappi,' she said as they joined the A70.

'Well, don't give up. The slow drip of water on rock.'

'The water runs off.'

'Not always,' Pappenheim said with an air of mystery. 'I've got something that might jolt him,' he continued. 'You too, perhaps.'

'You've got my full attention.'

Pappenheim told her about the incident on the B19.

Her eyes widened. 'You've got to be kidding me.'

'I'm afraid not. We have ourselves an interesting mystery.'

'You think it's *the* colonel?'

'I'm reluctant to commit, but it seems to point that way.'

At the word 'colonel', Müller had darted a look at Carey Bloomfield. 'What colonel?'

She held the mobile away from her ear. 'I think you should stop at the next gas station. You'll want to hear this. Do we need gas?'

'No. But I can top up the tank. Tell Pappi I'll call him as soon as possible.'

'Heard that, Pappi?' she said into the mobile.

'I've got most of it. Tell him OK.'

'He says OK,' she told Müller, as she ended connection.

'What colonel?' he repeated.

'Do you remember when we first met up, we found ourselves at an army base near Schweinfurt?'

'"Found" is an interesting word to use, but are you talking about Colonel Bill? *The* Colonel Bill?' Müller darted her another glance. This time, it was one of astonishment.

'Hear what Pappi has to say,' she said, 'then you tell me.'

She gave him a quick precis of what Pappenheim had said.

'Vogel said "the colonel",' Müller said, remembering, 'and was surprised to see a woman. They're going after *Colonel Bill*? But why? What's the connection?'

'I'm looking at one.'

'Come on, Miss Bloomfield,' Müller said. 'That's reaching, as you would say.'

'I never say that, but I admit some people do. They tried to get me yesterday. Why not Colonel Bill?'

'For a start, I do not work with him. And . . .' Müller stopped.

'"And", Müller?' she urged.

'He can hardly be considered as being close to me.'

'But what if something happened to him that required police involvement? Something big enough to get *you* involved.'

'A trap?'

'There are many ways to bait one.'

'That, I certainly do know.' A sign for the next service station hove into view. 'I'd better hear what Pappi does have to say. We'll stop at this *Tankstelle.*'

'Can I drive from there?'

'No.'

'Spoilsport.'

'Don't sulk. You're a colonel.'

'A *lieutenant*-colonel. That allows me some sulking.'

'If you say so.'

The service station came into view soon after. Müller pulled off the Autobahn, and up to the pumps. After topping up the tank, he found a parking bay well away from other vehicles in the uncrowded car park.

He returned Pappenheim's call, remaining in the car. He listened silently, as Pappenheim gave him the details of what the goth had found.

'So, do you think he is *the* colonel in question?' Pappenheim finished.

'It's a strong indication. He has a son who would be about that age. About twelve, the report said?'

'Yes.'

'I was twelve when my . . . parents . . .' Müller stopped. 'No. It could not be something so . . .'

'Why not? It would fit into their madness. Very symbolic. As we know, they go in for symbolism.'

'Miss Bloomfield believes it's a ploy to get me involved.'

'She could be right.'

'Perhaps they want to show me how far they are prepared to go. Perhaps they are saying no one is safe, if they put their minds to it.'

166

'And make you responsible.'

'There are other things playing in there as well, Pappi. He has not been in touch with the police, you say.'

'According to the report. Nothing official whatsoever.'

'Was the Volvo also carrying American plates?'

'That's the thing. It is locally registered, but there was no owner listed in the report.'

'Then it's his wife's car. I am certain of it. She is German, and perhaps being back in the old country, she wanted her car to have a German plate. An easily understood emotional thing. See if one of your many people can trace the ownership, without making even the tiniest of waves.'

'Funny you should say that.'

Müller smiled. 'I should have known.'

'As soon as I get it, you'll get it. As you're heading into the area, will you pay him a visit?'

'No. Not unless I am really dragged into it. Whatever it is, I'm certain the Americans will sort it out themselves. I'm continuing with my original plan.'

'You're the boss. I'll let you know.'

'Alright, Pappi.'

'And let her drive,' Pappenheim said.

'Don't you start.'

'Spoilsport.'

'Are you two telepathic?'

'I know there's a clever comment in there somewhere,' Pappenheim said, 'but I'll let it pass.'

The call ended. Müller put the phone into the small, lidded compartment on the central console. 'Did you get most of that?' he said to Carey Bloomfield.

'I got most of that.'

'Do you need the lavatory?'

'That's a non sequitur, if ever—'

'Not really. I won't be stopping again until we get to Baden-Baden. That means another three hundred kilometres, at the very least. I want to make the best time possible, before we go on to France. It is now –' he glanced at the clock on the main console – 'nine thirty precisely. I intend to be in Baden-Baden before midday.'

'I need to go to the toilet.' She got out and headed for the Autobahn services.

He watched her go, enjoying the slight toe-in of her walk. 'You've got a great walk, Carey Bloomfield,' he said softly.

He selected Clapton's 'Wonderful Tonight' on the CD changer, and continued watching, as the wailing guitar opened up, until she had gone out of sight. Then he relaxed in his seat and let the music take him.

Now dressed in lightweight suits, the two men who had rigged the explosion were in their hotel, which was not far from the one in which Carey Bloomfield had stayed. Close scrutiny of one of them would show he bore a remarkable resemblance to the 'policeman' who had tried to kill her the day before.

They were in one of the two rooms they had booked under assumed identities, and sat drinking vodka from the minibar. They were not Russian, neither were they German.

The one who had laughed silently after seeing the Wannsee boathouse explode, and whose room it was, put down his glass, and went over to look for something in one of the drawers of the bedside cabinet. His taller companion had been the 'policeman'.

'What are you looking for?' the companion asked.

'Can't understand what's happened to my dagger.'

'You've *lost* it? Are you mad?'

'I didn't "lose" it. It must be somewhere.'

'Just don't leave it here for the hotel staff to find. You wouldn't be very popular with certain people.'

'I'll make quite sure it isn't here. Perhaps it's fallen between the seats in the car.'

'I hope, for your sake, it has.'

On the outskirts of Berlin, two other men were sitting in the opulent splendour of a large mansion, looking out on an immaculately tended garden. They were having coffee.

'Odd,' one of them said. 'No public mention at all of the explosion, or the death of Vogel.' The two men in the hotel had acted on his orders, as had the men who had kidnapped Elisabeth Jackson.

'What of the colonel's wife?'

'There too, nothing is in the public domain as yet.'

'Müller's work?'

'I am certain he has put the embargo on the events in Wannsee. But not with the matter of the colonel's wife. By now, there should have been an alarm raised . . . at the very least. Perhaps the good colonel is playing his own game. His career records show that he is not unlike Müller in some ways. Likes to follow the unorthodox path.'

'The lone wolf?'

'In some ways, yes. This can sometimes make him the bane of his superiors. Again, as with Müller. It is not natural that a man who *knows* his wife has been kidnapped would remain silent for so long. It is even more unnatural when that man is Colonel Jackson. The colonel may be planning something; but we'll be ready.'

'I sincerely hope you are right.'

'It still continues to puzzle me how Müller got to Vogel.'

'No links to anyone?'

'None at all, so far. Damn that man, and his father! All these years after von Röhnen's death, the damage he did continues to hurt us. Now his son forces us to take the kind of action I would rather employ more . . . judiciously.'

'Are you saying he is manipulating our responses?'

'In part, yes. But he is also blundering into areas he should not. He has already received sharp warnings.'

'Which he ignores.'

'Just like his wretched traitor of a father!' There was an abiding anger in the voice.

'We got the father. We'll get the son. In the meantime, perhaps you should send some visitors to Grüber . . . in case Müller knows about him too. Send those two from Wannsee. They can use one of the helicopters . . .'

The other shook his head. 'Helicopters mean flight plans. Flight plans mean traceable. We cannot afford to be too visible. Time is needed to make flight plans invisible.'

'Are you prepared to risk that Müller might know of Grüber?'

'No. But they'll have to go by car.' The man in command of the killers took a sip of coffee. 'Looking forward to tonight?'

'Most certainly. It will be good to see so many of us among the crowd.'

The man laughed. 'And the crowd won't even know we're there.'

They smiled at each other. One of the men having coffee was a retired general and the other a man of the church.

In the hotel, the man who had lost his dagger answered his mobile phone.

'You will go to Grüber, and remind him of the virtues of continuing silence, as opposed to a permanent one,' the hard voice said in his ear.

'Do we fly?'

'You drive.' The connection ended. He turned to his companion. 'We're going for a walk in the Black Forest. Grüber needs a visit.'

'When?' There was eager anticipation in the question.

'Now. We're driving.'

'Then we'd better check out. It's a long drive, even the way I drive.'

'Fast? Or faster?'

They laughed; the shorter one silently.

Pappenheim picked up a phone and dialled a number. The person he hoped to speak to was someone he hadn't seen for years. He blew three interlocked smoke rings, and waited.

'Dietrich.'

'Ah! Detlef!' Pappenheim said, full of bonhomie.

'Yes? Who . . . wait a minute. I *know* that voice. My God. *Pappenheim?* How long has it been?'

'How many kids do you have?' Pappenheim countered.

'Four. The first is nearly ten.'

'There's your answer. You weren't even married then . . . not that marriage is necessary . . .'

'I was married . . .'

'I'm sorry to hear. How . . . ?'

'Oh, it's not what you think. She's very much alive. Got another man.'

'I'm still sorry to hear.'

'Don't be. I've got another woman.'

Pappenheim paused to take this in. 'I see. One of those rare amicable divorces we keep hearing about, but never are in reality? You seem to have made it.'

'Not a chance,' Dietrich said. 'It was a war zone. But life is peaceful. She never gets in touch with me; I never get in touch with her. I pay for the kids electronically. Nice and clean. The fourth one is with my new wife.'

'What a boon, this electronic world.'

'And you?'

'Alas. Not so lucky. She's gone. The worst of ways, for me. Cancer.'

'I'm the one who's sorry to hear.'

'Thank you, Detlef. But it was some time ago,' Pappenheim said, hiding the pain he still felt, even after all the years.

'Life goes on.'

'That it does.'

'So . . . who says it first?'

'I will. You have a report about a Volvo on the B19 . . .'

'My God! How do you . . . What *is* it that you do up there in Berlin?'

'Can't tell you. If I did—'

'You'd have to kill me.'

'No. Boil you in oil.'

'You sound like a strange lot to me.'

'You have no idea how strange,' Pappenheim said, thinking of Kaltendorf. 'About the Volvo. No traffic about it.'

'Don't investigate?'

'For now.'

'I'm a lowly *Kommissar*. My bosses might want to know why . . .'

'Refer them to me. I'm certain they will be able to make contact, one way or the other.'

'So, what are you these days? When we last saw each other, I had just got my three green, *Hauptmeister* stars, and you, your first silver. *Kommissar* Pappenheim! Mark you, we never thought you'd make it, seeing you gave the bosses so much grief. What have you got now? Three silver? Your first gold?'

'Alas, just two silvers.'

171

'Still aggravating the bosses, eh?'

'Someone has to. But I've got a boss who seems to like me. So, life's bearable.'

'You haven't changed, Pappi. I know when you're pulling my leg.'

'It's true. We work well together.'

'So who's this paragon?'

'You'll not have heard of him. Name of Müller. Now *he's* the one heading for his first gold star.'

'Müller? I *have* heard of him. Rumour at the time said that he barged into an American base, not far from here.'

'He never barges. Charges, though . . . sometimes.'

'Is this Volvo thing—'

'You're too quick for me, Detlef.'

'Why do I get the feeling you're not telling me everything?'

'Oh, I'm always telling something to someone, somewhere, sometime,' Pappenheim said.

'And now that you've laid your smoke grenade . . . OK, Pappi. I'll make sure the Volvo stays quiet. But if my bosses—'

'Blame me.'

'I will.'

'There you go,' Pappenheim said. 'Thanks, Detlef.'

Pappenheim put his phone down.

'Who'd have thought it?' he said. 'Detlef Dietrich, playboy of the *Länder*, has become a serial monogamist, and doting father. People *can* change.'

The phone rang. He picked it up.

'*Pappenheim!*' Kaltendorf's voice roared.

'Sir?'

'Have you heard from Müller?'

'Not yet, sir,' Pappenheim lied.

The line clicked.

Pappenheim again replaced the phone.

'*But not this one,*' he remarked with a sigh.

In the house where she was being held, Elisabeth Jackson was again bound hand and foot, and lying on the bed.

She lay on her left side, trying to be as comfortable as was possible. Ever since the man with the kinder voice had come to take the cup away, no one else had entered. She could only guess at how long that had been.

Then she heard the key in the lock. Her body tensed, despite her efforts to remain relaxed.

It was the man with the knife.

'Did you miss me?' he asked in a sly voice. 'It seems you are not missed,' he went on. 'Nothing at all from your husband.'

'I thought you said *you'd* be getting in contact. You wanted him to sweat.'

'That's certainly true. But we expected at least an alarm. You know, police rushing around pointlessly.'

'You claim to know about my husband. You don't. You shouldn't be fooled by his silence. It would be a smart thing to let me go before this gets worse . . .'

The man gave a chilling laugh. 'For *us*? Is that what you were about to say? On any balance, Mrs Jackson,' he went on coldly, '*your* situation is the more precarious. We can leave here at any time we choose. *You* can only leave here at the time *we* choose.'

'My husband is doing something.'

'Your husband does not frighten me.'

'You clearly don't know about him at all.'

'I could say I hate to disillusion you, Mrs Jackson, but I won't; because I do *enjoy* disillusioning you. You, clearly, have no idea what this is all about. Despite the fact that I have contempt for you for coupling with that . . . that . . .'

'Go on. Say it. Why don't you . . . if it will satisfy that small ego of yours?'

'*Don't* push me! I can give you so much pain, you will do anything I ask, just to make it stop.'

She said nothing.

'That's better,' he said. 'Much better. Just remember who is master here, and you and I will get along perfectly.'

He stroked her thigh once, slowly, and she forced herself not to flinch, in case that set him off again.

Then she heard him leave, and the key turn in the lock.

Ten

Berlin-Wilmersdorf. 11.30, West European Summer Time.
Hans Schörma – accompanied by Hammersfeldt – parked the
car in such a way that the main entrance to Müller's apartment, and the garage entrance to the building itself, were well
within view. The day had remained dry, and was warming up
nicely, but not as much as expected for July.

Both were in the usual civilian 'uniform' of jeans, trainers
and T-shirt, with the black, regulation leather jacket that bore
the shoulder-mounted green stars of their ranks. Each carried
a sidearm, but Schörma had augmented this with a big
Browning automatic pistol in a shoulder holster. He had carried
that pistol since his Legionnaire days, a gift from an American
fellow-Legionnaire.

Hammersfeldt was peering at the building. 'Nice place.
Nice to be rich. If I had his money, I'd be off to Majorca,
build me a huge villa and wait for all those summer chickies
to come flocking.'

'And here I was thinking you joined us because you liked
kicking some heads in.' Schörma gave a feral grin. His haircut
bore more than a passing resemblance to the brutal crop of
the Legion.

Hammersfeldt gave a distant smile. 'I'm fascinated by
him, though. I mean, he's got all that money, that car, those
clothes . . .'

'And don't forget the ponytail, and the earring,' Schörma
added, baring huge teeth. 'But don't let that fool you. He can
be as hard as nails when he wants to be. An old Legion friend
came here for a visit, and saw him walking by. "Bet there are
some people who think he's a weak tit," he said to me. "Let
me tell you about guys like this. They are dangerous. Knew
a cop like that once. The cruds on the street hated and feared

him." "Why?" I asked. "Because," he said, "they could never tell where he was coming from. He wrong-footed those suckers all the time." That fits your *Hauptkommissar* perfectly.'

'So, you have a lot of respect for him.'

'Oh yes. He and Pappenheim are the best pair of cops I've come across. Pappenheim is supposed to have taught him all he knows. I wouldn't put it quite like that, but the *Oberkommissar* is a character all by himself too. Tough bastard, if you ask me. Instinctive. I mean, look at what happened last May. Who would have ever imagined he would have decided to wear body armour that night? *He* did it because his gut instincts told him.

'That's the kind of thing that makes all the difference between cops like Müller and Pappenheim, and you or I; and I've been in real wars. Out there on the battlefield, trusting your instincts, and your buddy, to do the right thing at the right time, can mean the difference between getting your head blown off and taking it back with you in one piece. Müller and Pappenheim are like that; they trust their instincts, and each other. And it works for them. I've seen some cops I wouldn't trust if they were the last people on earth.'

'Anyone like that in our Ready Group?'

'Everyone's got the right stuff.' Schörma grinned. 'Even you, Hammy, our newest.'

Hammersfeldt looked pleased. 'Thanks, Hansi.'

'Now, don't let it go to your head.'

Hammersfeldt smiled, but said nothing to that.

After a while, he said, 'So, what do these people we're supposed to be watching look like?'

'We're not watching them. We're supposed to look after them. What do they look like? Well, they're an oldish – not *really* old – couple. The *Hauptkommissar*'s aunt, and her husband. They'll be driving a Mercedes coupe. She knows the apartment. I think we'll be able to recognize them,' Schörma added drily.

'Well, I think they're coming.'

Schörma looked in the direction Hammersfeldt was pointing. The Mercedes coupe was just nosing round the corner into the street that led to Müller's building.

They watched in silence as the car approached.

'Shouldn't we at least introduce ourselves?' Hammersfeldt suggested.

'Good idea. Let them know we're on the ball. Come on.'

They got out of their car and began walking at a rapid pace to where the Mercedes was pulling to a halt, just in front of the entrance to the garage.

They reached it just as the garage door began to roll upwards.

Aunt Isolde looked startled as the two policemen stopped by the car. Greville immediately climbed out.

'Trouble, officers?' he began in German.

Knowing instantly this was not Greville's mother tongue, Schörma said, 'Good morning. I speak English. No. No trouble. I am Schörma, and this is Hammersfeldt. We are from *Oberkommissar* Pappenheim.'

'Ah,' Greville said, then, reverting to English, 'All is now clear. The cavalry. Glad you speak the lingo, old man. Don't have to offend your ears with my quite execrable German. I'm Greville, and I'm certain you know this is *Hauptkommissar* Müller's aunt.'

Schörma nodded. 'Yes, sir. I do. Now we will leave you to your business. We just wanted to introduce ourselves. We will be out here, on watch. Not to worry.'

'No worries at all, old boy. Glad to have you.'

That was when everything changed.

Schörma had begun to turn, in preparation for heading back to the unmarked police car. His eyes popped when he saw the gun in Hammersfeldt's hand. Then they screwed up in pain as a single shot tore into his chest. He staggered backwards and, even though dying, had begun to pull at his own sidearm. He never made it. A second shot ripped next to the first.

Schörma was dead before he hit the ground, shock in his staring eyes.

Greville turned slowly to look at Hammersfeldt, who had a frightened look upon his face.

In the car, Aunt Isolde put a hand to her mouth.

Hammersfeldt lowered his weapon, but did not put it away. 'Quick!' he urged in English. 'We must go! Schörma was trying to kidnap you! I was afraid to do anything before. I did not get a chance until now.'

Greville stared at him. 'What do you mean "kidnap"?'

'I heard him on his phone to someone,' Hammersfeldt said. 'He did not know I heard. They were talking about you! He was supposed to take you, and kill me!'

Greville moved closer. He did so with unhurried steps. 'Calm yourself, my boy. Let's have this coherently . . .'

Greville considered he was close enough and acted with a speed that astonished Hammersfeldt, who had clearly thought he was dealing with an old and slow pensioner.

A chopping palm slammed into the upper arm of the hand that held the gun. Hammersfeldt gasped with the fierceness of the sudden pain. The hand opened involuntarily, and the weapon dropped to the ground. Greville swiftly picked it up, and pointed it at Hammersfeldt.

'Now,' Greville said, 'do let's talk about this little piece of theatre. Don't move a muscle, old boy. I am quite good with these toys.'

Hammersfeldt looked into eyes that sent shivers through him, and remained perfectly still, not even trying to hold, with his other hand, the upper arm that now hurt excruciatingly.

'Stay where you are, my dear,' Greville called to Aunt Isolde; then, with his left hand, he fished his mobile out of a jacket pocket and, keeping a cold eye upon Hammersfeldt, dialled Pappenheim's number.

'Pappenheim.'

'Ah. *Oberkommissar.* Greville here. We're at Müller's place.'

'Welcome to Berlin, Mr Greville . . .'

'I'm afraid the welcome has been rather thin. One of your officers is down. Schörma . . .'

'*What?* And the other one? Hammersfeldt?'

'Ah. That's the problem, Hammersfeldt shot him.'

A shocked silence greeted this.

'Go on, Mr Greville,' Pappenheim continued heavily.

'I've disarmed him—'

'*You?*'

'Me. I've now got him at the point of his own gun, pending further enquiries. He gave a cock-and-bull story about Schörma

177

planning to kidnap us. Rubbish, of course. But it does make one wonder about his own motives.'

'It certainly does, Mr Greville. I've already got people on the way even as we speak, and—'

It was at that moment that Hammersfeldt decided to make his move. He turned and ran, removing the leather jacket and dropping it as he went.

'*Stop!*' Greville shouted. '*Stop, I say!*' But he did not shoot, and Hammersfeldt escaped.

'*What was that?*' came Pappenheim's voice sharply.

'I'm afraid our man has legged it.'

'He *ran?*'

'Afraid so. Clean getaway. You have lost a second policeman, old man. Something tells me you won't be seeing him again in this particular uniform. He threw off the jacket he was wearing.'

'Exactly what happened?'

Greville gave precise details.

'My God!' Pappenheim said when Greville had finished.

'As well you might. Look. I feel rather exposed out here with a police weapon in my hand, and a dead officer at my feet. People are beginning to look.'

'Put the gun away and pretend you're caring for him. Some of my people will be with you soon. *Kommissarin* Fohlmeister is in charge. She'll take care of everything. As soon as she arrives, leave her to it, and get inside. Your part will be over. Just look after Jens' aunt, and yourself.'

'Will do, old boy. They can't get here soon enough.'

A few minutes later, one of the Ready Group's vans screeched to a halt, and Ilona Fohlmeister jumped out, followed by three male colleagues, who immediately began to attend to the dead Schörma.

She went up to Greville, hand outstretched. 'Mr Greville? Ilona Fohlmeister.'

'Glad you're here,' he said, shaking hands. He gave her the gun. 'This was Hammersfeldt's.'

Her lips tightened as she took the weapon, then turned to look as Schörma's body was placed on a stretcher, covered, then picked up to be put into the van.

'The little bastard,' she said, thinking of Hammersfeldt.

'Nothing quite as bad as the betrayal of one's own team,' Greville said with feeling.

Her eyes darted towards him. 'You say that with the voice of experience.'

'Oh,' he said. 'I've been there.'

'I can hear things that I know I should not ask about,' she said. 'So, I'll leave you to it, Mr Greville.'

He nodded. 'Yes. Sorry about your colleague. Bad business, his going like that. Any wife? Children?'

'None.'

'Still not much of a comfort, but worse if there had been. Sorry,' he repeated, and got back into the Mercedes.

The garage door, having reached maximum elevation, had remained open. A shocked Aunt Isolde drove in.

Baden-Baden outskirts, 11.45, West European Summer Time. Müller had made even better time than he had hoped. He had driven at extremely high speed, reducing Carey Bloomfield at times to long periods of silence as she had watched the road stream before her, marvelling that the car had remained on the road at all. Sections of the A5 Autobahn had felt so rough, with a regular thumping that was accentuated by the Porsche's stiffened suspension, despite the comfort within the car itself.

She now gave a quiet sigh of relief as Müller began to slow down, in preparation for the approach to the exit.

He glanced at her. 'Were you frightened?'

'Of course not!'

'Good run, wasn't it? We are here before midday. I enjoy these high-speed dashes from time to time. The car feels free; like a charger being given free rein.'

'It's a car, Müller.'

'It's four hundred and fifty horses,' he corrected, smiling, knowing she was trying to goad him.

'I'm happy for each and every one of them. So, where does this person live, who we've charged down to see?'

'Just outside Baden-Baden. We won't have to go through town. In fact, it's not far from the Autobahn. Very handy.'

They found the place less than ten minutes later. It was indeed close to the Autobahn; but the large house within its huge grounds was such a haven of peace, the traffic could scarcely be heard.

Carey Bloomfield stared at the house as it came into view at the end of a long avenue of tall trees.

'Oh wow!' she said. 'Müller, nothing beats the Derrenberg for grand style, but this ain't no log cabin. I didn't realize editors made this kind of money.'

'If you're paid enough to defame someone,' he remarked with some bitterness, 'you might be able to afford this. It will be worth many times more, perhaps, than when he was first able to buy it. So, he's made a profit too, if he ever decides to sell.'

'On the backs of your parents.'

'Could be.'

'Suddenly, this place doesn't look so beautiful anymore.'

'The place is still beautiful. It is a large *Herrenhaus*. But it was designed to look like a mix between the traditional *Herrenhaus* and a villa. Architecturally, it should have been a disaster. But this looks good. It's not its fault that the man who lives here bought it.'

As the avenue ended, the white building with its red roof seemed to rise before them in imposing majesty. A uniformed butler came out of the house to stand upon the raised, crescent-shaped terrace as the car came to a stop.

'My, my,' Carey Bloomfield said. 'Will you look at that. He's not sneering at the car, Müller. So, he must approve.'

'Behave,' he said, as the butler began to descend a short flight of steps, with all the poise of an emperor.

'If *he's* like that,' Carey Bloomfield whispered, 'what's his boss going to be like?'

'Behave,' Müller repeated, getting out of the car.

He drew himself to his full height, just as the butler reached him. Having lost the raised advantage of the terrace, the butler had to look up.

'May I be of service, sir?' the butler enquired.

'You may. My name is Müller, *Hauptkommissar* . . .'

The butler did not bat an eye. 'Herr Grüber knows all the

senior policemen in the area. I have never heard him speak of a Müller.'

Müller was rapidly becoming impatient with the man, and went for the big gun he tended to use on snobs like this.

'Then perhaps he knows von Röhnen. *Graf* von Röhnen.' Müller handed him a gold-bordered card with an embossed coat of arms.

The butler, a round man with a perfectly round head that was reminiscent of a football, blinked when he saw the card.

'*Herr Graf*! Of course! I will inform Herr Grüber at once. If the Herr Graf and the Frau Gräfin von Röhnen will please follow me.'

The butler waited until Carey Bloomfield, keeping a perfectly straight face, had joined Müller.

He bowed slightly. '*Frau Gräfin.*' Then he turned, as if on wheels, and began to go back up the steps carrying the card before him as if it were a laden silver platter.

'*What* did he call me?' she whispered to Müller. 'Did I just hear that correctly?'

'You've been ennobled. I think he assumes you're my wife, the countess.'

'I should be so lucky. Müller, you carry a *titled card*?'

'Behave,' Müller said for a third time, whispering. 'Let's hurry. I want to see Grüber's face when we're announced. I don't want him to have an excuse to avoid seeing me. If we're there, he can't pretend he's too busy.'

'I'm curious too,' she said.

They were led along a seemingly endless hall with a Kelim runner as long as the hall itself, on a gleaming surface of highly polished wood.

Carey Bloomfield looked up at the extremely high ceiling. 'Can you get vertigo looking up?' she whispered.

Briefly, Müller put a finger to his lips.

The butler finally stopped at the very end of the hall, and opened a door. He stood back, and again gave a little nod of the head.

'*Frau Gräfin, Herr Graf.*'

They walked through into a kind of antechamber that was again laid with expensive Persian carpets. Another terrace, as large as the one at the front, was accessed through a door in the floor-to-ceiling glass panels. The terrace looked out upon one of the most beautiful landscaped gardens Müller had set eyes upon.

Grüber, in an open-necked white shirt, sat at a large table with a white tablecloth, eating either a late breakfast, or an early lunch. He was alone. He was a thinnish man with lank, dark hair that he grew to neck length. Rimless glasses were perched upon his nose. He looked his age. He was sat in such a way that both the antechamber and a wide expanse of garden were within view. Even as he ate, his face bore an expression of extreme superciliousness. Müller disliked him on sight.

'I'm going to enjoy this,' Müller said as the butler went out to announce them.

Carey Bloomfield noted his expression. 'You don't like him.'

'Would you?'

'Knowing the background to this little visit, and looking at him . . . no.'

The butler had reached Grüber's table. Grüber made him wait, concentrating on drinking some coffee, and taking his time about it. He did not even look up at the butler.

'Jesus!' Carey Bloomfield said. 'What an asshole.'

'Manners of a pig,' Müller commented. 'Despite the size of this house, that's not the reason he has a butler. His type would have a butler even if he lived in my small place.'

She looked at him. '*Your* place is *small*? You could get half of Washington in it. I exaggerate – a little – but there's small, and *then* there's small. You should see mine. Your place does not fit into either category.' She returned her attention to Grüber. 'Oh look. The lord and master is finally looking up at his servant. Can he see us from there?'

'Depends on the reflections on the glass. Even if he can . . . it's too late for him to run. He's got to face me now.'

The butler was handing over the card. Grüber took it, read it, then looked as if he were about to faint.

'Well,' Carey Bloomfield said, 'you've got your effect. Time for the entrance?'

'Time for the entrance,' Müller agreed. 'Let us not give the butler any extra work. I am actually feeling sorry for that snob. They suit each other, those two. After you, *Frau Gräfin.*'

'Go boil an egg, Müller,' she said, as she stepped out on to the terrace.

He smiled. 'That's an expression.'

Grüber was looking at them as he would a pair of venomous snakes about to strike. The butler had wheeled himself away.

Grüber's mouth was open, and stayed open when Müller and Carey Bloomfield reached his table. They did not sit down, nor did he ask them to.

Finally, weak eyes darting from one to the other, Grüber decided to speak. His eyes looked as if they were staring at ghosts. The card lay face up, next to the fine china coffee cup and saucer.

'You're . . . you're like them!'

Carey Bloomfield glanced at Müller. 'What in—?'

'I think,' Müller began, 'he means my parents.'

'You're kidding. Is he out of it?'

'In a way, yes. Herr Grüber,' Müller began, 'I think you know why we're here.'

'How . . . how did you find me?' The eyes again went into their darting dance.

Müller just looked at him.

'I knew . . . I knew this would happen some day,' Grüber said, almost to himself. 'I knew . . .'

'How odd,' Müller cut in. 'That is almost what Vogel said.'

Grüber's eyes tried to leave their sockets. 'You have seen *Vogel*?'

'I have. He was very forthcoming. Alas, he is now dead.'

Grüber jumped. '*Dead?* You . . . you . . . *killed* him?'

'In my place, Grüber,' Müller said in a voice that must have chilled the man before him, 'wouldn't you? But no . . . I did not. He did it himself. Must have been all those years of guilt.' Müller's eyes bored mercilessly into the cringing Grüber. 'All I need from you are straight answers to my questions. Then I'll leave you to all . . .'

He waved an arm, glancing up as he did so. A face at a window darted out of sight. A woman. Grüber's wife?

' . . . this,' Müller finished.

183

'They made me! They made me write all that . . .'

'And paid well enough, looking at this place. You have lived high upon the backs of my parents. Who are *"they"*, Grüber?'

Grüber suddenly looked even more fearful, and said nothing.

'I am a police *Hauptkommissar*, Grüber . . .'

'I know that!' Grüber said; this was clearly old news to him.

'I can have you taken in.'

Grüber actually laughed, but it was a short laugh of bitterness, as well as of resignation.

'Yes. You can. Then what? Do you think they would let me live? Why do you think Vogel killed himself?'

'Guilt?'

'*Fear*,' Grüber corrected. 'Terror. Just by coming here, you have already killed me.' Gruber got to his feet.

'I can have you protected . . .'

Grüber again gave his bitter laugh. 'Don't be ridiculous! *You* will have me protected? Protect me from what? From whom? You want your revenge . . .'

'Yes. But on those who paid you. Not on you . . .'

'Because you consider I am not worth it? Your look tells me all. You look at me as if I were a bug just about to crawl under your shoe.' Grüber's mouth turned down. 'You "nobility". If you lived in a shack, you would still look down on people like me! Protect me indeed!'

'You've got a problem with status, Grüber. I look down on no one, except criminals.'

Grüber glanced upwards at the window where Müller had briefly seen the face.

'Tell you what, *Graf von Röhnen*.' Grüber emphasized each word. 'You think you know it all . . .' Grüber was suddenly becoming talkative.

'On the contrary. I know very little.'

'How little, you have no idea.' As if his loquaciousness had given him a new shot of courage, Grüber had his supercilious look back on. 'Did you know that the flight recorders were faked? The real ones are buried somewhere at the crash site. Who would look for them, when they had already been "found", all nicely scarred and scorched?'

Müller was staring at him. 'What?'

'There. Do you see? Graf. Von. Röhnen. Now all you've got to do is find those recorders.'

Grüber began to walk away, laughing as he did so. He headed for the garden.

'Give my regards to the Semper,' Müller said.

Grüber froze. He stood like that for several moments. Then he turned, slowly, a real fear now in his eyes.

'You have killed me,' he said in a low whisper. This time, he appeared to really believe it.

'You did that to yourself, Grüber,' Müller told him in a hard, unforgiving voice, 'twenty-two years ago, when you helped kill my parents and destroy their name.' He turned his head slowly, taking in the garden and the house. 'Enjoy this, which they paid for with their lives and their reputation, while you still can.' He looked at Carey Bloomfield. 'Let us leave this place of the dead.'

'Müller,' she said in the car. 'Remind me never to get on your bad side. If eyes were weapons, Grüber's body would be lying drilled to that beautiful terrace. You were so cold, you made *me* cold.'

'Sorry,' Müller said as he started the Porsche. 'I've waited years for this.'

'Hey, I'm not blaming you. In your place, I'd probably have shot the bastard right there on his big, beautiful terrace. And now? Where to?'

'Grenoble,' Müller said, sending the Turbo rushing down the tree-lined avenue.

In the house, the butler was on the phone in his room.

'They have been, and gone,' he said. 'You are too late.'

There was the sound of swearing. 'Did he talk?'

'He spoke. But I did not hear what was said. He was laughing at them, so perhaps he said nothing.'

'That's not good enough. We must be certain.'

'Then I shall be out when you arrive.'

'Make it a long outing. You have been paid well for your services.'

'I have indeed. I think I shall take a long trip.' The butler looked out of his window. It was a dry day, so far. 'Somewhere with less rain.'

'Wherever it happens to be, be certain to maintain your discretion. If not, you can be found.'

'Discretion is a word pinned to my soul.'

'Then see that you don't lose both. And give the rest of the staff the day off.'

'They will wonder—'

'*You* are the butler. *You* are in command. The house must be empty.'

'Then your wish is my command. And Frau Grüber?'

'Naturally, she remains. She will be leverage for Grüber's cooperation.'

Conversation ended, the butler hung up, then began to pack.

At about the time that Müller and Carey Bloomfield were hurtling down the A5 Autobahn heading for the border crossing, Jackson arrived at one of his destinations.

He had not gone anywhere near Stuttgart, and was, in fact, now within the Black Forest. He had left the Audi in a car park just off the road. He had changed into walking clothes; then, taking the backpack with the weapons and other equipment, had locked the car, and had set off. He had deliberately left the car where it was, as a marker.

He was now 5 kilometres from where he had left the Audi, and stood within some woods through which he could see a small lake. The ambient light made it seem a dark green that was almost black. It reminded him of his daughter's eyes. He decided this was as good a place as any to wait. He knew the area well, and knew where he could make shelter for the coming night. He tried not to think of his wife, and prayed that what he planned to do would eventually save her.

He put down his pack and sat down, propping himself against a tall fir. He took out a photograph. It was a family photo of his wife, Josh, Elene, and himself. They were standing, grinning at the camera, arms about each other's waists. The children were in the middle, the adults on either side. All were in walking gear. A tall fir behind them was the very fir against which he was now leaning.

He sighed, put the photograph away, and let his head rest against the tree; then he closed his eyes.

But he did not fall asleep. All he had to do now was wait for his plan to set things in motion.

'Are you hungry?' Müller asked Carey Bloomfield.

'I could eat.'

'Can you last till Besançon? That's about one hundred and twenty kilometres after we cross the border. There's a service station on the A36 autoroute. Good opportunity to fill up. But that's not the only reason. There's a cafeteria that has one of the best hams going, cooked-on-the-bone. At least, in my opinion. It's slightly reminiscent of the Swabian version. I stopped there once, late one night. They had almost closed, but the woman behind the counter took pity, and brought out this amazing ham. She gave me huge slices – more, I am certain, than the normal portion . . .'

Carey Bloomfield was nodding. 'You and the women, Müller.'

'She was old enough to be my mother.'

'So?'

'Well? Would you like to try it? Or don't you like the idea?'

'Why not? Your friend might still be there. See if she gives me a mean portion.'

'Sssss,' Müller said.

'Are you hungry? I've brought you something.'

Elisabeth Jackson recognized the speech patterns as belonging to the man with the kinder voice.

She nodded. 'Yes,' she replied in German.

'I must remain here while you eat. There is a knife, and a fork. You understand.'

'I understand.'

'I will untie your hands. No funny business.'

'No funny business,' she promised.

He untied her, then put a small plate in her hands, with knife and fork.

'It's *Schweinebraten*,' he said.

'Mmm. I can smell it. It smells good. Who made it?'

'Please. No questions. And watch the edge of the plate. You might spill some on yourself.'

She nodded then began to eat. After a while, she paused.

'You're not Bavarian, are you?' she said. 'I'm very good with accents. You are definitely not from around here. I don't mean wherever this house is. I mean where you . . . kidnapped me. I was born in the area, so I'd know. You have a north Rhine accent. Kölsch, perhaps. Well not so much the city itself, but perhaps the general area. Frechen? Kerpen, perhaps? Wesseling? Amazing, isn't it? When one sense is gone, as with this blind-fold, the others increase. I can hear better today than I did yesterday. It was yesterday, wasn't it, that you took me . . . ?'

'I think you should stop talking and finish your food. If the other person had been standing where I am, he would have taken the food away and tied you up again. Don't force me to do that.'

'Would you? I know you did not like the idea of taking me . . .'

A stony silence greeted this. The silence went on.

After a while, she continued eating.

The two men arrived at Grüber's house over two and a half hours after Müller and Carey Bloomfield had left. They had driven fast, frequently breaking any speed limits posted along the way.

They rushed in, guns drawn, and began searching every room. They did so painstakingly; but all that greeted them was emptiness and silence.

'Grüber's gone,' the one who had lost his dagger said, getting annoyed.

'Where to? He knows we'll find him.'

'Hiding then?'

'We'll get him . . . even if we have to take this whole fucking palace apart. Let's keep going. We haven't got to the master bedroom as yet.'

When they did, the man who had lost his dagger said, 'Shit! Bastard!'

They had found Grüber and his wife. Both were lying on their huge double bed. Both were quite dead.

The taller one went over to a bedside table, and picked up a small brown bottle. There was no label on it. It was also empty.

'Whatever was in there,' he said, 'is now in their bodies. Now we don't know what he said to Müller, if anything.'

'I think the bastard talked. Otherwise why do this?'

The other smiled wolfishly. 'He knew what we would have done to him to find out . . . whether he really talked to Müller or not.' He tossed the bottle on to Grüber's body. 'Pity. I was looking forward to that.'

'So, what now?'

'We report, then stay here for a while. We've got the whole fucking building and all that garden to ourselves. I always wanted to stay in a palace.'

'These things will start to smell.'

'We won't be here long enough. Anyway, I don't fancy driving any more for today. You call and tell them what we found. I'm going for a walk in the garden.'

Autoroute A36, near Besançon. Müller finished paying for the petrol, then drove over to the restaurant car park.

'Let's see if that ham is on the menu today,' he said as he cut the engine.

'It had better be,' Carey Bloomfield said. 'I'm salivating.'

'Then let's find out. How's your French?'

'Terrible to non-existent.'

'Oh sure. I think your French is better than you say,' Müller said.

'So's yours.'

They entered the cafeteria, and Müller was gratified to see a large ham on the bone, behind the counter. Two women were busy serving customers. One of them looked up as Müller and Carey Bloomfield joined the small queue. She brightened.

'It is Monsieur!' she greeted. 'You see? Your ham is here!'

'That should make you happy,' Carey Bloomfield hissed. 'She recognizes you. Oh wow!'

The woman came to them. 'So, Monsieur. The usual?'

'Yes, please. Kind of you to remember.'

'Not at all, Monsieur. Not at all.' She glanced at Carey Bloomfield. 'And Madame?'

'The same, thanks,' Müller replied.

'A pleasure, Monsieur.'

She beamed, and gave Müller a huge portion, on a generous bed of fresh salad. Carey Bloomfield got rather less.

'I knew it!' Carey Bloomfield said in a sharp whisper as they found a table some distance from the counter. 'She gave me a meanie! And, by any biological stretch, Müller, she's not old enough to be your mother.'

'You can have some of mine.'

'Are you calling me greedy?'

'No. It's just that I have rather a lot, which you're welcome to share, if you like it.'

'We'll see,' she said.

They were halfway into the meal when Müller's phone rang.

'I'd better take this outside,' he said. 'Do you mind?'

'Nope. I'm enjoying the ham. When I'm done with mine, I might start on yours.'

'Be my guest,' he said with a tiny smile that could have meant anything. 'Yes, Pappi,' he went on when he was outside.

He walked to where he had left the car.

'Where are you?'

'Aire de Besançon-Marchaux, enjoying some great ham.'

'Hate to spoil your fun, but the news is not good.'

The distinct lack of levity in Pappenheim's voice made Müller brace himself for the worst.

'I'm listening.'

'Hans Schörma is down.'

'What? How bad?'

'He'll be staying down.'

Müller looked heavenwards, shut his eyes briefly then passed a hand across them. 'My God,' he said softly. 'How?'

'I'm coming to that.'

'What about Hammersfeldt? And are Aunt Isolde and Greville OK?'

There was a silence.

'Pappi? Are you there?'

A heavy sigh sounded in Müller's ear. 'Hammersfeldt did it.'

'*What?*' Müller repeated, this time in horror. 'Can't the

idiot handle his own gun? What the devil was he doing? Playing with it with the safety off?'

'Oh, he can handle his gun perfectly. He put two shots into Hans, at close range. Deliberate shots. Then he gave Greville a ludicrous story about Hans wanting to abduct him.'

Müller realized he had his mouth open as he listened to this. He shut it quickly.

'Greville did not believe it, of course,' Pappenheim was saying. 'He went up to Hammersfeldt and disarmed him. No slouch, your Greville. Hammersfeldt then ran away. Greville could have shot him – he'd taken Hammersfeldt's weapon – but was reluctant to do so.'

'I can well understand. It would have seemed to anyone watching that he was shooting an unarmed officer.'

'Which, of course, mattered little to Hammersfeldt when he shot his own partner. Schörma was not unarmed, but he was certainly unaware.'

Pappenheim went on to give Müller a detailed account of what had occurred.

'Hammersfeldt was planted on us,' Pappenheim continued, voice tight with emotion. 'I think he planned to take Greville to whoever is really paying him, the bastard. There is no doubt it was he who set me up for that shot in May. I remember how he hung around me that night, on my way down. Someone was waiting, and he pointed me out. And, all this time, I've been thinking the little shit had saved my life. You do remember it was Kaltendorf who brought him in.'

'I certainly do. But, much as I have little time for him, he's not clever enough to be allowed deep into these people's organization. He's useful. That's it for them. I doubt if he even realizes what he's playing with. He has turned from a good policeman into a desperate networker. He's also now well aware that he's vulnerable. The people who will go to the lengths of killing my parents, attempting a hit on you, planting people on us, eavesdropping on our communications as they did last May, hunting Greville, kidnapping the wife of a senior American officer, will have little compunction about taking Kaltendorf's daughter again, whenever they feel like it. And he's well aware of that.'

'So, he gets a recommendation to add someone to our personnel, and he follows through.'

'Exactly.'

'Well, he's now got two colleagues down, and one absconder to think about.'

'I doubt we'll see Hammersfeldt again in this life,' Müller said with grim certainty.

'Meaning?'

'The people who hired, employed, or recruited him to their cause, don't like failure. He shot a police officer. He tried to take Greville, and failed. Sloppy work, by their lights.'

'So, you believe he'll be punished.'

'I believe our colleagues somewhere in this country, or perhaps our European colleagues, will be investigating another mysterious killing; this time, with Hammersfeldt as the victim.'

'Funny thing. I had the same thought. Good thing too, or you might have been investigating me for having my hands around his throat, and squeezing. Something else about Hammersfeldt. Remember that car he seemed to spend most of his time polishing? The Mercedes combi.'

'I know the one.'

'It's here in the garage. As he's never going to come back for it, it stays put. The forensics people found traces of mud, possibly no more than a day old. So, I sent a team to his apartment – certain he'll never return there, either – and they found that his bicycle had been used very recently, on muddy ground.'

'The cyclist at Wannsee?' Müller remarked softly.

'Certainly looks like it. Nice, eh? But nothing that leads to the people in question could be found,' Pappenheim went on. 'No fool he. But he overplayed his hand with Greville. He certainly did not expect Greville's response.'

'Greville did have long years perfecting them.'

'Which he certainly put to good use today. I've also thought of the way Hammersfeldt stared at Miss Bloomfield. He may well have been admiring her . . . but I think he had a more unpleasant reason . . .'

'He was marking her out,' Müller put in, 'for the fake policeman.'

'I'd bet on that.'

Müller was angrily silent.

'I can tell,' Pappenheim said, 'that you're mentally measuring his throat with your hands too. While you're enjoying that thought, I have some more news, neither good nor bad; just info. It's about the colonel's wife.'

'Yes?'

'Her full name is Elisabeth Elene Neusser-Jackson. The car is registered in the name of Elisabeth Neusser, and the address of the supposed owner is a Klaus Neusser, her cousin. Nothing wrong in that. I'm assuming that, originally being a local girl, she simply wanted to have her personal car registered in the same area. When she has to return to the States with her husband, or wherever they post him to, she probably intended to leave the car with Neusser. I'm guessing, of course, but I think this most likely.'

'I agree. What does this Klaus Neusser do?'

'Not what he does, but what he owns. Poor, he isn't. Neusser is CEO of a television company. A very successful one at that. Specializes in thought-provoking drama, thank God; both home-grown, and international. No mindless froth. And it makes him a lot of money. There's a moral in there somewhere. Do you want me to talk with Neusser? I've got a number for him.'

'Not yet. But he's definitely on our list, if this kidnapping starts getting close to us. I'm assuming you did not get any of this information from our local colleagues.'

Pappenheim's own silence was eloquent.

'I've got the picture,' Müller said. 'Anything else from Neusser?'

'Jackson's also got two mobile phones . . .'

'*Two?*'

'Two. One's his own, the other's one he borrowed from Neusser. It really belongs to Neusser's son Markus. It's an old card phone that the son no longer uses, and still has plenty of units. Now ask me why he would need two phones . . .'

'For which you've got the numbers . . .'

'For which I've got the numbers.'

'Alright, Pappi. Why two?'

'As if you haven't already worked it out, but I'll tell you anyway. He wants to be tracked with one. Lure his prey.'

'As you would say, great minds.'

'You know, of course,' Pappenheim went on with the kind of smoothness he tended to reserve for moments when he wanted to skirt around an awkward point in the conversation, 'that the GW will be screaming for your blood. He hasn't started yet. Probably still in shock. But, when he wakes up, he'll want to drink it . . .'

'And he'll come bellowing at you.'

'That he will. Where will you be?'

'Out.'

'I knew I shouldn't have asked. Two other things – Ilona has personally taken over the watch on your place, with one of her team. She seems to feel responsible somehow. And you don't have to tell me to tell her not to be so ridiculous. She's not having any of it. You know Ilona when she gets that bee.'

'I know only too well. Thank her for me.'

'Will do.'

'And the second?'

'Got a contact for you where you're going. Alphonse LaCroix. Retired gendarme. Quite senior. He knows people who should be known, and quite probably about the incident that's taking you there. I'll send his address and phone number to the car, along with Jackson's mobile numbers.'

'Good,' Müller said. 'I'll retrieve it all as soon as we're done. While I remember it, Berger and Reimer. This duty they're on tonight . . . tell them to be very careful. After what happened to Hans Schörma, we don't need more surprises like that. Tell them to watch their backs.'

'If they don't, they'll get a good roasting from me.'

'Alright, Pappi. Thanks.'

'Some days we're having.'

'Not good ones.'

'Do you think we've got more like Hammersfeldt?'

'I hope not. But just in case . . .'

'We watch, but stay quiet.'

'Precisely.'

When they had finished, Müller opened the car and switched on the communications system. He called up the information Pappenheim had sent. He read LaCroix's telephone number and address, and the mobile numbers for Jackson, then he switched the unit off.

The information had been automatically saved, and would be there for retrieval when he needed it.

He shut the car, and went back into the cafeteria. As he returned to his table, Carey Bloomfield looked up.

'Your girlfriend's gone,' she began, 'and I've been raiding your plate. This ham's good . . .' Her cheerful words faded when she saw his expression. 'What's wrong, Müller? News that bad?'

'It isn't good,' he replied as he sat down. He gave her the news from Pappenheim.

Face paling, she listened in complete silence.

'My God,' she said when he had finished. 'He fingered Pappi, shot and killed his partner, spied on you, and nearly got me killed. What a nice piece of shit. I want to shoot him myself.' She shook her head slowly as she thought about it. 'What a royal piece of shit,' she repeated. 'And I'm really sorry to hear about Schörma, Müller. Two of your guys down in less than twenty-four hours is not fun.'

'That it isn't. If you're finished, I think we should leave.'

'I'm done here. Nice as that ham is . . . suddenly, I've lost my appetite.' She began to get to her feet.

'So have I,' Müller said, following suit. As they got to the car, he added, 'You drive.'

She stared at him. 'You mean that?'

He squeezed the remote to unlock the Porsche, then handed her the key. 'See? I mean it.'

She looked at him warily as she got in behind the wheel. 'What's the catch?'

'No catch,' he replied, getting into the passenger seat.

Still giving him a wary look, she started the engine. As it barked into life, she continued to look as if she thought he was planning to change his mind.

'Ah,' he said. 'Remember there is a blanket speed limit of one hundred and thirty kilometres per hour on the autoroutes, so you'll have to resist the urge to do more.'

'I damned well knew there was a catch,' she said in frustration. 'Thanks for nothing, Müller.'

'That should not be a problem, should it?' he said. 'After all, you've got lower speed limits in the States.'

'Aah, shaddup!' she said. 'I just wanted to burn Hammersfeldt out of my head.'

'I am certain you'll still enjoy the drive.'

For reply, she sent the car charging towards the exit road. It did so with a powerful roar as it lunged forward, fat wheels gripping.

He shut his eyes briefly.

Eleven

Berlin outskirts, 18.00 hours. The gleaming BMW drew to a stop in the parking area provided for invited guests. It did not look out of place among the other examples of equally gleaming, expensive machinery already filling the allotted spaces. Parking attendants moved like marionettes, dancing between the cars as they directed the traffic. The house to which the grounds belonged was the same one in which the retired general and the visiting churchman had been enjoying their coffee, earlier in the day.

Berger looked at the gloved attendant who had directed them to their space. He was already engaged with the next visitors, who had arrived in a bright-red, burping Ferrari.

'There's a lot of money around here tonight,' she said to Reimer.

He glanced around. 'Enough to run many small countries for years.'

'All this stuff makes me heady,' she said. 'I suppose we'd better get out and enjoy the stratosphere. Ready?'

'As I'll ever be.'

Both were in evening gear. Berger wore a long dress, classically simple in style, with a long split on one side. Reimer wore a white dinner jacket over black trousers. His gun was in a shoulder holster, Berger's in her bag.

They got out, and Berger brushed herself down with quick, nervous hands. 'How do I look, Reimer?'

He looked at her, openly admiring her curves.

'Careful what you say,' she warned, 'or I'll fry both your eggs and serve them to you sliced.'

'As I said before,' he told her, 'you look . . . great.'

She looked pleased; but Reimer could not resist going on. 'Too great,' he continued, 'to waste on Pappenheim.'

Berger's face grew dangerous. 'Reimer!' she hissed. 'I don't know whether you're a part-time idiot, or a full-time one. I've told you before what goes on, or does not go on, with Pappenheim is another country to you. You *don't* cross that border! Don't look to me as a surrogate for your diet-freak girlfriend. Now put your brain back in gear and let's go do our job!'

'Look. I'm sorry. I was wrong. It just . . . slipped out. I . . .'

'Don't dig yourself further in, Reimer. Stick at "sorry".'

'Yes. OK.'

Berger's expression relaxed. 'And you look good. Who knows? Perhaps one of those rich little girls will take a fancy to you. Got the invites?'

'In my jacket pocket.'

'Right. Come on, then. Let's look as if we're rich and that car is really ours.'

They walked towards a wide flight of steps to where two further attendants were checking the invitations. A short distance from them, yet more attendants were standing around with silver trays laden with glasses of champagne.

They reached the invitation checkers, one of whom smiled a welcome while his companion beamed at another couple.

'Frau Berger, and Herr Reimer,' he intoned. 'Thank you. Enjoy the evening.'

Berger gave a regal, sideways tilt of her head. 'Thank you.'

She walked on, with Reimer following in her wake.

The attendants had a brief respite, and the one who had attended to Berger and Reimer whispered to his colleague, 'Guess who really wears the trousers.'

The other grinned. 'Yeah. But, with a body like that, I wouldn't care. She can wear my trousers anytime!'

Then they once more pasted on their welcoming smiles as more guests approached.

Berger and Reimer had reached the champagne barrier.

'Not for him,' Berger commanded as an attendant swooped. 'He's driving.' She neatly lifted a glass of champagne.

'Why can't I just have one?' Reimer complained in a low voice.

'Both of us can't be drunk.'

'You never get drunk,' Reimer insisted.

'You sound disappointed, Reimer,' Berger said, eyes subtly raking the milling crowd. 'It sometimes amazes me how people with real money throw it away on these things they call dresses. Let's mingle.'

'What are we supposed to be doing, anyway?'

'See that man over there? Talking to . . . you'll like this, Reimer. The man talking to that anorexic blonde . . .'

'We're watching her?'

'You wish. No, the man talking to her. We watch his back . . . unobtrusively.'

'Who is he?'

'A retired general. Pappenheim showed me a picture.'

'Why doesn't he—?'

'*Shh*, Reimer. He's coming this way! And the blonde with him. Your lucky day, after all, Reimer. And, whatever you do, *don't* answer questions about what we are, or whom we have met. You have undercover experience, so you should be smart enough to know it.'

'Hey. I'm not a rookie.'

The general stopped before them with a benign smile, greeting them as genuine guests.

'Frau Berger, Herr Reimer. So good of you to come.' He lowered his voice. 'Please do make yourselves completely at home. You don't look like police at all. Excellent. Enjoy everything. May I present my niece, Mary-Anne? She is part-American.' He gave a deprecating smile. 'The bigger part.'

He shook their hands warmly, and moved on to his other guests. Mary-Anne stayed.

'Hi,' she said, looking at Reimer.

Reimer cleared his throat, while Berger gave a tiny, knowing smile.

'I know I'm part German,' Mary-Anne continued in English, in the kind of voice expected of her, 'but my German's terrible. Tell me you speak English. Please?'

'I do,' Berger said in English. 'And Reimer here . . . well . . . he's OK. Perhaps you can help each other out.'

Mary-Anne gave one of her sunburst, multi-teeth smiles. 'Sounds like fun!'

Berger rolled her eyes upwards. Mary-Anne was so engrossed in Reimer, she did not see it.

'I'll leave you two to get acquainted,' Berger said, and began to move away.

'Er . . . wait,' Reimer began in German. 'Shouldn't we—'

'I'll be around. Just be careful with the general's niece. Generals don't like it if you mess around with their nieces.'

She hoped Reimer was sharp enough to pick up the double message. She did not believe for one moment that Mary-Anne knew little German.

As Berger moved away, Mary-Anne said to Reimer, 'You two are . . .' She paused deliberately.

'No,' he began. 'We . . . are . . . professional partners. Yes. Partners. Only.'

'Oh! That's good!' Mary-Anne put an arm in his. 'Let me show you around.' She grabbed a snackette off a passing tray, and put it into Reimer's mouth with a giggle.

From a safe distance, Berger watched the pantomime. 'Watch your step, Reimer,' she said quietly. 'She's setting you up for something.'

Half an hour later, Reimer found himself being cajoled into a vast bedroom. Mary-Anne, apparently drunk from too much champagne, was hanging on to him for dear life. She was giggling and snuggling up to him.

'Just . . . just a little rest, my strong Reimer,' she slurred. 'Then . . . then I'll be fine.'

Reimer closed the door. 'OK,' he said. 'But I must find my partner. You have a sleep. Yes?'

'Oo–kayyy,' she said, staggering.

They made it to the bed. Still giggling, she pushed him

so that he fell on to it backwards, and she on top of him.

'One . . . one little kiss, my strong Reimer. One . . .' She pressed her lips upon his. 'Umm. Nice, Reimer. I . . . like . . .'

'Your uncle. The general . . .'

'Forget . . . him . . . mmm . . .' She sat upright and began to squirm, eyes closed. Her hands moved upon his jacket, then beneath. 'Mmm! That feels like a big gun!'

Before Reimer knew what was happening, she had whipped the gun out with a speed and control that was not that of a drunk. She remained sitting upon him, but the gun was pointing unerringly at a spot between his eyes.

'And now, my strong Reimer,' she said in perfect German, 'some questions for you. You will answer them, and correctly.'

Reimer was staring at her, then alternated between her and the gun. 'What . . . what the . . . ?'

'Question one. Where is Colonel Bloomfield?'

'*What?* I don't . . .'

'That's not the kind of answer I want. I'll ask again. *Where is Colonel Bloomfield?*'

'Stop repeating yourself,' a voice said behind her.

Mary-Anne froze. 'Berger. Make the wrong move, and your partner is dead.'

'And, less than a second later, your spine will stop working. Take your pick.'

Tense moments passed. Reimer stared into the barrel of his own gun. He could feel the heat of Mary-Anne's crotch upon him. He could feel his own breathing, and hers.

She gave him a sunburst smile. 'Enjoying it?' Then she slowly put the gun down. 'Another time, lover. I need my spine.' She gave a final wriggle. 'To remember me by.' Then she climbed off him, and off the bed.

She turned to face Berger, who was looking at her just over the pointing gun.

'You've got the eyes of a hawk,' Mary-Anne said. 'Do you know that?'

'I know. I've been told.'

'Would you really have blown my spine away?'

'Oh yes.' The gun did not move.

Mary-Anne nodded. 'Yes. You *would*. So, what now? You shoot me?'

Berger did not reply. Instead, she spoke to Reimer. 'Pick up your gun, Reimer, and get off that bed.'

Looking sheepish, Reimer did so.

'I thought we were supposed to protect the general . . .' he began.

'By fucking his niece?' Mary-Anne said mildly.

'*Hey!* You pretended you were drunk. You dragged me in here . . .'

'God. Cops. You really are thick. You know nothing . . .'

Suddenly, with a strength none would have suspected, she whirled, grabbed Reimer, and shoved him towards Berger.

That spoiled Berger's aim.

Within those fleeting moments of confusion, Mary-Anne was moving swiftly. She ran towards a corner of the room, and pushed. A door, well camouflaged by the ornate decoration of the room, sprang open. They heard her laugh as she went through. Then the door shut firmly.

Reimer ran to the spot.

'Don't even bother,' Berger said. 'She knows this place. She'll be long gone. We could spend the night looking. Reimer,' she went on, 'how stupid can you get? Stop thinking with those eggs of yours. Use your second brain once in a while.'

'What do you mean? She was *drunk*! I brought her here so she could sleep it off. How could I know . . . ?'

Berger shook her head slowly. 'Men.' She got out her phone, and called Pappenheim. 'Chief? An interesting little story.'

She told Pappenheim what had occurred. The resulting bark was loud enough for Reimer to hear.

Reimer seemed to cringe with embarrassment. 'Did you have to tell him that part?' he whispered at her.

She looked at him blankly, and did not respond. She nodded in response to whatever Pappenheim was saying.

'OK, Chief.'

She cut transmission and looked at Reimer. 'You're not his favourite person right now, Reimer. He wants us to remain here, and give no indication about what just happened. Not even to the general. This time, Reimer, you stay away from the blondes. Can't leave you alone for one moment.'

'But . . .' Reimer began.

Berger was already out of the room.

Pappenheim got another call.

'You should watch some TV,' the voice said.

'What do you mean?'

'TV news. Now.'

The line went dead.

'OK,' Pappenheim said, putting down the phone and picking up another. 'TV it is.' He called the goth, whom he knew was still in the rogues' gallery, flying her simulator online. 'Enjoying the combat?' he said when she had answered.

'I'm winning a campaign.'

'Well, hold your forces for a while. I want you to check the news channels. Something interesting is supposed to be happening right now.'

'Will do, sir.'

'I'll be with you in a minute or so.'

'Yes, sir.'

As he hung up, Pappenheim killed the cigarette he had been smoking, then got to his feet. By the time he had made it to the rogues' gallery, Hedi Meyer had found the material he wanted.

'Very strange one, sir,' she began. 'If it is what you're looking for. I've got a video of it.'

'Run it.'

The goth did, and Pappenheim stared at the image of Colonel Jackson, as he listened to the message.

'Oh my God,' he said.

In a lot of places, all hell was breaking loose. Bad news had travelled fast. The colonel's taped message had been repeated with the speed of a virus replicating itself. The radio stations also had it.

On CAFA Base, Dales, himself in a state of shock, was fielding calls; the most dangerous was from the commanding general.

'*What the hell's this, Colonel?*' the outraged general barked. '*Have you any idea of the heat I'm getting? How could you have let him do this?*'

'Sir, it was difficult . . .'

'What do you mean "difficult"? Why do you think you've got those silver oak leaves? You're *supposed* to be able to make difficult decisions!'

'I had orders from my commanding officer, *sir*! Permission to speak freely, *sir*!'

The general paused. 'Alright, Jack. Let's hear it.'

'He left me a sealed envelope, sir, with letters: one authorizing me to take command. There's a letter to you – copied to me – stating that he takes all responsibility. There's another offering his resignation.'

'Offering? Not tendering?'

'Definitely offering, sir, if it all goes bad.'

'It can't get very much worse. If I have understood his message correctly, he's challenging those people to come looking for him. I don't want one of my best officers taking out German citizens in a private vendetta, no matter what the provocation.'

'Sir, that boy is your godson. What those people did—'

'Is abominable. I'd like to shoot them myself. But I'm a general in the United States Army, not a vigilante.'

'And if they kill Elisabeth, sir?'

The general went quiet.

'The colonel felt, sir,' Dales went on, 'that if he contained it to himself and these people . . . I am not saying he is right, but imagine if the troops got it into their heads—'

'I hope you've got that under control.'

'The colonel left strict orders, sir. We're carrying them out.'

'Well, I've got to tell you something, Jack. My superiors have activated a team to stop Jackson.'

'What does that really mean, sir?'

'It means they'll try to persuade him to stop what he's doing.'

'And if not?'

Again, the general fell silent.

'Who's leading this team, sir?' Dales asked.

'Lieutenant-Colonel Hagen.'

'*Hagen?* Sir, that man *hates* Colonel Jackson. They were rivals for Elisabeth. Not really rivals as such, since Hagen was never in the running in the first place. But he has never stopped hating Bill Jackson for it.'

The general sighed. 'I know. I tried to get Hagen removed, but was overruled higher up. I've got to live with that. If you know where he plans to set up his battlefield, you'd better tell me.'

'I can only guess, sir. I know he frequently went walking in the Black Forest with Elisabeth and the kids. They loved it there.'

'That's a hell of an area to search.'

'Best lead I can give you, sir. No certainty that he is there.'

'It's a start.'

'Yes, sir.'

'And Jack . . .'

'Sir?'

'Pray for Elisabeth.'

'I've been doing that since I first heard, sir.'

At the house on the outskirts of Berlin, the reception was in full swing. None of the guests were watching, or had watched television; with a few notable exceptions.

In a room sealed off from all the other guests, five men and a woman were sitting in deep armchairs of dark brown leather, watching a replay of the Jackson video. The men were the retired general, the churchman, a politician, a very senior gold-starred policeman, and a captain of industry, all in evening gear. One of them was not German. The sixth person was Mary-Anne. The general had been alerted by an urgent phone call, and he had unobtrusively gathered them together.

They watched the replay for the third time, in silence. When it had again come to an end, the general spoke first.

'It is an open challenge. Come and find me, he says, before I reveal what I know. He is daring us to come to him. The man is a warrior, and he wants a fight. And he has chosen his battleground, wherever that might be.'

'It is not what we expected,' the policeman said.

'Every endeavour has its element of risk,' the general said. 'Some can be minimized, others can be needlessly incurred. This is such a case.' An angry frown crossed his features. 'Dauermann was clumsy. He should have been more careful with his dagger. The boy remembered it. He should also have ensured that the boy's phone was switched off. And as for the idiot who spoke our name . . . Fools! They will not be allowed to get away with this incompetence.'

'Jackson could be bluffing,' the churchman suggested.

'I very much doubt it.' The general spoke with conviction. 'Though he did not mention *what* he heard, his tone leaves no doubt. In any case, we cannot ignore the possibility; and he knows this. He is offering us an exchange for his wife, or combat.'

'Then we cannot take the risk,' the politician said, 'if there is the slightest possibility of his knowing something.'

'Of course not. That is why we must silence him; or rather, have him silenced. An American team is on its way to get him. Before anyone says it, yes. I know. Killing an American officer so openly could have serious repercussions that would do us no good. However, we do have a damage-limitation programme in place.'

'We let them do the job for us,' the businessman remarked.

The general nodded. 'They won't realize they are doing so. But we take nothing for granted. As soon as we know where he is—'

'But how can we know that?' the churchman asked.

'I am a soldier. He is a soldier. He wants an exchange, or a fight. He has picked his battleground, as I have said. When he is quite ready, he will let us know where he is.'

The policeman stared at the general. 'How?'

'You of all people should know. Very simply, he will use his mobile phone to call the base, or someone else. He will not have anything of interest to tell them; but he will initiate the traffic, expecting us to monitor the call. I have already alerted some people. He will tell us how to find him. It's his plan. I am certain of it.'

'This man is a combat veteran,' the businessman said. 'He has elite-unit experience. You are asking for a bloodbath.'

'Not if this is handled correctly. Our strength lies in our invisibility. We do not need further exposure.' The general looked about him. 'Wherever he is, we will have people to call upon. Our people will shadow the Americans; but should they find him first . . .' The general shrugged. 'There are ways of ensuring the American team still receive the credit. And then,' the general went on with some emphasis, 'there's Müller. Müller will also go after him, to try and stop him. Müller will do this both as what he sees as his police duty, and to try to save the man from himself.'

The general's mouth turned down. 'Müller is fatally attracted to doing the right thing, or what he thinks of as the right thing. If he does not go to Jackson of his own accord, I am certain it can be arranged that he does go. When he eventually does so, he will no doubt be accompanied by Colonel Bloomfield.' He looked at Mary-Anne. 'And then, my dear, you will have them all.'

She ran a slow tongue across her lips. 'Warriors. I love warriors.' She stood up. 'I should get ready.' The redness of her lips was not due to lipstick.

'I think you should. Where are the two police officers?'

'Wondering where you are. They seem to think they are here to protect you.'

The general smiled. 'How kind of them. Too bad it did not work out with that young man.'

'She interrupted.' Mary-Anne's eyes blazed with a real hatred. 'Perhaps I'll get her to myself one day.'

'Who knows?' the general said.

The men all got to their feet as she walked out.

'Is she really your niece?' the politician asked as they sat down again.

'Oh yes. My brother, her father, was killed some years ago in the field, by a young and green lieutenant. He surprised him in a country east of here.' The general paused. 'His name was Bloomfield. So, you see, this is a family affair too. I think Mary-Anne wants blood.'

Within the Black Forest, Jackson checked his watch. If Klaus Neusser had done as promised, the hornets' nest had been poked. The clock was ticking. He could only pray and hope that Elisabeth would be alive when the ticking stopped.

In the house where she was being held, the man with the knife was shouting.

'Do you know what your crazy husband has done?' he yelled. 'Is he trying to kill you? He has gone on TV, *threatening* us! He's mad! Threatening *us!*' He stopped abruptly, breathing hard.

Wondering whether she should dare speak, Elisabeth Jackson waited for him to calm down.

After he had said nothing for a while, she began tentatively, 'What has he done?'

There was no reply. Then came the sound of angry footsteps and the door slammed. The key turned in the lock.

But she felt a surge of elation. Bill had been planning something; and now, he had gone into action. Whatever it was that he had done, it had clearly unsettled them. For the first time since she had been dragged from her car, she felt some ease.

The Porsche was just taking the roundabout near Lyon-Saint Exupéry airport, when Müller got the call from Pappenheim.

'You're talking,' Pappenheim said after Müller had answered, 'and I can hear the car. Don't tell me you let her drive.'

'I let her drive. She's been at the wheel since Besançon.'

Pappenheim let out a low whistle. 'Never thought that, one day, I'd hear that from your very own lips.'

'Remember there is a blanket speed limit of one hundred and thirty . . .'

'Ah ha. Method in the madness.'

'But that does not seem to have prevented her from wanting to drive. When the urge gets to her, she creeps above it . . .'

'Leave me out of this,' Carey Bloomfield interrupted. 'I'm concentrating on keeping to the limit.'

A chortling sound, mixed with a drag on a cigarette, came down the phone.

'As you're sitting so comfortably,' Pappenheim said, 'I'll let you have both barrels. The brown stuff has hit the fan. In a big way. And many things are beginning to fall into place like coins on a church platter.'

'Go on.'

'The good colonel made a video . . .'

'A *video*?'

'Ooh yes. And what a video.' Pappenheim went on to repeat Jackson's message to the kidnappers, word for word.

'A declaration of war.'

'Oh definitely. Does a name come to mind?'

'Neusser. The television CEO.'

'Oh, so smart, so smart. Yep,' Pappenheim went on, 'no prizes for guessing how he got the broadcast. It's been on radio too. Time to talk to Neusser?'

'Smother him with your charm. Let's see what our TV man knows. I have the feeling that Jackson sent a message to me as well; and I'm tied in, anyway, given the name he dares not speak for now. Then there's that knife or dagger, entering the picture again. Which puts me in, whether I want it or not.'

'Funny that. My own impression. Jackson's planning to hunt down the kidnappers, and he's chosen a battleground. So? When are you coming back?'

'We're only about an hour or so from Grenoble, if that. Not worth turning back for another long drive. As you've said, the stuff will be hitting the fan; but they'll have to find Jackson first, and that will take some time. We, on the other hand, have got Neusser. He should know where Jackson's gone to. So, we'll continue to Grenoble, then return tomorrow. I want to see where it happened, Pappi.'

'I can well understand,' Pappenheim said quietly, having a good idea of how Müller must be feeling. 'Regarding Jackson,' he continued, 'the question must also be how the kidnappers might react towards his wife after this video broadcast. He's made a very specific threat.'

'It could go either way. These are not excitable people. They plan coldly, as we know only too well. But that incident with the boy worries. One of their foot soldiers appears to have exceeded his brief. They won't like that at all, as it is the reason Jackson apparently knows so much; too much for their liking. If Mrs Jackson is still in the hands of the

208

actual kidnappers, those individuals may not be particularly stable, given the evidence so far. That is a very big worry.'

'Then let's hope for Jackson's sake – and his wife's – it does not turn sour on him.'

'Which does not bear thinking about. Call the base as well. He will have left someone in command. We may get something from him . . . On second thoughts, I'll call the base. You handle Neusser. I'm certain you can find the base number.'

'A mere bagatelle,' Pappenheim said. 'I have an interesting snippet about that event Berger and Reimer went to. You'll laugh. Not.'

'My ears await.'

'Berger found the exceedingly thin, but immensely strong Mary-Anne astride Reimer . . .'

'Astride?'

'Very much so, according to Berger, with Reimer's own gun pointing at Reimer's second brain. Not my description, you understand. Berger's. And you know Berger when she gets going.'

'I know Berger.'

Pappenheim went on to describe the scene that had greeted Berger's entry into the bedroom.

'What an idiot!' Müller said when Pappenheim had finished.

'That's very mild compared to Berger's accolade. Interesting that the murderous Mary-Anne so urgently wanted to know the whereabouts of Miss Bloomfield. Sounds like a definite, homicidal need. You should warn her.'

'I shall.'

'I'll get back to you with the number of the base.'

'Fine, Pappi. Thanks.'

'Pull in at the next *aire*,' Müller said to Carey Bloomfield as the conversation ended. 'After the *péage*. L'isle d'Abeau. I'll take over. You've done a long stretch.'

'I've enjoyed it, believe it or not. Even with the speed limit.'

'This car can be enjoyed at any speed.'

'You don't have to sell it to me, Müller. I've got the message. So? What was all that about?'

'I'll wait until we stop. There. That's it. The three-hundred-metre mark,' he added, as the green and white slashes appeared, indicating the start of the exit.

209

She pulled off the autoroute, and drove to a parking space well away from other vehicles.

They got out to stretch their legs and, as they walked, he told her all that Pappenheim had said.

'Jesus,' she remarked softly when he had finished.

'Jackson's video? Or Mary-Anne?'

'Both. Jackson wants a private war, and Mary-Anne wants my head. I can understand Jackson; but *Mary-Anne*? What have I done to her?'

'Perhaps she can't forgive that "scrawny neck" remark.'

'Hmm,' she said.

'Weak joke, was it?'

'Very.'

'Then think. Have you ever met her before? Anywhere?'

'No. I'm sure of it. No way have I met or seen her before. I would have remembered that creature.'

'Sounds of claws being unsheathed,' Müller said, as if doing a voice-over.

'Damned right,' Carey Bloomfield said. 'I can't think of any reason why she should have been screaming my name at Reimer.'

'There must be one. Somewhere. I'd advise you to be extra careful.'

'You don't have to tell me twice. Whatever that psycho wants,' she continued in a hard voice, 'she'll get it; but not the way she thinks.'

The mobile rang.

'Pappi!' Müller said into the phone. 'That was quick.'

'Quick. That's me. Are you in a traffic jam? I can't hear that racing engine.'

'We've stopped, but not in traffic. We're at a service station. Change of seats.'

'I see. I've got the direct line to the deputy base commander.'

'That was quick too. Name?'

'Dales, Lieutenant-Colonel . . .'

'Dales . . .' Müller repeated.

Carey Bloomfield was looking at him. '*Dales? Jack* Dales?'

'Just a minute, Pappi. You know Dales?' Müller said to her.

'If it is Jack Dales. Yes. The name is really John Dales . . .'

'But he's called Jack.'

'Yes.'

'Pappi . . .' Müller began into the phone.

'I heard most of that,' Pappenheim said. 'Yes. Our man is John Dales.'

'It is John Dales,' Müller said to Carey Bloomfield.

'If it will help,' she said, 'I can talk to him first. Make him less formal. More relaxed.'

Müller nodded. 'Good idea. Miss Bloomfield offers to talk with him,' Müller continued to Pappenheim. 'She knows him.'

'Every little helps. I'll send the number to the car, as before.'

'Fine.'

'I've also talked to Neusser.'

'And?'

'Very forthcoming. I pointed out to him the virtues of not having me interested in his life.'

'How considerate of you.'

'I think he appreciated its value,' Pappenheim said without shame. 'Interestingly enough, he confirmed that Jackson hoped to reach you. Apart from the fact that Jackson appears to have some respect for you, I believe the good colonel also hopes this will preclude a massive hunt for him by our colleagues. And . . . Jackson's got two mobile phones . . .'

'*Two?*'

'Two.'

'The cooperative Neusser?'

'The very cooperative Neusser. One of the phones belongs to Jackson, and the other's one he borrowed from Neusser. It really belongs to Neusser's son Markus, currently at his Uni. It's an old card phone that the son no longer uses. Now ask me why he would need two phones . . .'

'For which you've got the numbers . . .'

'For which I've got the numbers.'

'Alright, Pappi. Why two?'

'As if you haven't already worked it out; but I'll tell you anyway. He wants to be tracked with one. Lure his prey.'

'As you would say, great minds.'

A loud suck came down the airwaves. 'What it is to have

211

them. Regarding our colleagues joining the hunt,' Pappenheim went on, 'as I've already told our contact with the local boys to leave this one to us, there's been no fallout, so far. But it's only a matter of time before his bosses give a "what-the-hell" call to the GW, who continues to be conspicuous by his silence . . . again, so far.' Pappenheim sounded as if he expected the storm to break over his head at any moment. 'So, I really think you should be in place, so to speak, by tomorrow, if you possibly can. If you're asking for my advice, that is . . .'

'Taken.'

'And I'll hold off the hordes as best I can.'

'If anyone can, you can.'

'Such flattery the man has. The most likely place for our colonel,' Pappenheim continued before Müller could jump in with a dry comment, 'has also been sent to the car . . . with his phone numbers. That is Neusser's best guess. All info is with it.'

'Good work, as ever, Pappi. Thanks. I'll give Dales that call, then continue the journey. There's still plenty of light, but definitely not enough left in the day to check anything out there, after we arrive. So we'll use the time to meet with people, then do an early-morning foray tomorrow.'

'OK.'

CAFA Base. 'Dales.'

'Hello, Jack.'

'Who's this? And how did you get this number? The proper procedure—'

'This is Carey. David's sister.'

There was a stunned silence. Then, 'My God! Carey *Bloomfield*?'

'That's me.'

'Good God, Carey. Many years. Got told you were on the base last time with a German cop, but I was up flying at the time. Carey, you couldn't have called at a worse time. All hell's breaking loose around here, and—'

'That's exactly why I'm calling, Jack. We know about it.'

'*We?*'

'Someone wants to speak with you.' She passed the phone to Müller.

'Colonel Dales,' he began. 'My name is Müller. *Hauptkommissar*—'

'The Berlin cop?' a stunned Dales asked.

'Yes, Colonel.'

'He wanted to get in touch with you. He told me so, but didn't want to do it the ordinary way.'

'Given what I do know, I fully understand.'

'And how much is that, *Hauptkommissar*?'

'Nothing I'm prepared to discuss for very long, even on my own telephone, secure though it is.'

'I can also understand. What help can I give you?'

'First, I want you to know I will do my best to help him.'

'I think he already knows that. I think you're the only person in your line of work that he trusts right now. If you can do anything at all for him, Mr Müller . . .'

'I will do everything I can, Colonel.'

'Thank God. I have a pretty good idea where he may have gone . . .'

'You do not have to tell me, if it is a favourite family spot. I've already got the information I need.'

'You've got it in one. He said you were good. I'm impressed.'

'Thank you, Colonel. If there is anything at all that you believe might help us, call the number I will give you. It will put you in direct contact with *Oberkommissar* Pappenheim, who will pass it on to me, wherever I am. Talk to *no* one else. You can trust Pappenheim completely.'

'Anything I can think of, he gets it.'

'Exactly. Here's the number.' Müller gave it.

'Got it. One more thing, Mr Müller. You should know that a military team is also after Colonel Jackson. They have orders to bring him in, or . . .'

'Or what, Colonel?'

'You would not like the "or".'

'I see. Then I must tell you, Colonel, if I do meet up with that team, I will not allow them to commit what would in fact be a crime, on German territory.'

'In which case, I should warn you about what you're up against. This is an elite team, led by a man called Hagen. A lieutenant-colonel. I may well be speaking out of turn telling you this . . . but Hagen also holds a years-old grudge against Bill Jackson. He might not be too scrupulous about how he carries out his mission. You read what I'm saying, Mr Müller?'

'Very clearly. Why the grudge?'

'Hagen wanted to marry Elisabeth.'

'That is not good.'

'It's worse, because he never had a chance with her in the first place. He assumed something that was never there.'

'The worst of ingredients.'

'Yes indeed, sir.'

'Again, I can only tell you I will do my very best, Colonel.'

'I know you will, Mr Müller.'

'And please tell Sergeant Henderson, if you do see him, we are doing all we can. I remember he and Colonel Jackson go back many years.'

'He's Lieutenant Henderson, now . . .'

'Then please add my congratulations.'

'I will. And I'm certain he'll appreciate your comments.'

'Goodbye, Colonel.'

'Goodbye, sir. And thanks for the call.'

'Have you ever heard of someone called Hagen?' Müller asked Carey Bloomfield as he handed her the phone.

They were back in the car and about to leave. Müller was again at the wheel.

'I know a Major Hagen . . .'

'This one's a lieutenant-colonel.' Müller gave a brief smile. 'Must be the time of the colonels. Everywhere I turn, I run into them.'

'Hah-hah,' she said. 'Lieutenant-colonel?' she went on. 'That has to be a recent promotion, if it's the same guy. You know how it is. You get these things with the cereal packet, these days.'

'So, that's how it happens.' Müller started the car. 'I did wonder. And what is Hagen's specialty?'

'The one I know leads a retrieval team.'

'What's that in plain English?' he said as he eased the

Porsche out of the parking bay and headed for the slip road.

'They go after people. Did Jack Dales mention Hagen?'

Müller gently braked the car to allow a huge lorry to rumble past with a hissing of air brakes.

'Yes.'

'And Hagen is going after *Jackson*?'

'Unless I've completely misunderstood what Dales said to me, it certainly seems to be the case.'

'Just great. Hagen is known as a hardcase, and a nut. He's been doing that kind of job for too long. He enjoys it now. Even those who know him well think so.'

There was a clear run to join the autoroute, and Müller sent the Turbo darting on to it. 'There is an added ingredient,' he said. 'Hagen is supposed to hold a grudge against Jackson. It would seem they were once rivals in love. The lucky woman – or unlucky – was Elisabeth Jackson . . .'

'Oh great.'

'Worse, she was never interested in him in the first place, so there's an element of bitterness.'

'Better and better. Whose bright idea was it to use Hagen?'

'Dales gave no more information. I suspect some big general somewhere.'

'If Hagen gets the chance, and a good excuse, he would rather kill Jackson than bring him back in one piece.'

'That little thought had crossed my mind . . .'

'Müller?'

'Yes?'

'You're doing more than one hundred and thirty. Much more.'

'Really?' He did not slow down. 'Jackson is now being hunted by his own side, by the Semper, and, if Pappi fails to block it, a special unit of my own colleagues will enter the chase.'

Carey Bloomfield stared pointedly at the speedometer, but made no further comment about it. 'Then he could use some friendly support.'

'The best thing would be to get him away from there.'

'If he'll agree . . . which I doubt.'

'I very much doubt it as well.'

*   *   *

215

They made good time to Grenoble. On the approach, Carey Bloomfield stared at the great alpine ramparts with their sheer rock faces. The lowering sun bathed them in splashes of light where it could reach, while other parts lay in deep shadow, contrasting so sharply, it appeared that the play of dark and light had been etched upon them. High above, a piercingly white plume of cloud spread itself across a deep-blue sky.

'Wow,' she said. 'This is impressive stuff. Beautiful.'

'One's first view of Grenoble is always awe-inspiring.'

'I've been to some great places that literally take the breath away, but this is something else.'

'This,' he said, 'holds my memory of my parents.'

'Sorry, Müller. I didn't think.'

'No need to be sorry. I've been past here on a few occasions, going south. This will be the first time I will actually be going into the place itself. I've looked at these slabs of rock and have thought – *you killed them*. But of course they did not. People did.'

'Are you OK with this?'

He nodded. 'After all these years, I am ready.'

Müller decided that his first stop would be the home of the former editor and surviving co-founder of *La Souris Atrichque*, Jean-Marc Lavaliere.

Lavaliere's house was on one of the borders of a small square, in the centre of Grenoble. There was a statue, and a café with pavement tables doing a roaring trade. Remarkably, there were few cars, so free parking spaces were plentiful.

Müller stopped the Porsche next to one of the ubiquitous white Twingos they had seen on the approach to Grenoble.

'This is the address,' he said, 'and that car has a three-eight suffix. Grenoble. Let's hope it's his, and he is home.'

Carey Bloomfield peered up at the classic old building. 'This whole square looks pure eighteenth century.'

'Then let us see if the man I hope to meet is in his eighteenth-century home.'

They got out, and Carey Bloomfield looked about her. Beyond the buildings, the alpine peaks were omnipresent.

'Everywhere you look,' she said, 'there they are.' She looked at the café. 'When we're done, Müller, let's have coffee.'

He glanced at the café. 'Alright.'

They went up to the narrow, wooden door. There was a white bell pull that looked like a stop on a church organ.

Müller gave it a brief tug. Faintly, they heard a tinkling deep within the building.

'Did I say eighteenth-century?' Carey Bloomfield remarked, looking at the organ-stop bell pull with a critical eye.

A good thirty seconds passed and Müller was about to give it another tug, when the door swung open silently. A smallish man with wispy hair, and a mischievous expression that belied his true age, peered out at them. He wore his spectacles on the tip of his nose, rather like a fussy professor. Then the eyes that were peering above them suddenly widened.

'The boy in the photograph,' he said in awe. He spoke English. 'You are surprised by my English. LSE.'

Müller, astonished by the man's remark, said nothing.

It was Carey Bloomfield who spoke. 'LSE?'

'London School of Economics,' Müller said in a daze, staring at the man, who must be Lavaliere, he decided.

'And now a university,' Lavaliere said. 'I am Jean-Marc Lavaliere, as I am certain you have concluded.' He looked at Carey Bloomfield. 'Remarkable. You even look a little like her.'

'Hey,' she said. 'Don't spook me. Someone else has already said that.'

'American. Quite amazing. Nature copies when necessary.'

Müller finally asked, 'How could you tell who I am? You have never seen me before.'

'Oh, I have, my dear Graf. Please. Come in. I have been expecting you for some years.' He looked at the Porsche. 'Very unobtrusive.' He smiled with mischief as they entered.

'This is Miss Carey Bloomfield,' Müller said as they were led along a wide hall with a tiled floor.

Lavaliere shook her hand as they walked. 'A pleasure. Come. Let us go into the garden. I was there when you rang. We can talk in complete privacy. Would you like some coffee? Wine? Brandy? Something to eat? You have got your hotel?'

Müller smiled at this. 'Which do we answer?'

Lavaliere paused, and turned to look impishly above his glasses. 'All.'

Müller gave Carey Bloomfield a quick glance. 'Coffee would be fine, thanks.'

'I could eat,' she said.

'And some brandy for the Graf, I think,' Lavaliere said, adding, 'And the hotel?'

'We came straight here . . .' Müller began.

'Then it is settled. You will stay with us. There is plenty of room, and we have much to talk about.' Lavaliere paused once more. 'My garage is round the corner. Plenty of room too. I think you should put your car there . . . away from the curious. And if you are going to use it later –' he shrugged – 'then you use it. So. Will you stay?'

'If you're sure . . .'

'Of course I am sure.'

'Thank you.'

'I am the one who should be thanking you. I have waited for years for this day. You cannot imagine. Leave the young lady with me. We will go to the garden and wait. There is a door to the garage from there. I will have it open.'

'Which corner do I take?'

'To your right as you come out of the house. Turn the corner and a few metres later you will find a right turn into a short alley. It is a cul-de-sac. Its end is my garage.'

Müller nodded as he glanced at Carey Bloomfield. 'Won't be long.'

Lavaliere gave another of his impish smiles. 'Do not worry. She will be quite safe.'

'Are my thoughts so obvious?'

'Understandably so.'

Müller nodded once more, then went back along the hall. He went outside into the still-bright day. There seemed to be more cars, and more people in the square. Some were giving the car admiring glances.

He got in and, following Lavaliere's instructions, came to the garage, which was quite big, and already open, as was the access to the garden. It was spacious and empty, save for the usual household items stored there. Carey Bloomfield, and Lavaliere, could be seen waiting in the garden itself.

Müller drove in, and stopped. The up-and-over door began

to drop behind him, then locked itself. Müller got out and went into the garden, which was bigger than expected, and more like an orchard. It was surrounded by high walls, and not overlooked, except by the rock faces, which seemed closer than they really were.

A large square table of solid wood was already laid with tea plates, cups on saucers, cutlery, and assorted cakes. There was also some dessert wine, and liqueurs. Four chairs were at the table.

'Odile, my wife,' Lavaliere said as he shut the solid door to the garage, 'will soon be here with the coffee. She is delighted you will stay. She has also been waiting to meet you, Graf von Röhnen.'

'Let us settle one thing,' Müller said. 'Please call me Jens; or, if this is too informal, Müller will do.'

'You do not like your title?'

'It isn't that. I don't "trade" on it, if that's not too opaque.'

'Not at all.' Lavaliere looked his most impish. 'For an old left-winger like me, it sits well. I shall reciprocate, as I feel we have known each other for decades. Please call me Jean-Marc, or simply Jean, if you prefer.'

'And I'm Carey,' Carey Bloomfield said.

They all shook hands on it.

'I am certain Odile will also approve of the informality. Like me, she has been waiting to meet you for a long time, Jens.'

'How come?'

'Odile was a staff member of the *Souris*. That is how we met.' Lavaliere smiled deprecatingly. 'The old cliché. But, over the years, she looked into the incident of your parents with great determination; sometimes even more than I. It was she who found them.'

Müller stared at him. 'Found what?'

'Let us first have our coffees, enjoy some wonderful Grenoble walnut cake, walnut wine or liqueur, and generally relax ourselves before we get into what Odile and I believe really happened. Can you hold back your eagerness just for a little while?'

'We have come this far. After all these years, I can wait.'

219

'Good. Good! And here is the light of my declining years.'
Müller turned to see a tall woman, taller than Lavaliere himself, approaching. She had the walk and grace of a ballet dancer; long black hair with streaks of grey was tied in a bun. She seemed younger by several years than Lavaliere. She carried a covered tray laden with two pots of hot coffee, which she placed on the table.

'Odile,' Lavaliere began, 'at last you can see the adult, from the picture of the boy. This is Carey, and Jens, as he insists.'

She beamed at them, and shook hands with Carey Bloomfield. Then she turned to Müller. 'It is amazing,' she said, her English perfect. She took Müller's hands in both her own. Dark eyes gazed into Müller's. 'It is good that you have come.' She held on to them for some moments, before finally letting go.

Twelve

Within the Black Forest, the light was fading.

Colonel William T. Jackson began the next stage of his plan. He took out his mobile and dialled a number. It was the one belonging to his wife's mobile phone. He had not seen her bag when he had picked up Josh on the B19, and hoped it meant that the kidnappers had taken it with them, and thus the mobile which she carried in it.

The connection was made. He felt a surge of relief. At least they had not destroyed it. It rang, and continued ringing until the answering service cut in, and her voice sounded in his ear.

He squeezed his eyes tightly shut, and cut the transmission. The sound of her voice had stabbed through him like a knife. He breathed deeply, forcing himself not to descend into wild imaginings of what might be happening.

'Stay cool,' he said to himself. 'That's what Josh would say. Stay cool, Dad. Stay cool. Stay cool.' He said that again and again into the gathering twilight of the forest.

*　*　*

Berlin. In a roomful of monitors and interception equipment, an operator had watched a brief red pulse on a screen.

'Someone's just tried to contact a mobile phone at the house!' he called.

Three other colleagues checked their own monitors. None had seen anything, and nothing had been recorded.

'Are you sure you saw something?' one asked him.

'When I say I saw something, I saw it.'

'OK, OK. Keep your shirt on. Call the house. Tell them next time, pick it up! Then we'll see.'

The man nodded, and picked up a phone.

In the house where Elisabeth Jackson was being held, the man with the knife picked up the main phone at its first ring.

'Yes?'

'Where is Mrs Jackson's handy?'

'Where it was, I suppose. In her bag.'

'Get it. When it rings, answer it.'

'What? What do you mean?'

'Are you hard of hearing? *Answer it. And keep talking until you're told to stop!*'

The line clicked, ending the conversation.

The man looked round as he put the phone down. 'Where's her bag?' he asked the one with the kind voice.

'Where you put it.'

'Don't be funny with me.'

'Who's being funny? You asked me. I told you.'

'So *where* is it?'

'You put it in the room with her!'

The knifeman gave him a glare, then went upstairs.

'*Arschloch!*' the one with the kind voice said, when he knew he could not be heard.

The knifeman entered the room where Elisabeth Jackson was still tied to the bed.

'I heard my phone!' she said in English, not as yet sure who had entered. 'Where is it?'

'Right here. Would you like to use it? Call your brave soldier husband?'

'Oh. It's you again.'

'Yes. *Me*. The only person who can get you out of here . . .'

The phone began to ring.

'Shall I answer it?' the man asked with a vicious playfulness. 'Or should you?' Without waiting for her reaction, he took it out of the bag and barked into it, '*Yes?*'

A silence greeted him.

'What's the matter, Jackson? Can't speak? Your beautiful wife is lying on a bed. Do you know she's got beautiful thighs? Of course, you do. Oh. And she's got a tiny mole, just on the side of the right cheek of her ass. Ah. But of course you know that too. You've got two children, so you must have seen it when you made the babies.'

He was still greeted by silence.

'*Don't you believe she's here?*' he snarled. '*Do you think I'm joking?*' He went over to the bed, and put the phone near her mouth. 'Talk to him. *Talk! Talk, damn you!*'

'Darling . . .' she began after a while.

'Elisabeth!'

'*Bill!*'

The man snatched the phone away. 'That's enough! Well, Jackson?' he went on. 'Do you believe me now? *Eh?*'

But he was talking to himself.

'Damn you, Jackson!' he shouted. 'You're trying to get your wife killed!'

Downstairs, the men heard the shouting.

'He's losing it,' the one with the kind voice said.

'What do you mean "losing"? He was never right in the head.'

'I think he has ideas about her. I want no part of it.'

'What do you mean, exactly?'

'I don't think he'll stick to what we've been told. I think he has a fancy for her. In this situation, that's very bad.'

'For him? For us? Or the woman?'

'For all of us.'

In the intercept room, a bright yellow line now connected the two points: the caller, and the called.

The operator who had first spotted it now expanded the

caller's location several times until it was clearly identified. He sent the information on.

On the outskirts of Berlin, the reception was in full swing. The retired general and his four companions were still having their private conference.

There was a discreet knock, and the door to the room opened. A man in full evening dress entered, handed the general a note, then went out again as silently as he had come.

The general looked at the note. 'Gentlemen, we have identified Colonel Jackson's location. He has made his contact. Time for Pröll, and Elland. Mary-Anne will be joining them; but she'll do so in her own way.'

In Grüber's garden near Baden-Baden, Pröll, the taller of the two men, put away his mobile after receiving a secure call.

He turned to see Elland, he of the silent laugh, approaching.

'We've got a hunt,' he told Elland. 'We start tomorrow. It's not far.'

Within the Black Forest, Jackson forced himself to thrust what the knifeman had said about his wife out of his mind.

'I'll go nuts if I don't,' he muttered.

He began to busy himself, preparing for the night. He had eaten some field rations, and would not need to eat again till morning.

He was not going to sleep in the same location as he had made the phonecall.

In Grenoble, Müller said to Odile Lavaliere, 'Odile, if I eat more of your marvellous walnut cake, I'll burst.'

'Come. You can have another.'

'Oh no. You've already said that twice and each time I have yielded to temptation. Besides, it is time for Jean-Marc to explain his mysterious comment about something you have found.'

Her expression changed to one of concern, but she nodded. 'Yes. I think it is time.'

Lavaliere rose from his chair. 'I'll get them.'

223

He was soon back, carrying a sturdy cardboard box that had been sealed with brown adhesive tape. The box looked as if it hadn't been touched for years.

Lavaliere put it down with a slight flourish, near Müller's feet.

'Before you open this,' he said to Müller as he sat down again, 'I will tell you something about what I believe you have come all the way here to discover. That you have found me confirms that you have read the old *Souris* article. How you got hold of it I have no idea.'

'I am a policeman.'

Lavaliere peered at him with interest. 'That, I did not know. A titled man who becomes a policeman.'

'I am not the only one.'

'I'm aware of that . . . but it is still something that intrigues me. What kind of policeman are you?'

'An ordinary one . . .'

Lavaliere shook his head slowly. 'No, Jens. You are not. When I saw that picture of the twelve-year-old boy, I asked myself if he would grow up to be the kind of man who would want to know what really happened. You have. But, more than that, you want justice – closure, if you like – and, because of it, you are hunting out the murderers of your parents.'

'It is more than that.'

Lavaliere nodded, and settled back in his chair. 'I can well imagine.'

He did not expand, pursed his lips, and gave Müller a sideways look. Odile was also looking at Müller, but with the vague look of concern she had shown previously.

'I was born in one of the mountain villages in this area,' Lavaliere went on. 'We are an independently minded breed. During the war, the Grenoble area was a centre of resistance. The Gestapo were down here, but up in the villages people were doing things that could get them shot. One village is known for hiding the Jews of the time. I mention this to explain why Roger, Odile and I did not believe the official version of the crash. All three of us came from the mountains; so when we heard a whisper from there that the aircraft did not go down where the papers claimed it had, we decided to investigate.

'Roger died mysteriously and suddenly, we were having great difficulties keeping the paper going. Our offices were mysteriously broken into. It wasn't long before the *Souris* closed, despite some wonderful support from many quarters; even from those from whom, politically, we normally considered ourselves to be at the opposite end of the spectrum.

'I will give you a map of the area where we *know* the plane went down. It is very detailed, with full directions. I drew them myself. Odile and I have marked the location with two small crosses on a nearby tree; as a form of respect, as well as a marker. Unless you know of the crosses, you would find them very difficult to locate, if not impossible. The people in the mountains told us they had seen strange men burying something. At first, we thought they meant bodies. To this day, we still do not know what really happened, and why, and who was responsible. Perhaps what is in the box will help you. We have never looked in there since we sealed it. Now, you can open it.'

Lavaliere took something out of a pocket. It was a sheathed carpet knife. 'Here. Use this.'

Müller took the knife, removed its safety cover, then glanced at Carey Bloomfield, who appeared transfixed. With final looks at Lavaliere and Odile, he began to slice through the tape. The upper flaps of the box popped slightly open. Müller put the knife down slowly.

'I cannot even begin to imagine what is in here,' he said, half afraid it would be items of his parents' clothing, and was uncertain how he would react to seeing that.

He looked at each of them in turn, then with a kind of reverence, slowly began to raise the flaps of the box, peeling them back one by one until they were fully open.

Whatever was inside was protected by a padded covering. He began to lift it out. He had lifted it just clear of the box, when his mouth came open, and his hands, holding on to the padding, froze in mid-air. Looking as clean as the day they had been put into the box, were two bright, orange-red items. There were scorch marks upon them.

Müller closed his mouth slowly, staring at the contents of the box. At last, he put the padding down, near the box.

225

'My God,' he eventually whispered. 'The flight recorders!'

'The *real* flight recorders,' Lavaliere corrected.

Carey Bloomfield, who from her position had not been able to see inside the box, got to her feet. '*What?*' She moved round to look. 'Jeeezus!' she breathed.

All three watched as Müller put a hand into the box to touch one of the data recorders. He did so with a gentleness that clearly expressed the way he felt. He stroked each one slowly, as if they were animate. Face still, he did not speak for several minutes. No one disturbed him.

Carey Bloomfield moved a hesitant hand to touch him, but, as if thinking this too would disturb him, she lowered the hand and went back to her chair.

At last, a long shuddering sigh escaped him, and he began to replace the padding; then he pushed the flaps back down.

Still looking at the box, he gave a shaky smile. 'Well. I certainly did not expect this.' He cleared his throat.

Odile still had the anxious look. 'Are you alright, Jens?'

He nodded. 'I'm fine. I'm fine.' He cleared his throat once more.

Carey Bloomfield looked as if she wanted to hug him.

Feeling a heat behind his eyes, he did not look up. 'Odile, Jean-Marc, this is a very dangerous thing you've done. There are people who would kill—'

'We know,' Odile said. 'But we have had them for nearly sixteen years. The place where we dug them up is long over-grown. There is no reason for anyone to believe it has been disturbed. We wanted to wait until you came to us. We always hoped that you would, one day.'

Müller swallowed. 'Thank you,' he said quietly. 'Excuse me.'

He stood up and began to walk to the far end of the garden.

Carey Bloomfield began to rise.

Odile stopped her with a gentle hand. 'Leave him be. This is something for him alone.'

They watched as Müller went to the far wall and stood near an apple tree, head down, hands in his pockets. He remained like that for several minutes. Then they saw him wipe at his eyes.

Odile was looking at Carey Bloomfield's expression. 'You sense his pain,' she said to her. 'How long have you been in love with him?'

'Truth to tell, I don't know. It sort of . . . crept up on me.'

Odile glanced at her husband, who was smiling back at her. 'I think we understand.'

Then Müller was returning. 'Sorry,' he said. 'Needed to think.' His eyes seemed dry.

'Of course,' Lavaliere said.

Carey Bloomfield looked at him, hiding her emotions.

'Odile,' Müller began, 'Jean-Marc. I am reluctant to ask this of you, but would you mind keeping the box for a little longer? There is something we've got to do tomorrow, and I think the recorders will be safer with you for the time being. I'll come back for them.'

'But of course,' Odile said. 'We shall put them back where they've been hiding for all those years. They will be safe.'

He looked at the Lavalieres in turn. 'And *you* must remain safe. I am certain you understand me.'

'We do,' Lavaliere said. 'We come from a line of people who know how to hide from the hunters. Just as our parents did when the Germans were here. No offence.'

Müller gave a rueful smile. 'None taken.'

'And now,' Lavaliere said, 'I think we could all do with a marc.'

Much later, after an exceptional dinner prepared by Odile and Lavaliere, Müller stood at the window of his bedroom. It overlooked the orchard, and, directly beyond the wall it seemed, a perpendicular wall of rock gleamed in the light of a powerful moon. Somewhere, two male voices rose in laughter that echoed in the night air.

'Beautiful, isn't it?' Carey Bloomfield's whisper came from the window next to his. 'Beautiful, and eerie.'

'Yes,' he agreed. 'There is that element.'

Was it this slab of rock face, he wondered, that had smashed his parents' aircraft like a toy?

And downstairs, or wherever Lavaliere had hidden them, were the black boxes with some of the truth. At last.

'Beautiful as this is to look at,' he now whispered to Carey Bloomfield, 'we've got an early start in the morning. And I am the worse for wear from Jean-Marc's alcohol, and absolutely stuffed to bursting point with Odile's culinary masterpiece. I can see the mountain from my bed, so I'll watch it from there until I fall asleep. I'll say goodnight.'

''Night, Müller. Don't have bad dreams.'

'I won't. Not now.'

06.00 the next morning. Fully dressed, Müller and Carey Bloomfield were in the orchard garden, near the garage door. Odile and Lavaliere, in dressing gowns, had accompanied them.

'Many thanks for everything,' Müller began. 'The cakes, the dinner, the rooms, the early breakfast, and . . . the box . . .'

Odile briefly placed a finger on his lips. 'You do not have to thank us for anything. Find what you are looking for. That will be our thanks.'

'Odile speaks for both of us,' Lavaliere said.

Müller looked at them, and nodded his appreciation. 'I forgot to ask yesterday. Do you know a man called LaCroix?'

Both nodded. 'If it is Alphonse,' Lavaliere replied.

'It is.'

'A good man. In fact, he helped us a lot, which was probably why he got early retirement. He was gendarmerie.'

'I know.'

'Will you be seeing him?'

'Not this time. Once we have been to the . . . place, we're heading back to Germany. Something there needs urgent attention. When we come back for the box will be time enough. I want to do some searching myself.'

'I understand,' Lavaliere said. He held out a hand to Carey Bloomfield. 'Take care of this man.'

'If he'll let me.' She gave the pleasantly surprised Lavaliere a hug.

'And yourself, of course,' he added.

'Of course.'

Lavaliere turned to Müller, hand outstretched, while Carey Bloomfield and Odile embraced. 'You have no idea how it

228

pleases me to have met you at last. Your father would have been proud.'

'I would like to think he would at least not have been disappointed,' Müller said, shaking the hand.

'I am certain he would not have been disappointed. Not at all.'

Müller turned to Odile. 'Odile . . .'

She embraced him tightly, and kissed him softly on both cheeks, near the mouth. 'We expect to see you again, very soon.'

'You shall.'

As he opened the garage door, Lavaliere handed Müller a white envelope. 'Do not open it until you are well on your way back.'

'Sounds mysterious.'

'Not very. Humour me.'

Müller nodded. 'Alright.'

He stood back for Carey Bloomfield to enter the garage, then followed. They got into the car as the main door began to rise. Müller reversed into the cul-de-sac.

The Lavalieres raised their hands in farewell and stood watching until Müller had reversed into the street, and had driven away.

'They make a fine couple,' Lavaliere said to his wife, as the garage doors closed. 'Let us hope they enjoy a long life.'

The light at that time of day had a hint of steel about it, and there was no cloud.

'What a sweet, sweet couple,' Carey Bloomfield said.

'What an extremely brave couple,' Müller amended. He shook his head in wonder. 'They've been sitting on a pile of high explosive for all these years. I don't feel particularly happy about asking them to continue doing it.'

'They are not weak people. They would not have agreed if they'd felt offended. And besides, you are right about not taking the box today. We're going back to find the colonel, wherever he may be planning to make his last stand, Custer style, in the Black Forest. Imagine if, for whatever reason, you lost those things out there. The car gets broken into by one of the Semper . . . and bingo. If you're way out in the

229

woods, the car's sensors would not help, just make a lot of noise. Somehow, I don't think that would bother a Semper killer much. So, I do understand why you left them.'

'I'm still uncomfortable. The Lavalieres have been lucky for sixteen years. I just hope our visit hasn't changed that. Talking of which . . . you're air force. How strong are those things? And can the data still be retrieved after so long?'

'Let's put it this way,' she said. 'The data recorder has an impact tolerance of three thousand four hundred Gs. That's a hell of a lot of decelerative force, when you consider the top fighter jets can start coming to pieces in the low double figures, positive. Less capable jets start coming apart long before that. Negative is in single figures. The human body, by comparison – even protected – starts taking serious, terminal damage long before the best jets start to break. The recorder also has a fire resistance of one thousand one hundred degrees celsius, and can take submerged pressure at twenty thousand feet. The cockpit voice recorder has the same resistance. These days, people can still grab information from computer discs that have been wiped. I think untouched black boxes will be a walk in the park. Of course, these are older recorders and some specs have changed, but not by much. Your only problem will be to make sure whoever opens them is one hundred and ten per cent trustworthy.'

'I think Pappi will be able to find someone.'

'Talking of Pappi,' she said, 'he gave you the colonel's numbers. Are you going to call?'

'Not until we're back in Germany. I'm certain that all calls to Colonel Jackson, and all those he makes, are being monitored. It's what he wanted. I have no intention of letting the eavesdroppers know I've been to France. It might lead them to the Lavalieres; which would be disastrous. Time enough for the colonel. They won't get to him as easily as they think. I am more worried about Hagen and his team.'

In the Black Forest, Jackson had long been awake. He had bathed in a cold stream and, fully refreshed, was calmly eating his field-ration breakfast. He had checked all his weapons.

He was ready.

*   *   *

230

The road twisted its way up the mountain in loops and hair-pins that seemed to go on forever. In the early morning, the Turbo roared up the road at a speed that Carey Bloomfield tried not to check on the car's speedometer.

There were times when she felt certain they would be heading back down the mountain in a more direct manner, a lot faster than they came up.

'Enjoying the scenery?' Müller asked. 'Great, isn't it?'

She nodded quickly; too quickly for real enjoyment.

'Worried?' he asked.

'Not really,' she said. 'But this road is *narrow.*' Her voice ended in a weak squeak.

'Don't worry,' he assured her. 'We won't be tumbling down the mountain. Do you think I want to damage my car?'

'That's what's keeping me afloat,' she said, glancing at the flowing zigzag of the road far below. 'Now, this can give a gal vertigo.'

'Not so far to go now,' he said. 'We'll park somewhere, then go for a walk. Forty-five minutes there, forty-five minutes back. The Romans, in full marching order, could do twenty-five miles a day and still make camp before nightfall. And they were certainly not as healthy as we are.'

'Good for the Romans.'

'Come, come. Me, police *Hauptkommissar.* You, air force lieutenant-colonel. We are fit. At five kph – which we can easily do – we'll be leaving by nine.'

'Müller?'

'Yes.'

'It's too early in the morning.'

He glanced at her. 'You look a bit queasy. Too much wine last night? Are you alright?'

'Nothing that a good puke won't fix.'

'You've been up in jet fighters.'

'Yeah. And they've got puke bags in there too.'

'The road has made you carsick. Would you like to drive back down? Being behind the wheel makes a big difference.'

'No thanks. I appreciate the offer, knowing what it cost you. But I'd rather be sick than have you look worried every time we come to a corner; and boy oh boy, are there *corners,* not to mention suicidal little cars that seem to think this is a racetrack. Remember that one that tried to play chicken on a goddamned *bend*? I'll be fine once we stop. That Roman walk might actually do me some good.'

'Some music, perhaps?'

'No!'

They got to the top not long after, where the road ended. All other roads had branched off a good 6 kilometres before. There was a wide gravelly space within which to park, big enough to hold several cars; but there were no other vehicles.

'Hey,' Carey Bloomfield said as they got out. 'This is a great view! Wow!'

'Was it worth it?'

'It's worth it to come here to do what you came for. But this . . . this is a bonus. I feel better already.'

The ramparts of rock were all about them and, far below, they could see Grenoble, and the outlying villages and towns dotted across the landscape.

Müller spread Lavaliere's map on top of the car. There was a sketch attached to it.

'Take a look at this,' he said to her. And, when she had come to look, went on, 'This sketch shows where the media said the plane hit, with the dotted line showing the general area where the wreckage is supposed to have fallen . . . and where the fake black boxes were found. Now, the second sketch shows another rock face . . . there – the one we're going to. See where that dotted line points. Where they found the buried recorders.'

He passed a hand over his eyes. 'God. These bastards really worked at hiding what had really happened.' He looked about him, looked at the map, then looked around once more. He saw a barely visible trail. 'There,' he said. 'That's the one.'

He reached into the car, unlocked the glove compartment, and took out a Beretta 92R. He gave it to her.

'Put it into your bag. Just in case. Don't go shooting ibex, marmots, or whatever else runs around in these mountains.'

'What about the two-legged ones pointing guns?'

'If you spot one of those, you know what to do.'

'You're in France. You have no jurisdiction here.'

232

'They would be in France, and certainly have no jurisdiction here, either.'

'Unless they happen to be French Semper.'

'Let's cross that bridge when we come to it.'

She put the gun into her bag. 'You've got one under your jacket, I've got this one. Any more?'

'There's another under the rear seat squab. The one behind the driver's seat.'

'Pappi had one in his glovebox too. Would he have more stashed about his car as well?'

'That would not surprise me in the least,' Müller said with a smile. 'Now come on. We have a rendezvous to keep.'

In the house where she was being held, Elisabeth Jackson woke up to her second morning of captivity. She had been allowed to go to the bathroom the night before, but now, she needed to go again. She hoped someone would come soon.

Minutes later, she heard the familiar sound of the key in the lock, and hoped it would be the kind-voiced man.

It was.

'Hello,' he greeted. 'I've brought you breakfast. Two rolls, this time.'

'I hope it's not a hearty breakfast.'

'What do you mean?'

'There's a saying – "And the condemned man ate a hearty breakfast." Hope that's not me.'

'Oh. I see. No. It's not that. It's me. I added the extra one. *He's* out somewhere, if you understand me.'

'I understand. But, before I have your generous breakfast, I er . . . need to go.'

'Oh! Yes. Here, let me help.'

He freed her feet, re-tied her hands at the front, then led her to the bathroom.

'Don't touch the blindfold,' he advised, 'or you'll get us both into trouble.'

'I won't,' she promised.

And she meant it. Now that she knew Bill had planned something, she would do nothing to jeopardize her chances.

* * *

233

Müller and Carey Bloomfield had come to the spot where the Lavalieres had found the buried data recorders. It was beneath a low escarpment but, high above that, the soaring rock face towered imposingly; and terrifyingly.

Müller looked up at it for at least a minute, saying nothing. He imagined he could see a dark smear, where the plane had hit.

'Not possible,' he murmured to himself.

Any marks would have long been erased, he thought, by rain, snow, and ice.

But not the gouges in the rock. So, perhaps he *was* looking up at the spot where his parents had died.

Carey Bloomfield followed his scrutiny. 'See something?'

'I think I'm just imagining it.'

'What? That dark patch up there?'

'You can see it?'

'Sure. A chunk is missing from that rock.'

Müller felt something like an electric current go through him. 'But it can't be where the plane hit, surely?'

'Who's to know for sure? Unless you get up there and take scrapings for analysis. But it seems to match Lavaliere's sketch. He would not make a mistake like that.'

Müller kept looking up at the spot.

'If you'd like me to move away . . .' she began. 'Give you some privacy . . .'

'No. No. Stay. I want you to. It's alright. Really.' He traced a line downwards in his mind, moving his head until he was looking at the ground about him, and the surrounding vegetation. 'Can you see the crosses?'

'No . . . Wait. Wait a minute. Look over there, to your right.'

Müller looked, and saw a small clump of wildflowers. 'Flowers,' he said.

'Now look closer towards the base of the rock,' she directed. 'What do you see?'

'More wildflowers. Nothing but . . .' his voice faded.

'Now you've found them,' she told him.

Müller understood what the Lavalieres had done. They had planted the wildflowers as a marker; then, on the edge of the clump, two much smaller clumps of the blooms were positioned, close together.

Müller went over to them, squatted, and touched them very gently while Carey Bloomfield stood a little distance away, watching him.

He remained like that for a long time, almost seeming to talk to the flowers. Then he raised his head to look upwards and saw, hidden beneath an awning of low branches, two small crosses, side-by-side, cut into the lower trunk of a tree.

Müller bit his lower lip as a surge of emotion took hold of him. His shoulders began to shake.

Watching, Carey Bloomfield felt the urge to hold him.

'Damn you, Müller,' she said to herself. 'I'm going to do it, whether you want me to or not.'

She hurried over, got down next to him, and put an arm about his shoulders. She held it there tightly, until the shaking eventually subsided.

'Thank you,' he said in a low voice, eyes on the twin clumps of wildflowers.

'Hey,' she said. 'What are friends for?'

'We're making good time,' Müller said. 'We seem to have missed the second rush hour.'

The one-hour run from Grenoble had taken a lot less than expected, and they were approaching the toll gates just after L'isle d'Abeau, in under 45 minutes.

They went through, and Müller took the speed to a reasonably inconspicuous 160. At that rate, the distance was eaten up without drawing unwelcome attention. Many other cars, with the licence plates of various nationalities, were travelling far faster; but Müller chose not to be tempted. Being stopped, even though he could explain to a fellow policeman, would still cost time.

Less than four hours later, having once more been able to travel at high speed, they were approaching the Renchtal Autobahn service station.

'Time to call the colonel,' Müller said. 'We'll stop here for fuel, have a quick snack, then I'll make the call.' He peered up at the sky. 'Looks like rain. And soon.'

After he had filled the tank, and they'd had their snacks, they returned to the car. The rain still held off.

Müller took out the fat envelope Lavaliere had given to him. 'We're far enough now,' he said.

'Did you get the feeling he wanted you to be far enough away,' Carey Bloomfield said, 'so that you could not get back there quickly?'

'It did cross my mind.' He opened the envelope, and pulled out three documents, plus a handwritten covering letter. He glanced at the documents, eyes widening. 'They can't do this! I can't . . .'

He passed them over to her.

'Jesus!' she exclaimed. 'These . . . these are the deeds to their house . . . in French, German and English!'

'So there's no mistake, and all properly notarized. Both of them have signed it. And they did so years ago. They've been waiting all this time for me. They must have family to whom they could give the house. They can't do this! I can't accept.'

'Read the letter,' Carey Bloomfield advised. 'It might explain.'

Müller opened the single sheet, and began to read. It was in English. '"I know this will shock you, but we made up our minds years ago. We always hoped you would one day come to us. So, this is in the event of our deaths – natural, or unnatural. We bequeath the house and all in it to you.

'"This is not as mad as it seems. We have no immediate heirs, and some items in it are of greater value to you than anyone else. Beneath the box, you will find documents. Years of investigation and research, which will be, we hope, of great help to you. You will find everything beneath the kitchen flagstones, should we be gone next time you come.

'"Do not feel embarrassed by this. We feel we have always known you, from the moment we saw your picture as a boy, at that terrible time. I am sure you have now realized that Odile looks upon you as the son we never had. I think she adopted you in her heart that day. That is how closely we have lived with you. Find those people, and punish them for what they have done. Jean-Marc, and Odile."'

Müller slowly folded the letter, and put it together with the documents that Carey Bloomfield had handed back to him.

'Life never stops surprising,' she said.

236

'What should I do?'

'*Do?* Jens Müller, if you reject them – because that is definitely what it will be – they will feel humiliated. They will feel very foolish. Do you really want to do that to them?'

'Of course not!'

'Then you don't have an argument. And put those things somewhere safe. That's dynamite you're holding.'

'I think I'll call the colonel.'

Jackson was intrigued to hear the card phone ring. He let it ring three times.

'Jackson.'

'Colonel.'

'I know that voice. I've been expecting your call.'

'I got your message.'

'I'm impressed. But then, you're an impressive man, *Hauptkommissar*. You know your job.'

'So do you, Colonel. I'd hate to see that career go down the pan, as you would say. You should know that we are doing all we can.'

'I knew you would.'

'We should talk.'

'We're talking.'

'I mean face to face.'

'It will take you a while.'

'I am not in Berlin. In fact, I am quite close, depending on where you actually are at this moment. But I know the general area. If I say family . . .'

'You have done your homework.'

'I also have some news you will not like, Colonel.'

'I'm waiting.'

'One word. Hagen.'

There was a long silence. 'What about him?'

'Some of your superiors have put him on your trail.'

There was another silence. 'You know what Hagen is?'

'Yes,' Müller said. 'A friend told me. Not pleasant.'

'We agree there, Mr Müller. Hagen is a piece of shit.'

'I also know he will enjoy his mission.'

'Our problem, Mr Müller, is how to get you here, without

others listening in. I know Hagen will be monitoring. So will the people who took my wife . . .'

'Because you want them to.'

'Yes.'

'I think I may have a solution. My phone is secure. They can't hear, or trace it. They will, of course, still hear you. I will ask questions. You will say yes, or no. That way, you can direct me in. Example. Are you near water?'

'Yes.'

'A lake? A river? Or a stream?'

'Yes to the first.'

'I will give you some names.'

After three tries, Müller got a yes on the fourth. After that, it was easy.

At the monitoring unit, the operator who had locked on to Jackson's call to his wife's mobile saw the pulse of another phone in the same caller area.

'What do you think this is?' he asked a colleague.

'Someone else's phone in the same area? There are other people out there, you know.'

'Let's see if we can get sound.' He began tapping at his keyboard.

'We don't eavesdrop on civilians,' the other cautioned. 'Unless we're told to.'

'If it is a civilian, I'll stop.'

'Of course you will.'

'Look. Just let me do this.'

The operator worked at the pulse, trying for audio. After a while, Jackson's voice came through very clearly.

'Yes,' they heard.

'*See?*' the operator crowed. 'So much for the "civilian".'

'Notice anything?' the other asked slyly.

'What? What's to notice?'

'Listen.'

'No,' they heard. Then, 'Yes. No. Yes. No. No . . .'

It went on like that, then ended abruptly.

They stared at each other. 'What the hell was that about?' the operator asked rhetorically.

238

'Oh, I'm out there. I really know.'
'Comedian.'

Müller found where Jackson had parked his car, and left the Porsche next to it. Then he and Carey Bloomfield set off to meet with Jackson. They took all the Berettas with them, including the one under the rear seat, leaving Lavaliere's envelope in its place.

As they walked on, the first spots of rain began to fall.

'Looks as if we're going to get wet,' Müller said.

'Last time I checked,' she said, 'I didn't melt in rain.'

Hagen and his team of four – kitted out with headphones, mikes, and an assortment of weapons – were already in the forest, and homing in on an area that his briefing had given as a strong possibility. Earlier monitoring of Jackson's first call had also confirmed it.

Hagen had psyched up his team. 'Remember that this man is a highly trained soldier. Whatever you think you know, he knows better. Whatever the tricks you believe you have learned in combat, he knows them all. However good you think you are with weapons, he beats you hands down. Take no chances. Our orders are to bring him in. If he resists . . .'

Hagen, a tall thin man with a hard face and sunken cheeks, had deliberately let his words hang. His eyes were like those of a marine predator; cold, and merciless, and harbouring years of grievance.

Today, he had decided, was payback time.

Pröll and Elland were also in the forest, and were being directed by the monitoring unit. The rain had increased in intensity.

'Shit!' Pröll swore. 'I'm going to get my suit wet!'

Elland laughed silently.

Mary-Anne was also in the forest, and though, like Pröll and Elland, she was being directed by the monitoring unit, she was working independently.

She had been flown to Stuttgart on an apparent business trip, and had hired a car at the airport under one of her many aliases. She had worn a dark wig, a soft hat pulled down over her head, sunglasses and business suit.

The hair was again bright blonde under the hat. The sunglasses were gone, as was the business suit. She now wore jeans, and a denim jacket. A silenced automatic was in a shoulder holster. On her feet were combat boots. A big knife was strapped to her leg, beneath the jeans.

The rain began to spatter her hat. She ignored it.

Pappenheim was wondering about the continuing silence from Kaltendorf.

'Not like him at all,' he said to himself. 'He's up to something.'

Having earlier and satisfyingly hauled Reimer over the coals for the debacle with Mary-Anne the previous evening, he was now looking for a distraction.

It came in the guise of a phone call.

He had finished a cigarette and was in the process of lighting another, when the phone rang. He completed lighting the cigarette before picking it up.

'Fully lit, are we?' the voice said in greeting.

'How well you know me.'

There was a faint chuckle. 'And how many of those sticks for the day so far?'

'You didn't call to enquire about my addiction, and it's none of your business.'

'Pappi, Pappi. Give it up. I did.'

'One thing worse to a smoker, than a non-smoker – and that's a smoker who has become a non-smoker.'

'We are on form this unfine hour.'

'If you're talking about the deluge out there, brighten my day.'

'Phone calls were tracked. Vengeful husband to kidnappers' hideout. Would you like the location?'

Pappenheim came alive. '*Would* I!'

The contact passed on precise details of the house where Elisabeth Jackson was being held. It was over 200 kilometres from where she had been taken.

'I think an assault team would be in order,' the caller suggested.

'You think correctly,' Pappenheim said. 'Thanks!'

'Nice to do business with you.'

The conversation was over.

Pappenheim made some rapid phone calls to people he knew, using himself and Müller as the responsible authorities. Within fifteen minutes, the local force closest to the kidnappers' house had despatched an assault team.

It would take them half an hour to get there. They went in without sirens.

Pappenheim decided to call Müller.

'And where are you?' he asked when Müller had answered.

'Home ground.'

'Quicker than I expected. But good you're back. I have good news.'

'And I have news to put hairs on your hairs.'

'Now *that* is interesting. The kind that should wait?'

'Most, most definitely.'

'It sounds a doozy, as an Ami cop of my acquaintance likes saying. I'll curb my impatience till your return.'

'It is worth it, Pappi. Pure gold.'

'Successful foray, then.'

'Most successful.'

'Well, I'd better try and give you something in return. We have found the house, and an assault team is on the way.'

'That, Pappi, is excellent news. Particularly now. How?'

'One of my carrier pigeons. Tell you about that later too.'

'Excellent,' Müller repeated.

'You said "particularly now".'

'I did. We're on our way to meet with the man in question. I have spoken with him, and he's given us instructions. This will make his day.'

'Then everyone will be happy.'

'Let us not tempt fate.'

'Let's not,' Pappenheim agreed. 'Besides, there's always the GW. He's *never* happy.'

'Great news,' Müller said to Carey Bloomfield under the tree where they had taken shelter when Pappenheim's call had come. 'They've found the house where Mrs Jackson is being held. An assault team is on the way.'

Her eyes lit up. 'Fantastic. This is great. God. I'm so glad for him. He can go home before this whole thing wrecks his career forever. Maybe we can get him away before any of those assholes turn up; and I include Hagen.'

'Then let's keep getting soaked.'

The rain was now a downpour. Blinking against it, they hurried on their way.

In the monitoring unit, the operator was twitchy.

'Something's happening out there,' he said. 'I know it.'

The others looked at him with some exasperation.

Stubbornly, he kept his eyes on his monitor. Then a pulse appeared.

'*Yes!*' he said with glee. 'He's making another call.'

But only one pulse had appeared. There was no second pulse to connect to.

The operator contacted Pröll, Elland, and Mary-Anne, and gave them new directions.

Mary-Anne was loping her way through the forest, avoiding roads, farms and isolated buildings, and flitting between the trees with ghostly unreality. She was a wraith; an ethereal being. In the sheeting, pounding rain, she seemed to belong there.

There was something in her eyes. They were alive with fire, and her lips red as if she had fed on blood.

She was on the hunt.

But it was Jackson who had first blood.

Pröll had split with Elland, planning to come at Jackson in a pincer movement. They had been homed on to his phone signal. Pröll could not know he was being zeroed on to a phone that was tied to a tree. The first thing he knew about Jackson's presence was a hard arm about his neck, and a hand bending his gun arm back far enough to break it if he struggled.

'Move the wrong way, asshole,' he heard in his ear, 'and

242

you lose your arm just before you lose your windpipe. You won't be able to scream with the pain of it.'

Pröll remained very still; just before he lost consciousness.

Jackson lowered the body carefully. He took the gun, then did a quick search. No ID. No credit card. But plenty of cash. He ignored the money and found something far more interesting: a small knife, exactly like the one Josh had described.

'If you're one of the kidnappers,' Jackson said to the unconscious Pröll, 'you're in shit street.'

He quickly tied Pröll to a tree, and put a thin wire about the killer's neck. It was then secured to his bonds in such a way that if Pröll tried to free himself, he would end up sawing through his own throat.

Jackson left Pröll's phone on, then went into hiding to wait.

The water from the rainfall, streaming down the tree, eventually made Pröll wake up. He was very professional and immediately understood the predicament he was in.

He remained perfectly still.

Elland was beginning to worry. He had heard nothing from Pröll for some time. Both were supposed to keep their phones on.

'Pröll!' he whispered. 'Where the hell are you? *Pröll!*'

The monitoring unit was still giving him instructions.

'I can't find Pröll!' he said to them.

'Pröll is still active. Now do your job!'

Elland came to the same point as Pröll, and stopped to gape in the rain when he saw his partner in killing. Pröll seemed to be desperately trying to say something.

Elland stood there too long.

'You have two choices,' he heard a voice behind him say. 'Both bad. Drop your weapon!'

Elland was fast. Very fast. And he knew it. He also knew he was not going to surrender. He whirled, gun hunting with deadly precision.

Unfortunately, his target was not where he thought it would be. A crushing, painful blow to the right knee told him how badly he had miscalculated. His scream of pain came almost at the same time as the bark of the big Sig Sauer automatic pistol.

'I did warn you,' Jackson said.

243

'*My knee! My knee!*' Elland yelled in English, his accent not German at all. '*You smashed my knee, you bastard!*'

Even in the noise of the rain, both the sound of the shot and the yelling seemed to echo through the forest. Every droplet of water was an amplifier.

Müller and Carey Bloomfield heard it; as did Hagen and his team; as did Mary-Anne.

'It came from over there,' Carey Bloomfield said.

She pointed to the edge of a lake that could just be seen through the trees and the rain.

'It's started,' Müller said with regret.

Hagen raised a hand when he heard.

The four men with him stopped, listening.

'Alright,' he said in a low voice. 'We're very close. Fan out. You know the drill.'

The men nodded, and melted into the trees.

Mary-Anne paused briefly in her flitting rush, head slowly turning, a predator scenting prey.

Eyes on fire, she smiled, and rushed on.

Müller and Carey Bloomfield came to a screen of trees, through which they could see the still-yelling Elland.

'You stay here,' he told her. 'We don't know who else is out there, apart from Hagen and his crew. Watch my back.'

Without drawing any of his own guns, he went to where Elland lay screaming.

He walked up to the wounded man, and looked down, then up at the trussed Pröll, and back to Elland.

'You're in a bad state.'

'Is that all you've fucking got to *say*? It hurts, damn it!'

'Müller, *Polizeihauptkommissar*. I don't think you want to swear at me.'

Müller glanced up at Pröll, then again down at Elland, and saw in their eyes that both men knew of him.

Though he had nothing to go on, he decided to throw in a guess. 'How's the yachting?'

Both men could not help reacting. The trussed-up Pröll twitched, and Elland actually paused in his yelling.

'Gentlemen,' Müller said, thinking of Max Gatto and his team, 'I know some people who would love to meet you. And that's only the beginning.'

Then Elland was yelling again.

'I think I should shut him up,' a voice said.

'Be my guest, Colonel,' Müller said.

There was a thumping sound, and Elland stopped yelling.

Müller turned round and saw Jackson, in combat trousers, boots and vest, standing next to Elland's now quiet form.

'You did not kill him, I hope.'

'Just a knockout punch. Good to see you, Mr Müller.'

'Good to see you, Colonel. I'm glad you've killed no one.'

'It could have been worse. That's for sure.' Jackson held out a hand.

They shook hands in the pouring rain.

'Now that you're here,' Jackson went on, 'as the ranking man on this turf, I suppose I'd better hand over to you.'

'It would be wise. Especially when you hear my news.'

Jackson looked at him steadily. 'News?'

'We have located the house where they are holding your wife. An assault team should be there just about now.'

Jackson turned his head up to the rain and shut his eyes. 'Thank God. Thank God. Thank you, Mr Müller.' Jackson looked down again. 'I'm sorry I roped you in; but it was the only option I felt I had, given the circumstances.'

'The circumstances, Colonel, are far more complex than you would believe. We were manipulated, you and I.'

'I don't quite follow.'

'It's a very long and complicated story, Colonel. Perhaps, one day, we will talk about it over a drink. But right now, we must get you out of here, and back to your family.'

'How pally!' a hard voice said.

Hagen, looking triumphant, telescopic-stock M16 with 9mm suppressor held ready across his chest, strode into the small clearing. He looked at Pröll, stepped over Elland, and came to stand directly in front of Jackson. He ignored Müller.

245

'Colonel Jackson, I have orders to take you back. Your condition on delivery is immaterial.'

Jackson looked coldly back at Hagen. 'Enjoyed that speech, Phil?'

'Lieutenant-Colonel Hagen, *sir*! Are you coming quietly, *sir*?'

'Colonel Hagen,' Müller said.

Hagen turned cold eyes upon Müller. They fastened briefly upon his ponytailed hair, and his earring. 'And who are you?'

'Someone who can arrest you for carrying an assault weapon on German territory without permission. And call your men out of the woods.'

Hagen stared at Müller as if he could not believe his ears. 'What? *You?* Arrest me? You're a *cop*? Your rank?'

'*Hauptkommissar.*'

'Well, *Hauptkommissar* . . .'

'Müller.'

'Well, *Hauptkommissar* Müller, let's get a few things straight. I am under orders to take this man—'

'Colonel Jackson, Hagen. His name and rank. Or do your orders allow insubordination as well?'

'Now look here, you . . .'

'No. *You* look here.' Before Hagen quite knew what was happening, Müller drew the Beretta and jabbed it hard against Hagen's chest.

'I'll be . . .' Jackson said, staring at Müller.

'Now, *Colonel* Hagen,' Müller said coldly. 'I am arresting you for violation of the prohibited firearms . . .'

The little clearing was suddenly crowded as Hagen's men came out of the screen of trees.

Jackson looked at them. 'I don't know about you, gentlemen. But I, for one, would not like to be held responsible for the shooting of a German police officer. I would suggest you all put your guns down.'

'You will obey my orders!' Hagen snarled to his men.

Müller's gun was still against Hagen's chest. He looked at the soldiers. 'Whatever orders you were given, they have been overtaken by events. Colonel Jackson is returning with me. I would advise you to become no part of a diplomatic incident.'

'I have my orders!' Hagen roared above the rain.

Müller looked at the soldiers. 'None of you look stupid,' he said. 'I am escorting Colonel Jackson home. Objections?' The soldiers lowered their weapons.

'*No!*' Hagen bellowed and, despite having Müller's gun against his chest, still tried to bring up his weapon to bear upon Jackson. The years of resentment and envy had caused Hagen to lose all control.

A crunching sound forced Hagen's mouth wide open. Blood spurted out of it.

'*Jesus, Müller!*' Jackson cried. 'Did you do that?'

'*No!*' Müller was already diving to the muddy ground.

Jackson followed suit, rolling for cover. The soldiers scattered.

'Then who the hell . . . ?' Jackson hissed, looking to where Hagen, having fallen, was crawling around, the blood still pouring out of his mouth.

A second shot crashed into Hagen's head. He stopped moving.

'I don't know!' Müller replied, searching for a possible sighting of the unknown attacker.

The next shot took a suddenly terrified Pröll in the throat. His eyes opened wide, and stayed open. The blood began to leak slowly out of the wounded throat as he made strange gargling sounds.

Then a moan came from Elland.

'He's waking up!' Jackson said in a sharp whisper.

Then into the clearing walked Mary-Anne, bright blonde hair streaming in the rain, lips red, eyes on fire, gun pointing at Jackson.

'Come on out, boys, unless you want the colonel to get it. You've seen what I've done. You know I can do it. You will never get me before I kill him. So, come on out.' She giggled, then gave her mega smile. Even in the dark of the forest, even in the rain, it was a sunburst.

Jackson stared at her in horrorstruck awe.

'Come on, boys! I'm getting impatient!'

Reluctantly, the soldiers came out.

'Now,' she said, 'isn't that better? Drop the guns, boys. Goood. Now lie down. Not on your bellies! On your backs!'

They turned over, blinking in the rain.

'Much better.'

Gun still on Jackson, she inspected each of the soldiers, then stopped at one. 'Mmm. You're pretty.'

To the astonishment of Jackson, Müller, and the soldiers, she sat astride the man she had picked.

'Mmm,' she said to the soldier. 'Like that? Nice? Open your mouth, soldier boy. Open!'

Terrified, he did. She put the gun in it.

'Any one of you moves,' she said, 'his head gets blown off.' She looked down at the soldier. 'Nice?' she asked him gently. 'Warm? Sweet?'

Wide eyed, the soldier was not sure what to do.

'You can nod,' she said.

He nodded, fearfully.

'You like me?'

Again the nod.

'She wants to squeeze my scrawny neck. Did you know that? But closer to the bone, the sweeter the meat. Did you know that too? *Not like that pudding Lieutenant-Colonel Bloomfield!*' she yelled suddenly. *'Where are you, Colonel Bloomfield?'*

'Right here.'

Mary-Anne could not have expected it, but even so, her speed was cat-like. Her gun was out of the soldier's mouth, and she was leaping off him and whirling in one motion, it seemed.

But it was the Beretta which roared first.

The shot hit her squarely in the chest, throwing her violently backwards so that she stumbled over the soldier she had recently been astride, and toppled clumsily, screeching in rage. She actually tried to get up, so powerful was her hate. She was still gripping her gun, and it began to rise towards Carey Bloomfield.

Jackson and Müller stared in astonishment as Mary-Anne began to stagger to her feet.

Müller began to raise his own gun.

Carey Bloomfield stood her ground and waited, Beretta pointing unerringly.

Mary-Anne was on her feet; legs parting, braced. Gun still coming up, pointing now, zeroing on target.

The Beretta roared again.

Mary-Anne was pitched backwards like a rag doll. This time, she made no sound, and did not get up again.

Carey Bloomfield walked up to Mary-Anne's body, and looked down. 'Pudding? The more curves, the better.'

Elland had begun to moan again.

Carey Bloomfield looked at him. 'Shut up!'

Elland shut up.

Müller and Jackson got to their feet, Müller putting his gun away. Hagen's soldiers staggered upright, looking bemused, and giving the one that had been Mary-Anne's plaything strange looks.

Jackson looked at Mary-Anne's body. 'What the hell was that?'

'That,' Müller replied, 'was Mary-Anne.'

Jackson looked at Carey Bloomfield. 'Nice timing, Colonel. She seemed to hate you. Any idea why?'

Carey Bloomfield shook her head. 'None at all, sir.'

Then Müller's phone rang.

'Where are you?' came Pappenheim's voice.

Müller frowned, thinking there was something strange about it.

'Everything fine here, Pappi.' He gave Pappenheim a quick rundown.

'Move away,' Pappenheim said.

'What?'

'Just do it, Jens.'

'Alright.'

Müller walked towards the lake until he stood on high ground, looking down at the water.

The others waited.

Suddenly, a scarcely human sound came from the direction of the lake, echoing in the rain. Forest animals, hearing it, scuttled into hiding.

'*Semperrrr!*'

The soldiers stared at each other.

Jackson looked at Carey Bloomfield. 'What the hell. Was that *Müller*?'

'I'll go to him.'

She ran, fear in her heart, a puzzled Jackson staring after her.

When she got to Müller, he was squatting on his heels, phone in one hand, head hanging down.

Unsure of what to do, she said, 'Müller, you're scaring me. What's wrong?'

He looked up at her, eyes so haunted, she really became frightened.

'Tell me this,' he said. 'What do I tell him?'

'Who?'

'Jackson. That was Pappi on the phone. One of the kidnappers was a psycho. The assault team arrived too late. They found two of the men dead, killed by the psycho. They caught the psycho on the stairs. One of the assault team killed him. Then they went into the room where she was being held, and found Mrs Jackson. Dead. She had been violated. Now *tell me*! *What* do I tell him?'